ERNEST PICK

Acting in Love

Contents

1

Roger Meets Denise

Roger Williams is sitting on a green and white chaise longue. The air is so dry it seems brittle. From a balcony twenty stories high, he is overlooking a Bahamian resort. When he stands, a hand over his eyes filtering out the rays of the sun, he distinguishes cruise ships extending cables, then tethering to docks. Like a parade of ants, passengers descend gangplanks to the casino several hundred yards away. Farther, a circular water field surrounded by boulders has been carved out for dolphins. Dolphins are cavorting in the water, human masters whipping them in balletic quartets high into the air, urging them into back flips which bring them crashing down nose first.

He takes out a cigarette, taps out loose tobacco, and lights it. Blows smoke contentedly into the morning air. The day will grow warm, even hot as it progresses, but for now, the air is cool. He revels in it.

Roger is pleased with himself. He sits back exhaling a cloud of smoke. After a decade of playing community theatre, partaking of commercials featuring only his feet, barely noticed in cameo movie parts, he has made it on TV in the role of a young private detective in love with the daughter of the owner of the great stallion, Miramar. The steed has won six races before narrowly losing in the Derby under suspicious circumstances. Taping is over for the next two months and the young man can finally relax. One of his actor friends recommends Atlantis in the Bahamas which he claims will settle him down. "Just sailing there on a cruise ship," the man avers, "is a soothing adventure." His friend is right. "First of all, the boat is large enough to avoid detection." Shunning recognition on trips, he prefers to be undetected, spending his time focusing on an inner world of rest rather than adulation. The latter may come soon enough, he trusts, when he returns to Babylon Revisited in the fall. Concerned only about his weight. He has been taking in gobs without regard for his figure. And after all, his body should be well manicured if he is to thrive in his highly successful soap opera. Jason Fierst, his director, scoffs and tells him to munch away, to consume tons of lard and steaks, down quantities of liquor and eat morning bagels with eggs and cream cheese. "For how can you unwind if you are constantly fretting about the food you eat?" Roger remains unconvinced. Nothing should deter from the attention he has received from fans of the soap. When he returns to tape again in the fall, his first scene will find him in prison playing opposite Ari Bloom, one of the mainstays of the soap who, he understands, will now finally meet his end on Babylon. Might as well be dead for real, he chuckles.

Only one thing troubles him in paradise. Fruit. There is little on the island. More precisely, to purchase a simple banana at the downstairs bar costs upwards of four dollars. Something wrong with this, he mutters to himself, but the entire island is costly. A simple plate of spaghetti and meatballs runs $40. He hadn't counted on spending so much for even the simplest meal.

In the moment, as he dresses, he is considering strolling the quarter mile or so to the dolphin exhibit. Dons shorts, a t-shirt with a pocket for his Larks, hitches up his suspenders, descends the elevator twenty floors and walks sprightly through the swinging front doors. Now turns left. In a few moments, he arrives at the dolphin area. Before a sandy area, he spies a coffee stand where he partakes of a latte which will set him back six dollars. Six dollars! He is beginning to rue the day he descended into heaven. But pays anyway. He wants a coffee badly. Walks to a covered trellis by the exhibit and awaits the next show. Finishes his drink. Puts down the Styrofoam cup. Dozes. Then a startling roar invades sleep. The crowd is approving the first of the dolphin pirouettes. Someone is narrating in an incomprehensible cackle through a loud speaker. Roger listens but cannot grasp more than the gist of the man's words. Doesn't care. Likes to watch the mammals flying in obvious graceful, pleasurable leaps and turns. One of the trainers, her arms the signal flags for the dolphins, is a young woman dressed in appropriate wet suit gear. Black hair. Wide eyes. A broad smile. Lips part slowly in wonderment as she observes her charges flying above her.

"Who is that woman?" he asks the barista.

"Don't really know much about her," the man replies without looking up. "I believe her name is Denise."

The dolphins are now in full motion cruising on the rim of the water until, upon a single command, Denise has them cartwheel into the air one after the other back into the water. A loud roar of approval from the observant crowd. The woman turns slightly and places a hand over her chest to receive an accolade. Five more minutes' pass and the show is ending. The dolphins start to feed from buckets of fish. Denise is wading through the cool water towards shore, her wet suit dripping, her dark hair resplendent in the reflection of the morning sun. Flecks of brilliance blaze from her hair as she agitates water out of it. Mesmerized, Roger thinks she displays an aura around her, an indescribable halo. He puts down his cup, his mouth open. Gets up. Hitches up his shorts, ties the string tighter. Ambles towards her. They meet somewhere near the center of the path.

"Quite a show," Roger remarks as she passes, regretting that he has nothing more interesting to offer.

She smiles, shakes her head once more to eliminate water drops which have crept into her ear.

"Wait", he says as she proceeds beyond him. "Can I buy you a cup of coffee""

Now she stops and turns to him, sees something she likes. Maybe it's the blond unruly hair swirling above his head like a Medusa.

"Sure," she responds. "I have some time now and I wouldn't mind a coffee. But let's not buy it at the stand," she cautions. "I'll bring out two cups from the employees' station...and" she laughs, "both will be just as delicious. Maybe even tastier because they're free."

She returns with two brimming, steaming cups.

"Wish I had some fruit," she laments after a sip.

He laughs. "Exactly what I was wishing for. But you're an employee. Don't they feed you properly?"

Lays down her cup. "Not ever enough fruit," she sighs.

"I'm too cheap to pay for it on the island," he confesses.

"I don't blame you. But," she adds, "if you leave the island, I am told there is a grocery store on the other side of the bridge where you can buy all the fruit you want at reasonable prices."

"No shit", he says.

"No shit," she repeats, laughing.

"So, let's go".

She looks at her watch. "I need to be back by two for the next show."

"How far can it be""

"Better than a mile," she says. "And I'm not exactly dressed for hiking."

"Do you want to change?"

"No."

"What's your name"?

"Denise" she says. They start out for the bridge. "Denise Rosen."

He is looking at her in profile as they walk together. They are passing a fleet of yachts docked on the pier by the restaurants. On the largest yacht, four people with caps are playing cards aft. "Keep going," she says. "We need to pass through this area to get to the bridge." From the corner of his eye, Roger examines her. He does not find her beautiful. Maybe pretty. Exotically pretty. The girl's look wafts, grows or dissipates, depending on her way of speaking, whether she is excited by something, or simply calmly reciting the obvious. But she exudes a vibration. A je ne sais quoi. It's a femininity, a sexuality redolent in her entire body, the way she moves, the swing of her arms, her bottom shifting slightly upwards as it glides forward, lips which give way to a romantic pout, her white teeth barely revealing themselves in this moment, breasts shifting in motion just a tad, just enough so that Roger is aware of them.

"I'm here only through the season," she says. "Then I return to the states."

"To do what?" he asks.

"I'm an actress." Lamenting now, she looks at him with eyes lowering. "Not a very good actress," she adds.

"How do you know that?" he questions her.

"Because I am not getting roles," she replies.

"What a coincidence," he says and now begins to talk about himself, revealing his role on Babylon Revisited.

She giggles slightly. "I thought I had seen you before. Although," she adds: "To tell the truth, I'm not a fervent watcher of your soap."

They're nearing the beginning of the bridge and now car traffic has accelerated in earnest. They scamper onto the bridge and begin to climb. At the apex of the bridge, half way across, ships, some bearing cargo, some with lounging, waving passengers in shorts pass underneath into the Atlantic.

"It's longer than I thought," she says, fretting.

"Getting tired?"

"No." A drop of perspiration appears above her lips.

They forge onwards descending to the other side of the bridge. As they reach the bottom, there is a street to be crossed. On the other side, three black men are standing idly on the corner.

"Does this mean trouble?" he questions"

"I don't know. I don't think so," she replies cautiously.

"Just keep on walking".

The three black men are dressed similarly in jeans. One is smoking. They are staring. Not only at the woman, Roger notices, but at him as well. He wonders why.

"Good morning!" one of them speaks up agreeably.

They respond in kind, tension dissipating. A few yards up the street, there is a broken fence of a grassy field. A young black boy in beige shorts wiggles through the fence. He is smiling. His teeth are blindingly white.

"Can you tell us where we can find the grocery store?" Denise asks him.

"Sure," he says. "I take you there. Come with me."

Now the three of them walk up the street. On either side, small brick buildings once occupied, many vacant. The air hangs acrid here.

"Are we being stupid?" Denise whispers.

Roger shrugs. "Come this way," the boy repeats. "It only a few blocks away. Large store with many things."

Suddenly, out of one of the buildings a middle aged black woman emerges, a woman of considerable girth. She sizes up the situation quickly and begins to walk next to the boy. "Thomas," she says, "watcha doing?"

"Takin' folks to the market," he says.

"Takin' me too," she says. She has said nothing to either Roger or Denise. Now the four of them are walking stride for stride up the hill.

Three minutes' pass before they come to the next intersection. "Look to the right," the boy points. "There's the store."

Roger reaches into his pocket, pulls out a Bahamian dollar and hands it to the boy. "Thank you", the boy says, checking out the bill. "You come back tomorrow and we walk some more," the boy says. Roger takes Denise's arm and heads towards the store. Turns once. The woman has her arm around the boy's neck. The two are quietly watching them enter the supermarket. The market itself is large, cool and filled with fruit. Bananas cost forty-five cents a pound, Roger notices with pleasure, and buys a bunch. Denise scoops up strawberries and blueberries.

"This is worth the hike," she gushes. They also buy chocolate bars before leaving the store. It is only then that they notice they are the only white people on the premises.

When they return to the island, Roger asks Denise to dinner. She laughs. "Better still," she responds. "Come to my place. I can make you a plateful of spaghetti for nothing, and even give you a bit of wine with it. You deserve something after the caper we just pulled off."

He relishes her spaghetti. The taste reminds him of dinners at Muggiano's in Boston. The wine feels off, but he drinks a glass anyway. They spend the evening chatting away. Chatting about acting and what it takes to be celebrated. "Luck," he says. "No," she responds. "It must be more than that. If it's only luck, then I might as well never think about it. No, there must be something in you that affects, even changes people. If you have that certain gift, they respond."

He shrugs. "I have no answer to that. But I do believe in luck if you are ready for it, if you take advantage of it".

"And how do you do that?" she asks.

"Take the shitty roles. We are never so full of ourselves that we can afford to turn anything down. True, once we become megastars, maybe then we can choose what to reject."

She grins. "I would be happy to take any cruddy role that comes my way."

"Maybe I can help," he says to her. She looks up at him now, smiles and begins to scrape dishes. "Wait," he adds quickly. "This is your moment to take advantage of your luck, your good fortune. I am in a position to help. Possibly. I can't guarantee anything, but I do have a little pull with Mr. Fierst, the director of the soap. Maybe I can squeeze you in there."

"I would kill," she responds throatily, her eyes sparkling.

"No need to do that," he responds. "You don't even have to sleep with the messenger."

"Hmm," she says. "Could be a first. What's your angle?"

"Just trying to help a fellow thespian," he responds. "Besides, if you get the gig, then we'll have a lot of time together, and I might even enjoy that."

"So, I don't have to fuck you to get this gig"

"No," he says.

"Even if I want to?"

"I never fuck on a first date," Roger giggles.

"Pity," she sighs.

"I realize I'm a bit odd here, but I like to get emotionally connected to the piece of ass I'm fondling. Slow childhood development, I fear. Maybe even bad, late toilet training."

"That is odd," she laughs. "Should I really take you at your word?"

"No strings. No hidden agenda."

Denise comes around, loosens an apron, plants a kiss on his cheek. A long, soft kiss. With her napkin, she smooths away a trace of lipstick. Grinning, he does not reply to her touch.

"How about some dessert?" he pleads.

"I thought that was what I was offering," she pouts.

2

The Play Begins

From the wings, through a small aperture in a velvet curtain, Roger studies the first rows. Clients are murmuring. Always a seething hum before the curtain rises. The public has already settled in, but they're edgily expectant. Churning, babbling, shedding garments in their seats. To while away time, they chatter to one another. Sounds of squirrels nibbling away at acorns. In France, Roger recalls that the beginning of the play is announced by three thumps on the stage. Then everyone quiets, eyes lift towards the stage. Here, only the raising of the curtain silences the audience. What are they doing here anyway? he asks himself.

They are at the Ostrovsky Theatre on 44th Street. The play is new. Entitled *Wars of Independence*. It has received several scintillating reviews. Critics praise the repartee. Some appreciate the plot, reveling in its unusual twists. Others compliment the wealth of emotion expressed by the principals. Biglar of the Post, however, abhors it. He calls the play crap, claims that it rehashes old ground mined throughout the ages by playwrights much worthier than Arnost Geryk. "Asshole," Roger reacts, angrily. Of course, he agrees, nothing is new under the sun, but there are contrivances, new connections, new ways of expressing ancient situations. Biglar apparently has never heard of poetry. Biglar particularly loathes the characters. He believes them unfaithful to their words. Roger shrugs.

Behind him, a girl is tapping him on the shoulder and urging him to break a leg. He smiles his peculiarly affecting smile at her, and she dances away with a short giggle. Now Denise comes up to him and plants a kiss on his cheek. "You'll blunt your lipstick, he chides her. But she puts one arm around his neck and draws him near. "Let's have real combat tonight in our wars," she whispers, and now he catches her by the waist and twirls her around playfully.

"You read Biglar's review," he asks her.

She shrugs, pulls up the collar around her neck. "It's a small thing."

"He has influence," Roger says.

"The house is full," she responds. "So much for his influence. Stop worrying."

"Yes," he concedes, "the house is full."

And now the curtain rises, spotlights illuminating the stage. Roger slowly steps forward to a welter of applause. Applause ripples at first front to back, then up to the balcony where there are several people standing and cheering. Must be my relatives. I haven't said a single word, Roger thinks mystified. He does not acknowledge the applause. Instead, he stands front center planting himself.

He is just a tad over six feet, a thin sapling of a young man with wild, blond, curly hair that somehow seems ill fitted to crown the shape of his body. His voice is rich, melodious, practiced. It sings out with power and grace. Even Biglar remarked on the fluidity of his voice. Roger is a romantic at heart. An introvert, who when induced to leave his shell as he is about to

11

do, becomes comfortably brazen. Stands with authority hiding vulnerability, self-doubt, the sapling giving away nothing. He loves this moment. It shunts aside an octave of nervousness and brings him into full compliance with the text in his soul. He was always meant for this moment, the opening stanza of a play, to speak boldly, gracefully, and convincingly to a group of people he has never encountered, to draw them into his character, to deprive them of any will but his.

From the corner of his eye, he observes Denise preparing herself, her skirt rising and falling as she fluffs it into place. Denise is his age, dark-haired, black eyed, Jewish, sultry, impenetrable, and sensuous at the same time in a pattern he has never encountered. As Roger speaks, he is moistening his dry lips. They are always dry as the play opens. In a moment, he knows, all will revert to normal.

Act One

(He is standing stage right. Addresses the audience)

"So, there we were, I her Professor, she my student. Not just any student. Full lips in a sensual mouth. The hint of breasts rising and falling behind her pullover. Graceful hands. Feminine, oh yes, truly feminine." Pause. "Pretty banal, eh? Beyond banal. Corrupt. We teachers have power, authority to change people. We attract our charges by the virtue of our prestige. Dubious prestige! Take Marcella. But this is no spring chick. The lady is married. Stupidly so, I wager." (With this, a light comes up on the woman sitting at her desk, her glance unwavering. She looks at Benjamin as if she were enthralled)

12

"Look at that smile," Benjamin grins. "She's vacuuming me in."

(He turns away from her and appears to be lecturing to an invisible class) "So was the Revolution worth it after all? Rioting by a middleclass who had already had their cake and now were intent on eating it as well. What else do you do with cake, eh? Where were the downtrodden peasants? They were the ones yearning for food, for a modicum of advancement. Instead, the power-hungry bourgeoisie took over, hardly concerned with the absence of bread and sausages."

(He turns to the audience) "You see what I mean? A little history. A little baloney interpretation, just look at her sweet face. She's captivated. She's also making me hot."

"How long has it been? I guess we have known one another for three years, but this is the first class she's taken with me. History of the Revolution. She's absorbed. She has her cute little face tipped upwards as if she were sucking in manna from heaven. My little student!"

Now Marcella arises and faces the audience. While she does do, Benjamin sits and rifles through papers.

"He's something, isn't he? My professor! He knows so much. Bright and quite learned. I value learning, don't you? He's kinda cute when he gets rolling with his subject. His face gets flushed with history. Love that golden mop of his! Listen to him talking about heads rolling on the Place de la Concorde." (She exits right)

(Benjamin arises and speaks to the audience) "Danton, Robespierre and Saint-Just, the Angel of Death, they condemned hundreds to the guillotine, brought them out at dawn in tumbrils while the people of Paris trailed the carts and jeered. But what happened to these revolutionaries? They met the fate they had prescribed for others." (He exits stage right momentarily and returns with a cart which he wheels to center stage with Marcella in it. Marcella gets out)

"Who are you?" she asks with dread.

"I am your murderer," Benjamin declares, donning an executioner's mask.

"Your name, sir"

"Benjamin Perls."

"How did you come to such a profession, sir?"

"My lady", Benjamin replies, "why ask about me? These are your last minutes on earth. Have you no prayer? If not for your children, your lovers, then for yourself...."

"Pray? she asks, exhaling slowly. For life everlasting? Hardly! I pray that the crowds may love me after my death. I have searched endlessly for love," Marcella continues, now kneeling. Angrily: "I could never find the love that transcends all peace. If I regret anything, it is the fact that I remain untouched by the many rather than the few."

Benjamin raises her, leads her to the stocks and places her head on the half-moon.

"I shall take your life. The country's just trying to get a head," he cackles. "Liberty, Equality, Fraternity."

"My breasts hurt," she moans. "Be a good executioner and rub them with ointment."

"Prepare to abandon them for the Revolution."

"No one will ever love me again," she croons. "Will you allow this to happen? Perhaps you yourself could honor a dying request. (She points towards the audience) Tell them to stop clamoring. They will have their blood lust satisfied soon enough."

(Benjamin removes his mask, addresses the audience) "Is this my fantasy or hers? A public execution in which her murderer

14

fondles her breasts as he decapitates her. And Marcella: what is she striving for in this last moment? A momentous orgasm, for the little death and the big death to climax together. Will this allow her to forget the legions who have never groped her?" (He moves to the table and chairs and sits facing the audience)

"I recall where we met. In the school cafeteria. I was sitting down for a sandwich at her table one day, and once her girlfriend disappeared, I spoke to her or she spoke to me. Probably the latter. I'm not so bold. She might have asked me to pass the mustard. Perhaps I asked to caress her cheek. Wish I had. I was attracted to her and quickly caught up in the attention she showered on me. She said nothing about herself. That I had to infer from later conversations. I ladled out my life and she would spoon back a thought, a memory or two. I learned that she is married, but primed for divorce. Nothing new in that. We all seem to be ready to move on. As if, a year or two after the ceremony, we remembered what lust, love or some other silly motivation had blinded us to. Yes, she says, I remember…"

(Light on Marcella. She stands facing the audience). "I can't go on like this. I'm lying to him by hanging on. I love someone else."

(Benjamin turns to her and speaks cynically). "Naturally! We offer fidelity to our spouse and then we rush to love somebody else. It's in the order of things."

(She turns and speaks petulantly). "Why do you say that? I love Jamie. He is a man who simply no longer cares for his wife. Yes, he has children. Did I tell you that he was once a priest? I imagine him in his vestments raising the chalice, transfiguring wine into blood. It feels like blood in my veins. He has that effect on me. Chilling!"

"Quite chilling, Benjamin quips. "Even intoxicating! But does

15

he intend to leave his family for you"

"No," Marcella responds hesitantly. "I doubt that."

"So, you want what you cannot have," Benjamin sighs.

"I want him alone", Marcella sings out. "He is dashing and young. Did I tell you that he has become an investment broker?"

(Benjamin turns towards the audience and begins to walk the stage). "No difference between the revolution and our time. What we desire we pursue. In the 18th century, we sat around and discussed our dreams rationally, we thought them through. And when that didn't pan out, we started killing one another. In our time, we don't think anymore. Discussion seems a waste of time. Let's get down to what we really want to accomplish. We feel urges and we strive to satisfy them, and thus we break in twain the fidelity we promised others. Of course, murder is never entirely out of the question."

Speaks to Marcella. "How long have you been lovers?"

"Three years. But it's over now. His wife uncovered letters I sent him."

"Silly of you," Benjamin admonishes her. "Don't you know that the first rule of illicitness is never to commit anything to writing?"

"He was in Tokyo for a year," Marcella says. "I had to write to him."

"But it's over?"

"Not in my heart," she sighs.

(Benjamin to audience) "Surely it is over and one of the signs is that she is coming on to me. (To Marcella who has now returned to her desk). In the 18th century, people rarely spoke of love. Lust, naturally, but not love. Think of Les Liaisons Dangereuses. Romance awaits the next century. So, what did we do instead of romancing? We intellectualized about things we thought meaningful. Posterity! Let the future judge our acts. If we disturb the even flow of life, there is reason behind chaos. It is called premeditation and it is the base of history."

(Marcella holds up a sheet which she has produced from her purse) "Look at this last letter he wrote me. A few lines to express his feelings. He writes: 'I've never been more spellbound by anyone, but it is time for us to end this affair. We are both married, have you forgotten?' My wife will not let me brush our marriage aside. Neither of us must forget that we owe ourselves to someone else."

(Benjamin comes over to her and takes her hand) "I've never been more enthralled by anyone," he says with sincerity.

She looks up at him with scorn. "I could never abandon my feelings for Jamie."

3

Benjamin and Marcella Connect

(To audience, continuing to relate the story) "So this is how it began. I didn't see her for a while. Then, three months later, we found ourselves at a party. I was playing bridge. Marcella brought me a cake for it was my birthday. She sat behind me, the cake on her lap. (Facing the audience, Benjamin takes his place at a table with three others, Marcella behind him) She was rubbing my neck much to the consternation of those at the table who knew both her and her husband. Then, after a while, just as I got a spectacular hand with 24 points, and was bidding six no trump, she moved her chair forward, placed the cake on the ground and reached between my legs to rub the inside of my thigh." (She does this languorously)

(Benjamin rises) "I'm the dummy." (He takes her hand and they move downstage left away from the players)

A player says: "I can make a little slam."

"Benjamin's working on a big slam," another player retorts to great merriment.

Benjamin whispering to Marcella: "You have to be more careful."

"It no longer matters," Marcella grins. "I've decided to divorce."

Benjamin pauses momentarily. "One down. But what about

those feelings for Jamie"

She looks a bit misty-eyed. "I'll always have feelings for Jamie."

Sarcastically, he says "Before or after you rub my thigh?"

"Shouldn't matter. I am attracted to you," Marcella replies. He kisses her. A long kiss filled with meaning, passion. "I feel dizzy."

"So am I," he responds.

"I'm such a mess," she groans, looking away and pursing her lips.

"You could have said a sexy mess."

"I'd be happy with sexy," she whispers.

"I think I made my slam. I could fall for you, Marcella."

"I'm so glad," she intones wholeheartedly.

(Benjamin returns to the table, but stops short, turns to audience. Marcella exits left. Benjamin's tone is again narrative) "A word about my past. Mother is French, father American. They met while dad was on scholarship to Lyon. They fell in love, they married, and I was spawned soon thereafter. Talk about banality. In a manner of speaking, they are still together. She speaks, he listens, and they survive tenuously…this is the conjugation of marital bliss.

I was raised in France while my father took on a teaching position. I was sent to the best all boy schools. In the beginning, they were fun. Later, despite my inclinations, I became militarized. Seemed kinda nuts. Walked around with a rifle on my shoulder and began to hate it all. I wanted to walk linking arms with Shelley or Keats. I did make a friend, however. His name is Pascal. Like me, he was somewhat of a rebel."

(Enter Pascal in uniform with a rifle on his shoulder. Good looking young man with a moustache)

(Benjamin speaking to Pascal) "Tiens! There you are. You are a flower of the war movement. Looking dashing in your kepi and boots. But, aren't you the one fiendishly opposed to combat?" he asks.

(Pascal speaks playfully. Parades) "No, my dear. You are confused. You are the one who hates war. I loathe peace. I like to thrust my bayonet into soft flesh."

"I had forgotten what a terrorist you had become. You are right. One of us hates war, and the other despises peace. But why do you need the constant strife, the fighting, the killing?"

"Aah, my naïve friend, this is the key to the human condition. I was the one who was raised gently, happily. Consequently, I grew up bored, lacking stimulation. I need excitement, tension, preferably unbearable stress, to re-right the balance. Everything in life is re-righting the balance. Hungry? We eat. Thirsty? We drink. Horny? We fuck. However, you were brought up with an American father and mother who didn't dote on you, and so they sent you hither and thither so long as it was far away, the farther the better, from home. This was daily combat, my dear, and so you are tired of it, and thirsting for peace.

"That's true", Benjamin says. "Attention! (Pascal snaps to) Do we love one another? The two boys who balance one another out? Is that what happened to two young man in an all boy's school who were young and randy."

"We love one another," Pascal responds loudly in a military response, sir, perhaps because there was no feminine flesh into which we could plunge our bayonets, sir."

(Benjamin sits contemplatively) "It's time for mess. I have to change into uniform. At ease. Dismissed! (Pascal relaxes, leaves, turns and finds a bed stage left and climbs into it. Benjamin accompanies Pascal to the bed and pulls a blanket around his shoulders. Now to audience) At night in the dormitory, when lights were extinguished and the sleep walkers had broken free of their restraints and settled into their unbridled frolics, when the epileptics had ceased foaming at the mouth and were strapped to bed with restraints on their legs and swizzle sticks tied to their tongues, then Pascal and I would pay one another nocturnal visits. Friendly they were. On our fours, we would scamper under beds to pay our respects." (He gets on his knees and soon encounters Pascal in bed. A sleepwalker passes slowly from stage left bearing an American flag in his pajamas. He passes with tranquility and then exits).

"Attention!" Pascal says, propping himself up.

"I am at attention," Benjamin responds still on the floor.

Pascal peering. "So, you are."

(Out of his bed) "I'm shy, you know. (As he rises, Benjamin also gets up, Pascal exiting left. Benjamin addresses audience). So, it was no surprise that when I met Manon who had long black hair and breasts and was the first girl I had dared to feel up, that we fell in love and married. And now we are in the States adult and married while Pascal is in the Foreign Legion buggering the Africa Corps from secretary to field marshal.

(Manon enters in apron from right. A pretty woman, some-what overweight. Benjamin speaks to her sternly) "What are you doing?"

"I am cooking," Manon says, bringing Benjamin a drink. "How are you?"

"I've had a hard day in the classroom. What's for dinner?"

"A small steak," Manon responds pleasantly, compliantly. "I hope it's filling. I don't want you to be hungry."

"I am always satisfied with your cooking. You are a fine cook. Did you see my Ipad" (She brings it to him. He speaks to audience) Why did I ask her for the Ipad which I wasn't interested in opening. As an exercise to keep the little darling hopping, to see how endlessly I could bend her to my will. To determine whether she would demur. Ours was an old-style marriage. The woman served me in every respect. I should have been completely satisfied, but I wasn't. I felt bound and gagged by my little woman who, as months went by, appealed less and less to me. Within a few years, I became profoundly bored."

(Manon exits left, A young female student, Heather, enters right and sits next to Benjamin. He rises and speaks to audience) "Then began the procession of students. Heather was not the first, were you, sweetie?"

"Just the best," she responds, smiling.

"So," he says, "to be fair, she wasn't bad. (The lights dim) We had finished a session of history at my house, an evening class it was. Heather stayed on ostensibly to help me wash wine glasses."

"Thanks for the help," he says to Heather, taking a dish rag from her. "Do you want another drink?"

"Yes, Dr. Perls."

(To audience) "I never earned a doctorate, but I loved it when they called me Doctor Perls. I would always respond with my first name. False humility leaves its mark. (To Heather) Benjamin! Please!"

"You have a lovely house," she says.

"My wife takes credit for that."

"Where is she tonight?"

"With friends on a shopping trip to New York. She'll be back tomorrow. Vodka all, right?"

"Yes, thanks", she responds. "I'm glad I stayed behind. I wanted to ask your opinion about a career in teaching."

"Teaching history?"

"I do love the past and I'd be good sharing it with others," she says. Her tone is turning coquettish as she speaks.

"Then maybe teaching is right for you. You do understand you won't make a fortune in history…although, you won't go hungry either."

"I don't care about that," Heather responds.

(Brings drink for her. Sits next to her) "Cheers! Here's to your career, then."

"It's warm in here. Can I open a window?"

He follows her to window. "Of course, it is hot." (He stands behind her, now beginning to caress her).

"Please! Dr. Perls!"

(Benjamin laughs turning to the audience) "A protocol demurral to show me she's not easy. (To Heather) My name is Benjamin! (She turns to him and they kiss. He motions her towards the stock in the middle of the stage. She places her head in it while on her knees. Lift your skirt. (She complies. He stands behind her and they simulate erotic gestures and noises)

(To audience while in the act). A lesson in history. Heather, sweet Heather was lonely and offered herself like some fat, ripe swan and here came the redoubtable Dr. Perls, man of the hour, up to the task of rescuing her from innocence. (He groans. Heather removes herself slowly from the stock. They straighten up. To audience) By the end of term, she was preparing herself for bigger and better things." (Heather returns to the sofa. Benjamin remains standing).

"So, you're ready for summer break?" he asks her.

"Yes, she says. I have a job as a cook in a diner on the west coast."

(Takes her hand) "Will you call me? Text me?"

"Of course, I will," she says (She gets up, smooths her skirt, kisses him, begins to exit) "Have a fine summer, Dr. Perls. (Stops, turns) Benjamin!"

"I waited expectantly. I was true to her, but she didn't call me. She didn't text either. I was fucking outraged. By the end of the summer, I was sure I'd never hear from her again. Nevertheless, she did return to school, and I was first on her list of people to see."

(Heather enters, speaks to Benjamin) "I frankly didn't have the time to call. Or text."

"You didn't have time to call me?" he says, reproachfully.

Pause. Now she turns to Benjamin. "If you must know," she adds almost angrily, "I hardly thought about you at all."

(This admission takes Benjamin aback) "Not very flattering," he simmers.

"I wanted experience this summer," she responds. "I was fascinated by...I can't tell you, she says demurely.

"Please!"

(Sheepishly) "All right! I wanted to experience a lot. Sexually, I mean. Didn't matter whether it was demeaning or not. I liked doing it with you, cheating on your wife. I had never cheated on anybody before. Felt good, just right. It excited me. When I left, I wanted more. I wanted to try sex with another man, you understand, because I was green then. But what happened was that it kinda spiraled out of my control. I experimented with one man after the other. I would finish work and spend the next hours on my knees before many men. I couldn't stop. (Brighter) But now I'm back. I'm glad to be back and I'm glad to be back with you."

(Benjamin can hardly believe his ears) "And that's how it was. (Takes Heather to stage left and acts the following out) I wiped Heather's mouth with my handkerchief, waved goodbye to her, watched her back up with a thin smile on her face. Shortly afterwards, I took up with Shirley. I think it was Shirley. She was the one who would only screw with her bra on because she said she lacked breasts." (Heather exits giggling)

4

An Audition with Jason Fierst

Denise enters the marble-clad lobby of the 55th street studio. Intercepted by a guard, she opens her purse for inspection.

"You have business here?" he asks, non-comital.

"Yes. An audition," she replies. She is almost surprised to hear her own voice. Now she realizes how very nervous she is.

The guard calls upstairs. Nods. "Ok, he says to her. Then: —Good luck!"

She smiles.

Wearing a blistered rose petal dress. It seems to make her dark eyes come alive, sparkle. Seems younger, elfin-like. All to the good, she says into her mirror while making-up for her audition. In the ladies' room, tries on several lipsticks. Settles on something full, but not too heavy. Crimson. Highlighting the dress. Shoes with heels. Pirouettes once to feel her feet. Accustomed to those. Fidgets. Underarms? Odor-free, dry! She has already experienced auditions, she repeats to herself. As ready as she will ever be.

Gives her name to the receptionist. The girl checks her monitor, finds what she is searching for, nods, motions Denise to a seat near the door. "Be just a moment," the girl says, without looking up. There are four other women sitting across from her staring.

Denise wonders whether Roger will be there. Of course, he will, she thinks. The thought braces her nerves. Door opens. A girl in a mauve dress and green hair motions her inside. They walk together down a hallway. She wants to make conversation with this woman, but cannot quite make eye contact.

"It's in here," the girl points not really speaking to anyone, then closes the door behind them.

Denise enters a middle-sized, round room. It is, in fact, a small theatre. There are seats below a stage. Maybe seventy seats, she gauges. Several people sitting. One stands. A man with red hair. Walks out of the row and onto the stage, motioning her over with a finger. Suddenly, to her relief Roger appears ambling towards her smiling, accompanied by an older man with silver hair.

"Denise, Roger says, this is Paul Scudery. Our Ari Bloom."

"I recognize you," she says breathlessly. "Always been a fan."

He takes her hand in his, squeezes it. "I appreciate that, but you'll have to shift your support to some other guy" he adds dourly. "I'm about to be snuffed out."

"Such a pity," she pretends to gush.

"And this red-haired breath of fresh air is Jason Fierst, our estimable director," Roger continues. She turns to a man with a wide, open face brimming with wrinkled signposts. "Charmed," he says to her with a high-pitched voice. "At least, I think so. Turn for me, please. Yes, I'm a scumbag. I want to see the entire package before I decide whether to open it or not." She turns slowly. "Good," he acknowledges. "I appreciate a woman with form. You have a speaking voice also?" he inquires.

"Of course," she avers, smiling. The rapidity of the thing

overwhelms her. The audition has already started before she can process two deep breaths as she promised herself she must.

"I'd like to run some lines between you and Paul. You said you had seen Babylon before?"

"Several episodes," she acknowledges. Tries to unbridle her muscles by breathing more deeply.

"So, you know he plays the part of Ari Bloom, a financial investment type."

"Yes, I recall," she says tentatively.

"Don't be afraid, girl," Jason prompts her, taking her arm, positioning her close to center stage. A teen-ager comes forward with a fresh script which she hands to Denise. "You'll be playing the part of Denise...he laughs...we are creating the part for you and plan to use your proper name. Ok with you?"

"Fine. Great. At least, I'll remember it", she adds.

"Promising," he replies without a smile. "You are auditioning for the role of secretary to Ari Bloom. In this scene, Ari is concerned about a certain Indian gentleman who wishes to conduct illicit business with him."

"Ok," she says, opening the script, scanning pages.

"All right," Jason exclaims to everyone. "Let's jump into the pews and allow the actors to perform the service. Momentary hush."

"You ok, miss?" Paul Scudery asks.

"I'm fine." Her breathing is shallow.

"Haven't seen you around," he says wetting his lips.

"First time here," she answers.

"You have a fine figure," he bleats unexpectedly.

The comment unnerves her. It is not in the script. The line is entirely askew. Paul is supposed to say: You look as if you can handle the work. Still, she stammers a thank you. Chatter in the seats. "All right, Jason croaks from below. Everybody hide in their cocoons and let's move forward. Quiet, please."

"Denise!"

"Yes, Mr. Bloom."

"Call me, Ari. Everyone does."

"Ari."

"Here's what I need from you. I have some dealings with an Indian man named Daitja Ganesha. Somewhere in the mess of folders on the desk there is a file on him. I need to see it. Can you obtain it for me quickly?"

"In a jiffy," Denise replies. She turns just as someone hands her a file. She presents it to Ari.

Opening it. "Just as I thought," Ari comments. "This man could jumpstart my career, but he is also a bit of a shyster. Crap. Now I don't know what to do. He has approached me about a rather large series of deals based on advance info. If we make the deals, I'd become rich, and the brokerage will earn gobs of money. But this is a scam, you know, and if anyone finds out, I could get fired or worse, go to jail. What to do?" he asks nobody in particular.

"You should do the right thing," Denise offers.

"Stop. Please stop," Jason trumpets. (To Denise) "You're acting like you don't care. Your voice is too mellow here. You need to have fire in the belly at this moment. Incensed that your boss may be entertaining devious conduct. Fire, Denise, got it?"

She rubs her belly although why she does this she does not rightly know. "Do the right thing!" she erupts.

"Fire, Denise, not arson. You are also expressing some sympathy for his dilemma."

"Do the right thing!" she exclaims with some passion.

He turns on her angrily. "And what the hell would that be,

young lady" I've been around for a very long time. I'm 70 years old, you know, and I still haven't always figured out what the right thing is. What is right for you may be all wrong for me. Pause. Sorry, I've flustered you."

"Just thought that you were looking for the ethical answer instead of the one that most appealed to you," she replies somewhat angrily.

He laughs. "That is absolutely true. If truth be told, I'm somewhat of a wimp. I don't have a lot of gumption when it comes to dilemmas. This means that if I never do a grand deal, I'll just limp along earning enough money to feed myself, but not enjoy a spectacular life. To hell with that," he trumpets. "I've played it safe for the last time. All right, I just decided! I'm going to trade with the Indian."

"Stop. Stop!" Jason Fierst calls out." We're going on to the next scene, Denise. Quite a few weeks later than the one you just played. But don't grovel so much. Ari Bloom is a nobody. Women love him because he is vulnerable, but you need to be a bit more forceful so they can distinguish his character from yours. Can you lift the hammer over Ari?"

"I can," Denise says forcefully. "I shall."

Jason grins. "Good. Ok. Second scene. Get on with it. Everybody quiet as church mice."

"Denise," Ari cries out in tears. "Step into my office. (Denise in his office.) Look! he says. Look! I have a corner office with windows. On one side, Broadway. I never thought I'd be looking out over Broadway. I love the stream of yellows cabs down there. For a moment, I felt like the King of Broadway. Just for a moment! The city could have been mine for the asking. I just needed to do the grand deal while evading the law." He sobs. "Now, I've not only lost Broadway. I have lost New York."

Denise comes over and puts her arm around him. "Ari, what's wrong?" she asks sweetly. "You can surely confide in me."

He lowers his head. "Earlier today, I had a visit from someone with the FBI. They know about the trades I handled for Daitja. They also know about some deals I made through my girlfriend in Canada. All illegal, he gushes. Any one of them can land me in jail."

"Surely, it can't be all that bad," she says, holding him tightly as he continues to shake and sob.

"Yes, yes. Good sympathy, girl", Jason speaks up. "I'm virtually awash in tears."

"I'm afraid I'm about to lose everything. Not only my job, but my freedom, and if I judge Daitja's purpose correctly, even my girlfriend."

"You have to buck up," Denise replies forcefully. "Defeatism isn't going to do you any good. Be a mensch, Ari!"

Jason elbows Roger who is sitting next to him but leaning forward. "She'll do. Not a great actress, he murmurs, but she has a sturdy, purposeful look about her, and I think the public will find her believable. Still she should puff herself up, present a tad more Batman to our effacing Ari. Can she puff up, Roger?"

He smiles. "You had better ask the lady."

"I can be tough as nails," she shouts down to him.

"Smells right to me," Jason yells. "I think she will puff up a storm. She drips with a little sexy edge that will tickle our viewers provided she doesn't use it against Ari." Now he turns to Denise. "This role is temporary, of course. You do get that."

"Temporary?"

"Yes. We intend to say goodbye to Ari Bloom in the near future. As he surmises, he is going to jail, he adds," and after a bit, Jason continues with no change in his voice, "we are going to murder him there. Then, poof," his hands thrust upwards, "no need for a secretary."

Denise appears shocked. Looks around for Roger.

"Roger didn't bring you into the picture? Sorry about that. Your role, of necessity, is small, temporary. But if the audience relates to you, we'll fit you in to Babylon one way or the other. We add or subtract all the time, adding pieces to the jigsaw, and removing them when they have fulfilled their purpose. That's up to you, my dear. Still you do have a nice voice, and you cut a curvy figure on stage. As long as the female audiences don't find you threatening. They've got to see you as endearing, you know. Tough, but loyal. Tough, but endearing."

"I can play tough and endearing," she avows.

5

The President of the College has a Message for his Staff

Near the central administration building, the red stone and white marble music hall looms prominent. Inside, it features a good-sized auditorium, and it is in this facility that President Jager has decided to convoke his faculty. But only his faculty. No staff. And, certainly, no students. President Andres Jager is fifty years old. A short man, he has sprouted a black moustache to parallel his slick black hair. At one time, in younger years, he taught philosophy. Frustrated with the pace of administrative change as a decade transpired, he joined with rebellious managers of the college and, intently, rapidly, climbed up the ladder to the presidency. Only his wife of twenty years, a boozer of renown, interrupted his life of easy grandeur, ruptured the genteel and modest customs which the president espoused. Before his faculty, Jager, presidential, immobile, and taut, awaits the closing of the doors by his sergeant at arms. Hands on lapels, he begins:

"I've asked you here to discuss a vital issue. There have been reports of liaisons between professors and students, both male-female and even female-female which transcend the normal, acceptable scope of contact. Pause. Jager arches up over his spectacles to make the point that what he has just imparted is deadly serious.

"One such case you are already aware of, that of Professor Lawson, who virtually kidnapped one of our students to entice her into immoral activity. The girl's parents have removed her from the institution after this distasteful incident. Not only this girl but, in addition, her twin sister with whom, Professor Lawson swears, he fell in love after an initial physical encounter, leaving the first twin in emotional distress. Lawson wished, he alleges, to marry this young thing. That is, the second twin to whom I am referring. Parents were understandably outraged. They could well have filed suit against our institution, he adds," and now stops momentarily for effect. "To placate their ire, Lawson is presently under indictment by the state attorney's office. Ours is a woman's institution, and young women may easily be swept off their feet during this period of post-adolescence when hormones often rage." Jager looks up again to emphasize the point.

"To engage in any relationship outside of strict teacher-student contract is a violation of State law. That is the State, I am taking about! And if the State doesn't get you, I will. No more hanky panky at this institution. Is that understood? I am addressing mainly male faculty, you understand, but let it be known that no one is exempt from this policy." Murmur of approval mainly from the female professors most of whom have banded together in a corner of the auditorium near the stage.

Nonetheless, there is also a murmur from the male faculty interspersed throughout the hall. "'Twins' one chuckles. Got to hand it to Lawson. I didn't know he had the balls." Another voice: "Swine. He didn't share with any of us! Can't use more

34

than one at a time unless you're a glutton!"

(Benjamin enters stage right, faces the audience) "But that is not why I abandoned my playmates. As I got older, they became less challenging and, in fact, banal. I was bored. Never considered while I was screwing one or the other, I would be thinking about grading papers. As for Manon, my about to be ex, she left for the east coast. Last I heard she was seen shopping at Bloomingdales.

Now why do I say things like that? I recognize that I treated her miserably. She was a good woman whose only goal in life was to make me content. That was my goal as well, but as an inexperienced young man I chose to find happiness elsewhere. I've rarely regretted anything more than my dreadful treatment of this woman."

(Manon enters, faces the audience) "He used to tell me that my conversation wasn't scintillating. Or stimulating. I tried to find different words. I read exotic books and texts, bought sexy underwear to bring him closer to me, but he had already made up his mind that I was creatively hopeless. True, I wanted nothing but stability with a little tabasco sauce now and then. I loved my husband and he wounded me terribly."

(Benjamin walks over, hugs her momentarily. Manon disengages) "I made the mistake of telling her about my affairs one night. An effort to soothe my guilty conscience, I suppose. That night, I was so pleased that she accepted my mea culpas, my explanations, in good grace. Naïve little dork that I was. The following morning I was shaving in the bathroom when I heard what I thought were plates breaking."

(He turns to a mirror pretending to shave when he hears the plates. Manon is walking purposefully towards him with a pair of scissors she has raised above her head. Benjamin quickly disarms her, and she falls to her knees weeping. Turns to audience) "Fool that I am, I should have let her separate my private parts from the rest of my body.

In those days, when I was young, I couldn't discern the difference between hormonal activity and real love. Stupidly, I abandoned our house for an apartment across the street from the emergency room of the hospital. A furnished apartment I had found quickly. It was all I could afford. Shortly afterwards, Manon instituted divorce proceedings. She didn't ask for alimony but once."

(Manon rises) "Benjamin, if I leave for New York, it will take some time for me to find work, to get settled.

"You know what I earn on a teacher's salary, Manon."

"You'll just have to share some of it with me."

"I don't want to see you starve, dear, so I'll offer you a lump sum settlement. I can afford four thousand dollars, but that will break me entirely."

"The court will award me alimony if I ask for it," she persists defiantly.

(Threatening) "Bad thinking," Benjamin responds. "If you let them soak me for money I can't afford, I'll hurt you."

"Hurt me? You?" She smiles. She had never heard anything remotely threatening from Benjamin in all the years they knew one another.

"You are perfectly capable of supporting yourself, and if you value your body parts, you won't make an issue of this again".

(To audience now) "She didn't, although my threat was spurious and Manon undoubtedly knew this."

(Manon exits with more sadness than anger) "Someday, you'll regret what you've done to me."

"I laughed at her, relieved that I had gotten away so cheaply, and years went by without the slightest remorse on my part. In fact, I was to grasp much later that she was by far the honorable one in our relationship. Manon did find work. In fact, within a year she was earning considerably more than I…but she never remarried, a testimony undoubtedly to my sterling influence. It took some time, but finally, once I myself had faced rejection, I began to hate myself for what I had done to her. Correction: not for what I had done because I thought it right that we were not together. But the way I did it. (Pause) And this from a woman who had only the kindliest instincts towards me. Thank God for guilt. It eventually reminds our dark side how potent, how self-deceptive and callous it is." (He exits with Manon together).

(Marcella enters from stage left, faces the audience). "I have no story, not really. Everything in my life was super…well, adequate at least. A house in the suburbs, plenty of family, food, friends. I came out of an Italian family from the West Side. My mother was a combination of primeval elements: loud, aggressive, sometimes terribly playful to exhaustion. I recall her dancing with me when I was a child. But she was not the guiding force in my young life. That belonged to Daddy. Here he comes now. Hi, Daddy!"

(Alberto smoking a pipe enters. A man in is forties, a little Italian man who seems laden with the trivia of the world) Hi, chicken. Where's your mother?" (He walks around to find an ashtray)

"Changing, I think," Marcella says. (To audience) "Daddy served in the army when I was born. I hardly saw him in my early years. He was back and forth to the Middle East and places like that. I missed him. I remember when he came home on furlough we would treat him as if he were royalty, love him up. We wanted him to be a king in his own house. I thought that if he liked us well enough he would never leave again."

"I've got a new assignment, chicken."

"Where are you going this time?"

"Back to Iraq. They need good dentists at the front. You can't believe how soldiers neglect their teeth, at least those that aren't shot away. Guess they are concentrating too hard on the rest of their bodies."

"So, after a week or two of doting on him, we would pile into the car and drive to the train station, and we would wave at Daddy's non-smiling face hanging out of the window. "(We hear train noises) Marcella is waving. A series of windows with a series of grim face in green uniforms and hats all waving. Lots of cigarette smoke clouding the moment. "And we would yell goodbye and then go home feeling that something was awry, but never saying it aloud 'cause mother thought that speaking the hurt would jinx daddy. Every time he left, she would cry like crazy and we would all join her like mad, but we were forbidden to talk about it because Daddy would surely get shot up or killed over there. I hated him because he left. I hated him when he was home because he would be leaving any minute. He'd never tell us in advance, just the day before. And I hated him for deserting us even though I was a pretty girl who behaved and sat on his lap while he read the paper or watched TV, and I would just sit there for hours on end waiting with dread for him to say to me: 'Chicken, I've got a new assignment and I'm leaving tomorrow'. And hoping to God I would not hear it!"

6

A Gig for Denise

Nervous! She sits twiddling hair ends. Door opens: Jason Fierst bids her enter. Determined not to stumble over her long dress trailing just a bit above stiletto heels she is wearing. Breathes a sigh of relief as she manages the short distance to the front of his desk.

Jason has taken his place behind the ornate, Louis XIV desk with its gilt ornaments, the burnished acajou, the curved legs. He notices her glance. "It is old," he tells her. "It also has a secret drawer." Reaches to the side and presses something underneath the trestle on which the desk is supported and the side magically opens revealing a hidden compartment. "I don't keep anything in it," he adds. "I just enjoy knowing it's there." Picks up a file. "Denise," he begins, "you played moderately ably as assistant to Ari Bloom before the latter was hurried off to jail and finally offed." Pauses. "Paul Scudery was a friend of mine who died in real life under peculiar circumstances. Did he discuss any of this with you?"

"No," she says. "What peculiar circumstances?"

"He was infected with mad cow disease; few people know about this terrible thing. It has little, maybe nothing, to do with cows. He may have eaten tainted meat which started the disease, maybe not. There are cases, doctors believe, which rise spontaneously. Anyway, once you have it, you have but a year left to put your affairs in order. Paul had been a regular with us for some twenty years. We hated losing him. Pauses. But you seem to have gotten along well with him, right?"

"Yes. We didn't chat much outside of our script exchanges, I'm afraid."

"He was busy at the end," Fierst acknowledges, "and a sick guy to boot. Anyway, that's unimportant. Let's get back to you. Now that Ari has passed, I've given your situation some thought. At first, some considered phasing you out completely. But there are amongst our group those who believe you can bloom into a larger screen presence. I think you needed a more significant role in the show to see how well the public may glom on to you."

"I think so too," Denise answers.

"Thought you might. Anyway, after considerable screwing around and fudging of the script, we have a whole new avenue for you."

She sighs. "You mean I'm not fired?"

"Why would I ask you to change your hair color to red if you were fired? That would have been bizarre…although, if truth be told, I have done some looney things as director of Babylon Revisited."

"I hoped that was the case," she says tentatively.

"Ok, here's the deal. We extract the mouse out of you and convert you into a little sexpot. Can you chrysalis into a seductive, sexy slut, Denise?"

"Are you asking me whether I have sexy in my vocabulary?"

"No," Fierst crows. "No, no! I'm asking whether you can make men salivate when they see you walking down a hall, whether they get boners when they ingest your scent. If they brush against you, does their fantasy world morph into rainbows."

Blushing, Denise says. "I have had that effect on some men."

Jason looks at her intently. "I fucking bet you have. You may not be the bees' knees of pulchritude, but you certainly are pretty. The dress you are wearing perfectly complements your shape, your skin color, your make-up is right on. Looking at you, I am dampening urgings I last felt ten years ago.

"Thank you, sir," she says blushing still.

"We have an idea. We'd like you to play against the guy who brought you to my attention, your friend Roger. We have made of his role a focal point, a centrality. He will continue to play a private dick but we intend to cultivate the role, make it shimmer so to speak. Now, the story line: I won't tell you the whole thing. We don't entirely have the whole text under our control yet, but here's the nub. Something is about to happen which causes you to visit Roger."

"I'm concerned about something."

"Yes, you are, my dear. Yes, you are. And this will lead you and our viewers smack into the middle of outrageous conflict. He smacks his hands together joyfully. I'd like to run the first scene tomorrow. Can you absorb lines that quickly?"

"Of course," she responds.

He hands her a script. "Not just to recite. Lines learned without thought, without introspection, are meaningless. You might as well throw away the cupcake and eat the packaging. Remember, sweetie, in this script you are no longer a quaking duckie. Instead, you are full bodied person, a Venus flytrap simmering with sex, shedding leaping pheromones. To be near you is to cause lips to tremble, to force saliva into the mouth. Longing! Make us long for you, sweetie. Can you make us need to fuck you? If every stuntman, every cameraman wants to rip your pants to shreds, then we are on the threshold to achieving our goal. How will the public react to you? Men will pant. Women will be curious at first, then jealous, and, if we are on target, eventually murderous. They will find fault with you. So much fault! Yes, my dear, they will write us analyzing each and every imperfection. Ha! The more the better. They will microscope each and every strand of your hair. They will notice if your boobs are sagging. They will pray that you become bloated one week, and the next, that your waist disappears and you evolve into a straight as a rail hipless loser, thereby blunting your appeal to the men in their lives. But above all, they will find in you a model to emulate provided jealousy doesn't discard you first. Not that they themselves will be tossing off pheromones every five minutes. No, they wouldn't permit themselves to venture that far. But they will savor every conquest you make even as they roundly condemn your behavior. That is the conclusion we wish. If women view you as a love-hate object, then we will have scored bingo perfection."

"I'll certainly try," Denise says somewhat troubled by this recital. She has never thought of herself in this fashion. And yet, almost instantly she connects within herself to a spark that she knows she can produce, may light into a smoldering flame. Sensual I can do, she thinks, and sensuality will be the base of my sexuality.

"Don't try," Fierst responds, watching her work through her dilemma. "Live it. Breathe sex. Connect to the ring of longing that encircles all men. Nature programs men to fuck any feminine object that moves. Men's eyes should bulge when they see you. They will forget about fucking their wives, their mistresses, anyone else but you. We crave their bulging eyes. We are desirous of their wet pants. Men in your life will either have you or have their dicks singing their praises to you. Get me?"

"Yes sir," she says swallowing hard.

The following morning, Roger spies Denise practically running, catches up to her on set. "You're moving awfully fast," he says to her.

Smiling. "In a hurry to start my new role, Roger," she replies. "I've got to get to make-up."

"No more Roger," he smiles at her. "My shamus name is Armand, the French private gendarme."

She spins once around. The dress is tighter, revealing more of the curves, the boobs, the legs. "What do you think?" she asks him. "A rather sharp transition from my world with dolphins."

"Gorgeous", he responds.

"I have hardly seen you in the past weeks. I thought you were avoiding me," Denise responds with a pout.

"Not avoiding you. Working on the new role, a new structure, the new direction of the soap."

"Ok, Armand," she responds smiling. "By the way, my name now is Keely. How about dinner? We can talk about the new direction over a burger."

Two weeks later, cameras above her both left and right, Keely is standing outside a hospital bedroom, clearly nervous, anticipating the worst. Today, she is wearing jeans and a black turtleneck sweater. The hospital corridor is active. Nurses filing by chatting together, a stretcher with a young boy sitting up, smiling, waving. The sound of a computer squeaking life sounds.

Approaching her, Doctor Dextra, a young intern, removing a mask. "I really can't tell you much right now. At first, I thought she was ailing from the flu. But your sister… what's her name,

Alexandra?"

"Yes."

"Alexandra may not have the flu at all," he says studiously. "After a couple of days, she appeared to be improving, and suddenly declined into respiratory shock. We've been pumping her with oxygen ever since. We've also launched a battery of tests to determine her illness. But clearly, and here I just don't want to give you any premature bad news, her condition is considerably more serious than a simple flu." At this point, the doctor's face looks blank.

"But surely, you have some understanding as to what this is, doctor?" she demands.

"I'll let you know as soon as the tests come back." With that, he strides off. Keely enters Alexandra's hospital room. The young woman is attached to an IV and is breathing through an oxygen mask. The room is dark, quiet except for the occasional beeps emanated by the machine that governs her vital signs. Alexandra is twenty-eight years old. Keely knows her as generally a fit person, capable of withstanding a great deal of adversity. The young woman is wearing a light green hospital gown. Looks pale, her brow wrinkling now and then. Her present ailment has debilitated her more than anything Keely has ever witnessed in her sister.

"Hi, Alex", Keely begins quietly. She takes her sister's hand in hers, kisses her on the troubled forehead.

Alexandra opens her eyes. Her mouth moves without issuance of words.

"Try again," Keely whispers.

"I hoped you would come," Alexandra says with some difficulty.

"Don't get too excited", Keely cautions. "I don't want you

moving any part of you other than your mouth. Can you lie still?"

"Yes."

A smiling nurse enters with equipment, places a thermometer on the night-stand. She whispers into Keely's ear.

"Nurse," Keely remarks impatiently, "can you not see that my sister is feverish? Her forehead is hot as blazes. Don't you have a wet cloth to cool her down?" The nurse runs to the sink, retrieves a wet cloth and places it on the girl's forehead. "Good," Keely remarks pointedly. "Finally!" Then to her sister in a more soothing tone. "The doctor says you are going to come out of this fit as a fiddle," Keely lies. "They are running tests now. Can you tell me what happened?"

Alexandra tries to sit up. "No, no," Denise cautions her again. "Just lie flat."

"I can't tell you much," Alexandra offers through blistered lips. "God, I'm so happy you are here. I wondered whether the doctor or nurse would find you. Several days ago, I began to feel fluey. You know fever, muscle aches, that sort of thing. At first, I didn't think anything about it. Just thought I'd let it zip through me until I got better. But after a day of feeling ok, I had a relapse, trouble breathing and so I drove myself to the emergency room. They admitted me at once. That was a couple of days ago, I think. Time has a funny way of disappearing," she adds.

"Yes, Alex. How are you feeling?"

"Rough right now. Thirsty! Still feel awfully achy, still have trouble breathing on my own."

"You have an IV for fluids. Be a good patient," Keely admonishes her. "Stop fidgeting, and be still as you can be until they figure out what's behind this."

"Pneumonia," Alex prompts.

Keely shrugs. "I have no idea. But I'm not so sure the doctor knows either. I hope we don't have a newbie."

The smiling nurse re-enters and pulls around a soft white curtain. (The scene ends)

Later, still at the hospital, the next scene opens: Doctor Dextra finds Denise sitting on a bench. "I've got some news," he says. His voice seems a bit less fluid than before. Denise looks up. "Tests came back?"

"Yes," the doctor says. "But the news is not particularly good. Your sister has contracted hantavirus."

Keely stands up somewhat unsteadily. "What the hell is that?"

"We don't see a lot of this in our part of the world. Out west, it's a bit more frequent. Occasionally there is a run of it somewhere, but rarely in this area".

"Tell me what it is," she speaks forcefully, rubbing her eyes.

"It is a rather rare virus which, at first, simulates the flu. That's why it's often badly diagnosed. But after a while, it affects the respiratory system so egregiously that it can be only a handful of things."

"How did Alex get this?"

His hands rise idly. "We don't have the foggiest idea. Usually spread by contaminated mouse feces you either touch or possibly sniff. The virus can even affect you by breathing it in."

"That's absurd," Keely snorts. "Alexandra is one of the cleanest persons I know. Fastidious to a fault. No way she would allow mice in her apartment, much less contaminated with a potentially serious disease." A moment later, she adds pointedly: "I'm somewhat concerned that you and the hospital have not done everything possible to avoid this calamity."

The doctor does not respond to this. Pauses. Thinks a

moment, then speaks in a hushed tone. "I don't want her to know this, but it is possible that this disease is fatal."

Now Keely sits with a thud. "Fatal? You must be kidding. From mouse droppings? Doctor, this is impossible!"

"I am simply reflecting our experience," the doctor says looking at Keely fixedly.

"Hold that thought," Jason Fierst cries out. Cameras cease their whirring. "Actors relax, sit." Jason comes stampeding onto the set. "Look, Keely, your sister is a very sick person. Maybe going down the tubes, if you catch my drift. Do you?"

"Yes, Jason."

"So, your reaction is too tepid for the audience to believe in her morbidity. You are reacting to the news as if somebody informed you your horse lost the second race at Belmont. I do like your defiance of the doctor, however. He's not the god he would like us all to believe. But what happened to the smiling nurse, anyway? Contrast triumphs here".

Distressed, Keely looks up searching for a correct response. "You mean I ought to cry."

"Would help. Can you?"

Keely scoffs. "I can cry at the drop of a hat."

"Ok, then, run the scene again from the moment the doctor drops bad news on you."

"…. it's possible that this disease is fatal," Dr. Dextra repeats.

"Oh, my God," Keely says shaking and, unable to control her legs, slumps into her seat. She begins to weep. "From mouse droppings?" Don't we need a second opinion, doctor? This diagnosis is outlandish!" A nurse in a brilliant white uniform walks by giggling as she listens to her phone.

"Afraid our diagnosis is correct", the doctor responds quietly. I fully understand your alarm, your anxiety, and your sorrow.

I'm so sorry to have to tell you this, but the tests confirm our understanding. We'll do everything in our power, of course, to ease Alex's concerns."

"Thank you, Doctor," Keely says, trembling in her seat, and fluttering her eyelids as she continues to weep. She begins to dab at her eyes with a handkerchief.

"Much stronger," a voice echoes from off set. "Much more convincing. I am having trouble keeping myself from sobbing."

7

Artie the Carpenter

(Off-stage) "A letter from Daddy, girls. He's all right." Gabriella announces.

(Marcella center front) "And I didn't know how to react to that. (Pause) Overall, my childhood was wonderful. Hardly any pressure on me to do anything but be girly, do my chores, go to school. A time when girls expected to marry and marry early and, if you did, that very fact became a badge of distinction. Look at my engagement ring, we would cackle, thrusting it into the faces of our friends, and the ones who didn't have one would ooh and aah, and we knew who was jealous of us, particularly if the ring was big, shiny and a bit different-looking.

I never finished college because I met Rolf. He was good look-ing and came from a fine family and was Catholic, important then, and touched me where and when I wanted him to and, besides, he was generous. He designed buses for transportation systems, and even though his work bored me as he described this schematic and that ever-evolving blueprint, I knew he loved me and that was enough, wasn't it? Sure, it was.

For a while. And then, once the business grew, expanded, we moved into the shell of a grand new house and hired Artie Columbus to construct the insides while Rolf was at work. I stayed at home to help or sometimes just watched Artie do his magic."

(Benjamin enters from left) "What was he like?"

"Artie? A craftsman, not terribly good looking, maybe twenty years older than I was then." (She walks to a rear wall and fingers the wallpaper)

"So, he didn't appeal to you physically?"

"No, he didn't. But as I was wallpapering, from the corner of an eye, I could see him staring at me".

"And that was enough to turn you on?" (Under a nightstand, he locates a hammer, a two by four and a handful of nails. He brings them over to the center stage.)

"I had gotten used to the sounds of hammers on nails. In the heat of an afternoon, all I could really feel was masculinity. Artie would be standing in the afternoon sun sweating, the hammer rising and falling, rising, and falling in rhythmic blows."

(Benjamin takes a hammer and hits a nail)

"Artie, you must be hot." (She brings him a glass of iced tea)

(Benjamin as Artie) "It is a hot day," he says taking a hand towel and swabbing off the sweat from his chest. "I'm almost finished with this joist and then I'll get to the tea".

(Benjamin as himself) "He knew that you were looking at him. Why lust for such a man? How did he appeal to you?"

"I don't know," Marcella responds. "I was just sitting next to him with a swatch of wallpaper (She sits next to Benjamin on the floor). And he seduced me." (She wipes Benjamin's face with a cloth).

"He seduced you?"

"Yes."

"This fifty-five-year-old with a wife and three kids whose toad face was so plain that no woman other than his wife ever looked at him more than once. This is the man who seduced you?"

(Unbuttoning Benjamin's shirt) "You must really be hot."

(Benjamin slaps her face and rises) "He's a common laborer who finds himself day after day with an attractive, horny woman, but he never seduced you. He wouldn't have had the nerve. You, my dear, just couldn't keep your hands off him."

"That's not the way it was," she reacts sharply. (She arises, speaks to audience) "We had an affair. How? Why? I don't recall. One minute he was sweating carrying a 2 by 4 up a ladder, and the next he was removing my pants. Sex lasted just a month or two and then he was finished with his work and he…he was gone. Heartbroken, of course…. Yeah, I was heartbroken. That is until I met Jamie, some months later."

"Could have been anyone."

"Don't analyze me, Benjamin, you know nothing about it."

"I smiled at you in class, you returned my smile, but I also could have been anyone." (He gets up and, with his hand moves her face so that she is looking at him directly)

"I hate what you do to me. I don't want you touching me again," she spits.

(Turns again to audience). "Yes, Benjamin! We were acquaintances for a couple of years. He had a bit of a reputation. Lothario. I was intrigued, of course. I wanted to know more about him. I finally got up enough courage and took his class. He was great. In command. He had style, panache, something beyond what I had ever encountered."

(Shaking his head) "Could have been anyone!"

(Remembering) "He was wearing tight jeans. There was a stain on the right knee."

(Brings her face to him again) "Do you even remember my name?"

(Marcella is bewildered, still in her past). "Your name?"
(Shaking her) "My goddamn name".
"Benjamin. Yes, it's Benjamin. You are Benjamin."
"Shit." (He is disgusted and leaves stage right)
(Marcella turns to the audience) "I know what he's thinking. He thinks I'm fickle. But I don't really have men in my head, not half the time. How could I? I have my job and I have my child. Baby lives with her father now. But I still have to provide for her, nurture her, don't I? I have to go to the store this afternoon for nail polish, the right kind, the dark red rather than the pink. It suits me better. Oh, Jamie, what was the style of the polish you used to rave about? Which one was it? (Exits)

8

Armand, the Private Eye

"I'm so sorry," Dr. Dextra says, his eyes cowled. Keely reaches instinctively to take his hand. He can feel the moist warmth of this impressive woman. He pulls his hand back slowly. In his in mind, to touch anyone on duty feels improper, and he shrinks from it.

"Less than two weeks ago, Alex was in perfect health," she blubbers unnerved. (Shakes her head, begins to weep, her body heaving).

"We did everything, of course, but sometimes the infection is too advanced."

"I'm not blaming you," Keely says, sitting down. "And yet, I have a hard time believing the hospital did everything in its power to save my sister."

Dr. Dextra demurs: "I wish we could have done more. Of course, you are terribly upset. But you need to look to your sister herself for clues. This virus doesn't appear out of the blue. Somehow, she herself must have handled it, breathed it in. I'm terribly sorry, but we did all we could." Pause. "You can pick up her effects now or later," Dr. Dextra adds. "There will be a bit of paperwork as well at the desk."

"Thank you, doctor," Keely says. "It's just so inconceivable…."

Hesitates before leaving. "If you would permit me one last bit of advice," the doctor continues.

"Of course."

"There is something extraordinary about the way she became infected. We just don't see that sort of thing here in the east. So unusual, my colleagues concur that it may involve something other than a natural event."

"What do you mean?"

"I mean that someone may have induced the droppings into her apartment," he says putting up a hand in defense. "Of course, this is only a wild guess without anything solid to base it on. I probably have no right to discuss this at all, but I suspect the police will see this event as a natural passing. They often don't care to be bothered with what they don't understand. We are not so certain. You may want to take some time and look into the matter."

Nervously trying to grasp the meaning of what the doctor is conveying. "And how would I do that?"

The doctor shrugs. "Not entirely sure. You can, of course, press the police to investigate. Or, if you want to probe the matter by yourself, hire a private detective."

Keely looks at the doctor, her lips trembling. "You are implying that she may have been murdered."

"I'm not implying anything. Just telling you what I would do in your circumstances." As the doctor is turning to leave, a boy on a stretcher is wheeled towards the operating theatre. When he passes Denise, he holds up two fingers in a victory sign, but Keely is too cratered into her own thoughts to react.

For several days, she does nothing but work out the funeral arrangements. The event of her sister's passing seems unfathomable. Cannot get a grasp of it. She decides to go toward those things in her life over which she has some control. The funeral itself will be simple, limited to family and a few close friends. Alex will be cremated as she requested. Days pass before Keely emerges from the shock of the event. Unsure as to how she should react to the doctor's final words to her. Who would ever want to kill my sister? she thinks. She had no enemies. A sweet girl without antagonisms. The suggestion is insane!

Nonetheless, a week later, she calls the offices of Armand Desqueyroux and obtains an immediate appointment.

Armand welcomes her at the door. A tall, thin almost skeletal man with a short black and silver beard. Notices that he has no secretary. He intercepts this thought. "Never needed one," he says. "Of course, in the old days when we had a land line, somebody had to man it, and if the investigator was out of the office, a secretary or somebody else had to be around to answer the phone."

The office is paneled in a fake mahogany. She also notices that this man's desk is clean. All of this concerns her. Maybe I haven't come to the right place.

Then she scans Armand with his black and silver mane. Appealing enough, she thinks, although the man is dressed in jeans, a cardigan, and wears suspenders. She thought that only old men used suspenders. Shrugs as he begins to question her. "Start from the beginning?" he prompts.

Keely recites the events leading to and through the death of her sister. Armand is taking notes. Looks up from time to time as if he were about to interrupt Keely, but then stops until she has concluded her description.

"You think she had no enemies?" he asks.

"None that I knew of."

He scratches his light beard. "Everybody has an enemy or

two".

She looks up quickly. "Not very optimistic, are we?"

"No," he asserts. "Not very. Boyfriends?"

"Not recently."

"And you've been in touch with her to know this for a fact?"

"Yes, we were close?"

"Former boyfriends she ousted?"

"I'll give you their names. Only two. One lives in Europe now as far as I know. The other may be in town."

"Good," Armand says. She had a job?"

"Yes. Alex worked in a laboratory for the Pharynx Corporation."

He nods. "A lab. What kind of lab?"

"Drugs," Keely says. Throws up her hands in dismay. "But I don't really know much about her company."

"And her job?"

"She was a receptionist for the lab professionals. Made appointments for them, took messages, dictation, that sort of thing." Keely laughs. "Not really her style at all."

"Still she worked at a lab."

"Yes, but only because it was the best job she got without a college education."

"Ok," Armand says. "Talk to me about the people in the lab."

Keely looks up again. "In the lab? I maybe met one or two of them. But most of them I don't know. I think she said there are about fifteen who work on the floor, some of them with assistants."

"Got a name where I can start?"

"Yes. A Dr. Goldsmith. He's the one who hired her."

"Good. I'll start with him."

"What do you think?" she asks, beginning to stand.

"Whether there has been foul play? I have no idea. But I am intrigued by one thing. Your doctor says Alex must have been infected with mouse droppings. The doctor says no one has reported infected mice in this area. And then, unexpectedly a pharmaceutical lab appears in our story. Don't labs often use mice to run experiments?"

Keely falls back into her chair. "Yes, of course. I hadn't considered that."

Armand smiles. "That's why you came to me. Not that you couldn't see the connection because it is rather obvious as a starting off point, but because you are too decent to put the two together. Fortunately for you, I suck at decency. I almost always expect the worst."

"I guess that's important for your work, although to tell the truth I never thought I'd hear myself say anything like this."

9

Marcella and Benjamin Meet in France

(Jason Fierst in wings with Benjamin) "Roger, remember you are about to turn love-sick. You do get love-sick, don't you? Better prepare yourself for the 'sick' part. Gnashing of teeth is paramount in relationships because love almost always turns into something like milk turning sour."

"I have been love-sick," Roger answers.
"Yes, but I craver to see your eyes red, drops of spittle at the corner of your mouth and, of course, the piece de resistance, a permanent erection."
Roger laughs. "Should I run home for my Viagra?"
"You do get my drift, don't you, lad?"
"I do."
"Ok then, play the scene."

(Benjamin enters from left, to audience). "That fall, the school awarded me a sabbatical. I'm still not sure why. I did get a hint from President Jager. He called me in one day a few months before my award to ask about one of my students, a girl named Wendy who had graduated a few years previously. I remembered her very well. She had been my assistant and, if truth be told, we had been close. But not so close that I wanted anything from her after she left. She used to call me from Asheville and ask me whether I would like to spend the weekend with her, but I always declined. Politely. Still, I declined. Somebody we jointly knew claimed she had fallen in love with me. Then I learned that one day riding in Central Park, she had been bucked off her bolting horse and broke her neck. Died on the spot. She had received an inheritance from her father's estate, a legacy which remained virtually intact and which mysteriously she left entirely to the college. Jager was enormously pleased, and attributed the windfall to my charm. So maybe this was my reward for a job well done. Of course, I took credit for it. Strangely enough, despite Jager's problems with faculty and students enjoying improper relationships, this one he didn't question or seem to mind. In fact, he even coyly asked me how close Wendy and I had been…but did not press me for any of the details. So, thanks to Wendy's infatuation, I was on my way to Paris to write a book on the French revolution, and the connection of the revolution to our war of independence. Marcella drove me to the airport. Sobbing. (He picks up a suitcase)

(Marcella entering just behind him, weeping)

"Thanks for the new suitcase, Benjamin says. It's perfect. Just what I needed. Walk with me to security. (To center stage)

"I can't handle it, Marcella says. "I hate to say goodbye."

"We won't be apart long," Benjamin responds sweetly. "You'll fly over at Christmas and I'll be home in a couple of months after that."

"It'll be endless," she pouts.

A crowd of revelers forge their way between them jostling one another to the security lines.

"Isn't it important for us to see how we are for a time without each other?"

"I know I'll miss you terribly," Marcella says.

"Me too." (They hug)

(Benjamin to audience as he waves goodbye to Marcella) "I hated leaving. We had now been intimate for months, and I could honestly say that I had fallen in for her. Despite my resolution to take it slowly, I was in love. I remember times when we were intertwined, I almost fainted from the ecstasy of the moment. Boy, was I hooked! I just caved, didn't I? As time went by, there was less and less mention of Jamie. I thought Marcie was getting over him and really connecting to me. Like all men, I thought I had something exceptional to offer which would make her forget former lovers. I thought of myself as someone who had lived purposefully, who had contemplated life in all its peculiarities, who had survived love and its loss. Survived even loneliness and lovesick despair. So, what would this woman, any woman, require other than an exemplar like me?" (Marcella turns before exiting) "Goodbye, Ben," she calls out. "Take care of yourself and watch out for the French floozies!" (Exits)

Benjamin lowers the suitcase. "Can you imagine anyone having a lousy time in Paris? Sure, I did my work. I had begun to write a book on the psychology of space in the French novel of the 18th century. I sat in the Bibilotheque Nationale mornings, took a bus home to my little studio in the arrondissement of Montmartre, did some writing before dinner and, evenings, incessantly walked the streets. I was hungry to digest the city completely. Couldn't get enough of it. Hours on end, up to Sacre Coeur, down from the Basilica to Pigalle and along the Clichy accosted by tourists, trollops, or transvestites on every corner. But when I tucked it in at night, I could not sleep for thinking about Marcie. I emailed her every day. Heartfelt longing for her. At first, my texts were returned with fervor. Time passed, and things changed. As time passed, I began to receive some very general, disappointing, sporadic correspondence from her. Emails became flighty, vague even, as if she were watching a show on TV while texting or emailing. I became upset about it." (Moves to left wing)

(Marcella entering from right, reading an email) "He says he can't live without me. Can I live without him? I'm doing exactly that right now. I have my work. Do I even think about him except for these daily emails? Sure, our first weeks together were intense. But since then…. yes, the emails are sweet enough, they flatter me, he writes damned well. But underneath, do I truly care?"

(Benjamin returning to stage) "Here's the latest excerpt. (Takes out a sheet from his pocket). 'I got up this morning and did my nails except for the pinky which was kind of scraped. I went to work without painting it. Looked funny, pink, and stubby'. (Benjamin looks up) Is this romance?"

(Marcella to audience) "He wants me to fly over at Christmas. Of course, I will. I do want to see him, but I know what's on his mind. Commitment. I'm not ready to get remarried. I'm not even divorced."

(Benjamin pacing and banging one fist into the other) "What the hell is she thinking?"

(Marcella sitting, speaks to audience) "It takes forever to balance a checkbook. I wonder whether Benjamin is better at it. I've never told him this, but what I dislike most about the man is that he chews popcorn loudly in the movies. Distracting and embarrassing."

(Benjamin to audience) "Time dragged. Suddenly, despite my

inner turbulence, Christmas finally arrived. I found myself at the airport. Her plane was delayed, and I was smoking Gauloises a mile a minute, and knew if she smelled them on me, she'd be furious. And then there she was just as I remembered her. Despite her fatigue, she looked stunning. She had made herself up carefully before going to the baggage claim. She had also brought a gift. A new tablet for me. (Marcella enters) We hugged speechlessly, and then we both talked at once. I picked up her bags and rode the taxi to my studio holding hands. We had stupid shit eating grins on our faces. Her hand was tiny in mine. It never stopped moving, a soft nail exploring the center of my palm. Took the elevator upstairs, opened the wrought iron gate, turned the corner to my little apartment."

"I like your studio," Marcella remarks. "Small, but it has a cute kitchenette. And that funny, flecked, heron and eagle wallpaper in the bathroom. It's so precious."

(Benjamin removing bits of her clothing. Hat, scarf, jacket) "It's been three months, three long months. (Kisses her neck)

"You've been smoking those awful French cigarettes. Your hair reeks of black tobacco."

(Turns her and kisses her) "I was nervous. I needed to touch her, to connect with her flesh."

"Look at the bed, Marcie. It's like a postwar French car held together with rubber bands."

(Marcella up and down on the bed) "Am I the only woman who's touched this bed'" she asks grinning.

(Diving onto the bed with her) "It's a virginal bed. (They kiss again). "It needs to be deflowered," I said.

(To audience) "We made love. Then and again later. That night once more and also the following morning. Occasionally, we would set out for a restaurant, drink some Saumur wine, and then decide we needed a nap to recover. We would dash home and find ourselves in one another's arms. Or we'd start out by the Seine, but couldn't resist longer than twenty minutes before we had to return home to enmesh into the other."

(Marcella to audience, smoothly, lovingly, a hint of amazement in her tone) "He was a changed man. Hardly any talk. No philosophizing. No analyzing. Thank God! Just lovemaking. He did it ferociously and, each time I sank deeper and deeper into the spell of flesh, as if there was no bubbly city of lights out there, nothing else but the cigarette scent of his body, the touch of his hair grazing me, his aura. After a couple of days, we were exhausted, almost speechless, but we continued as if nothing else mattered. Like two teenagers. There was a moment when I looked down to see him across the end of the bed kissing each of my toes. (Benjamin does this), and the hair on my head curled up as if nothing else mattered in the world but our physical union. Suddenly, I felt an all-embracing warmth. (With wonderment) Damn! It sure felt like love."

(To Benjamin, still at her toes) "I think you missed one."

(To Marcella) "Then I'll just have to start all over."

"This was a hungry man. I developed a new respect for him. I always sought out his mind, for the way he used it intrigued me, but all at once he morphed into a body on fire. He loved me the way I needed to be loved. Then, just as it felt as if we had achieved a new beginning, the week ended."

(Benjamin sitting up on a bed, pleading). "We'll change your ticket back. Just three more days."

"But I should go back to work," she protests.

"Isn't this better than work?"

"Infinitely, but neither of us can keep this up much longer. I'm walking bowlegged, and my nipples are bursting through my sweater. Everyone in Paris knows what we've been up to."

"Three! No, just two more days," he pleads.

(Lovingly) "Finish your book. I'll be at the airport when you come home in a couple of months. (Playfully) "But if you come home stinking of Gauloises, I won't let you touch me."

(Benjamin, to audience) "A happy moment. I felt I had triumphed. Waged war against her indifference, and had won. I couldn't stand it ending. (To Marcella) By the time I come home, your divorce will be final."

Marcella kisses him on the neck to end the scene.

10

A Picnic in the Park

"What are you doing Sunday?"

"Running lines as usual. Just trying to keep up with the show's requirements. Pretty stringent at times. I could use a little work on the blocking as well."

"Good," Roger responds, "you'll have hours for all of that, but let's take some time together Sunday. How about a picnic in the park?"

"Fine," Denise responds. Confused, she hesitates to say more. On the one hand, she has made it plain to Roger that she would like to have a more significant physical connection, and yet each time she alludes to it, each time she brushes up against him or shows him skin or affection, he seems to miss the signals or, worse, avoids a response. Still, he is not distancing himself from her. Clearly, he wants to spend time with her, and that deepens the frustration, the confusion. Occasionally, he has suggested they go to dinner. Or to a movie. Or, this day, a picnic. So, he wants to spend time with me, she says, but not physically? I'm not in the habit of offering myself repeatedly only to be rebuffed over and over. "All right," she relents, at last. "A picnic. What shall I bring?"

"A bottle of red."

"Done," she says. "What are you bringing?"

"KFC chicken, fries, corn, muffins, and napkins. If you don't mind, we'll eat with our fingers."

She smiles. "I don't mind at all. I could even poke at the food with my beak, if you like," she adds gaily.

Roger has brought a large picnic basket and stuffed it with food and napkins. They are moving slowly together through the grass towards a picnic area. From time to time, Denise glances over at Roger. What does this guy want? she ponders. Apparently not me...maybe just a small slice of me. She stifles a giggle as she imagines herself slicing pieces off for him.

"What's so funny?" he asks her.

"Just remembering something from my childhood," she lies.

They find a well-worn table, brush off a tiny colony of intruder ants. Daffodils are blooming near them behind a low wrought iron fence. The day is clear, bright, cool but not cold. Denise removes her sweater and places it underneath her. She is wearing scotch plaid shorts. Always had good legs, she thinks to herself as she examined them that morning. Could be Roger needs to see my set of pins. Up close! She looks over at him: jeans, a t-shirt without imprint (Roger hates to give free publicity to anyone), loafers without socks. Relaxed. He pulls open the wine carefully. Pours it into plastic glasses.

"Elegant, eh?" he smiles at her.

She chortles. "The Ritz!"

They consume the chicken, fries, some bread. He has neglected to bring a dessert and she chides him for the omission. "I like sweet things you know", she confides.

He pumps himself up. "Present." With a smile, she pretends to slap him across the face.

"So, tell me about the role. You've been at it for weeks now.

66

Do you feel like you're fitting in?"

"I think it's meaty," she responds. I'm even beginning to get some fan mail."

"A lot more if you stay with it," he responds.

"Sometimes, I wish I had more direction".

"From Jason?"

"From anyone. I'm not always so sure of myself that I feel I'm doing a good job."

"He would tell you," Roger snorts. "Trust me on this, if he felt you were fucking up, he would be all over your ass. You would be the first to know."

"Then I'm glad…and relieved."

"I didn't know you were so fragile."

"I'm an actress," she responds. Isn't that an admission of vulnerability?"

"I guess it is," he smiles, "although there are several who seem to hide theirs effectively."

"But there is something else," she continues. "Something else I would like to know." The air around them crackling with the odd prattle of children playing and adults calling out to them now seems dramatically hushed. As if some deity had sucked sound from the planet.

"I'm listening."

"It's about you and me."

"Oh," he says, his eyes darkening. Pause. Moistens his lips, rubs his eyes slowly. "I wondered when that subject might arise."

"It's between us always. Even when we picnic."

"What do you want to know?"

"How you feel about me."

He is looking down, to the left, then to the right. She takes his chin and positions his face towards her.

"You are asking why I don't hit on you."

"Yes. You're not secretly gay, are you?" Then she chortles at once, her words stupidly hollow, even meaningless.

"Not at all. But I do things my own way."

She seems somewhat bewildered by this response. "Is that an excuse which you hide behind...like I really don't like this chick, but instead of telling her what between actors may seem a bit ruthless, I'll fib. I'll pretend that I am an iconoclast.

"This is what I mean," he says now speaking with authority: "I take events in my own time. It rarely coincides with anybody else's structure. I am aware of that. I like you, Denise. I care for you. I worry about you."

"Worry about me." Really?"

"You bet. I brought you into the circus. I feel responsible. Caring too," he adds.

"But you don't want to kiss me".

He glances across at her sharply. "I didn't say that."

She looks up at him in wonderment. "Explain yourself."

"I do want to kiss you, but I don't want it leading to a premature situation."

"So, kissing is ok, but sex is out of the question?"

"It's a timing issue. Things have a way of leading to the other and suddenly the whole world is out of kilter."

"So, I should wait for you."

"I didn't ask you to do that."

Now she is angry. "You don't want me to wait, but you tell me you would like to kiss me. I'm confused."

"I often have that effect."

"You are fucking strange," she says, biting her lower lip.

Now, he reaches over, takes her face in two hands and pulls her close to him. He kisses her, a sweet, lovely, prolonged kiss.

Relishes it at first. "But there is no passion behind this," she says, recoiling somewhat. "It's sweet without pushing any limits."

"You can't be asking me to give what I don't want to give," he says.

"The picnic has come to a dramatic end," she responds controlling her voice, modulating her anger.

"I'm sorry you cannot take me in stride. I have never asked you to do anything, least of all to wait for me to come around. I'm a trifle slow in that department," he adds. "I'm fully aware of that. So, if you are dating others, I kind of expect that."

"And you?" she asks, standing with the blanket, and folding it. "Are you dating others?"

"Not right now", he avers. "Not now."

"But you would like to."

He shrugs. "If I met someone in whom I was interested, probably yes. I don't feel that I am committed elsewhere."

"You have made that abundantly clear," she says with steel in her tone.

"Please don't be angry with me," he says, opening the picnic basket. "I didn't say that well".

"There is a garbage can by the fence," Denise responds, pointing to it. Roger packages the debris and deposits it. "I'm angry with myself," she says, when he returns. "I misread you. I took your interest in me as personal. Like when a boy sees a girl he wants to be with."

"But it is," he claims quickly, "it truly is. I think you are beautiful, splendid. Of course, I value you as an actress as well. I'm watching you grow into a part I hoped you would take to. I'm fascinated."

"But not horny", she adds.

"Just careful", he answers. "I've had bad effects from jumping too quickly into love. I don't need that kind of crushing existence."

"So, you have been in love?" she asks.

"Yes. Dramatically."

"Away from the theatre?" she persists.

"In it, away from it, above it, under it. Everywhere. I was young once and terribly innocent and giving. I got my heart thumped several times. I learned that people don't always know what they say they crave. They seize the moment. Sometimes that is good, sometimes it wounds. Sometimes it cripples. I had a tortured heart. So, I learned not to indulge every time I had a hard on."

She shakes her head in wonderment. "Unusual for a guy," she says almost scoffing. "The men I've met stem from the same pattern." Once they spy legs spreading even a tiny bit, they go for it, they can't be stopped. Reason surely never prevents them from pursuing sex even when abundantly clear that they will never reach their goal."

Walking out of the park onto Columbus Circle. "If you think I am worth it," Roger confides after a momentary pause, "then wait. I give no guarantees. I interact, I observe, and then and only then, I act. It may be in the fashion you want, maybe not."

"Pretty fucking reasonable," Denise scoffs. "Yet there are dimensions on earth beyond reason", she pouts.

He kisses her again lightly on the lips. Opens her eyes. "I liked that."

"So, did I," he concludes. "So, did I". Smacks his lips slightly.

"Sure, you haven't overcome your inhibitions right now?" she asks hopefully.

He looks as it with slight disdain. "You heard me, sweet girl.

You heard me loud and clear."

"Nothing wrong with my hearing," she replies sadly.

11

Benjamin Returns Home

(Marcella, lovingly to Benjamin) "Finish writing your book. I'll be at the airport when you come home in a couple of months. (Playfully) But if you come home stinking of Gauloises, I swear I won't let you touch me."

(Benjamin to audience) "A happy moment. I felt I had triumphed. I had waged war against her seeming indifference, and had won. I didn't want it to end (To Marcella). By the time, I'm home you may already be divorced."

"It's about final now," she says. "Just some paperwork is incomplete." (She gets up, walks to stage right).

(Benjamin arising, to audience) "Those last months in Paris passed quietly for me, even happily. I thought I had won Marcella, had triumphed on the bedding field. She would call me each week and sounded the way I thought a woman in love sounded. Desperate. When I returned to take up my teaching duties, to share with classes the research I had done, she was there. (Benjamin moves to stage right)

(Marcella is at a desk. Benjamin speaks to his class) "If we had bought cheaper British tea, there might not have been a revolution. At least not at that time. But what was it we Americans wanted"

"Independence from a tyrannical, colonial empire," Marcella recites dutifully.

"A pretty straightforward notion, Benjamin agrees. "You want me to pay taxes, then I'll have to agree to pay them and I'll have certain expectations of my own. But if you levy taxes against my will, what other than force obliges me to pay? You can't influence the will of a people by threats, not over the long run." Ok, so let's take a short break."

(Class finished, Marcella gets up. Benjamin speaks to her) "You and I need to talk. I've been back a couple of months and every time I bring up the subject of us living together, you avoid it. Frustrating. It's frustrating the hell out of me."

"I know."

"But that's no answer. Are we going to live together or not?"

"Benjamin," she intones softly, "I need more time."

"What for? Either you want to do this or you don't. Doesn't living together make sense for us?"

"It's more complicated," Marcella responds. "You know that I like being with you. I think about you much of the time, but what happens if you move in with me? You know my life; how active it is. I have my child, I love to go out and see friends and do things. While you, well, you're more scholarly, even isolated. You stay at home and read. It's what you enjoy doing. You'd like me by the fireplace with you, preferably on the floor by your side, but that's not my way."

"You're selling me short, Marcella. I want this relationship, and I'm more than willing to do what's necessary to make it work. If that means developing into a social butterfly, then I'll buzz along with you flower to flower."

"I need to think about that," Marcella responds. (She sits down slowly at the desk)

Benjamin addresses the class: "Dictators have learned one precious bit of information from history. If you intend to plunder your society without repercussion, you must keep the citizenry afraid and hungry. A society grubbing for edible roots doesn't have the time or energy, not to speak of military resources, to strike back at you in a violent way. Too busy scratching for essentials. But once you provide them the staples of life, then watch out. People are greedy for their own account, and with time and energy to demand more, you can be sure they will."

(To audience) "What was she afraid of?" I've been back for three months from Paris and she's stalling. A relationship that doesn't move forward will crawl to a halt." (Walks to edge of wings right and returns with two epees).

"I've learned that I need more than bare necessities," Marcella intones to the audience. "He offers me love. I do need that. And yet, isn't love a rope that binds your body, inhibiting acting freely?" Don't I finally have an opportunity to experience my womanhood? Crap, I'm really confused."

(Benjamin gives her an epee. The walk together to center stage. He holds his epee upright covering his face) "We'll begin with thrusting."

"What fun," Marcella shouts.

"Lunge at me," Benjamin commands.

"Hmm... you have more practice at lunging than I do."

"Be serious," he admonishes her. "Try it once. Aim for my heart. (She does and he deflects her sword) Thrust and parry!"

"I feel awkward," she says. "You thrust and I'll parry."

(Lunges and her, she deflects it) "Don't worry. I would have missed you."

(Looking at epee, Marcella pouts) "I'm not quite comfortable

74

with this."

"One more time," he says with steel in his voice. "You do it. (She drives the epee to his chest. He does not try to stop her) You could have pierced my heart had you wanted to."

"I'm beginning to enjoy this game," Marcella laughs. "But you made no effort to parry. It's not fair."

"Just practicing." Once again, he encourages her. "Bend your knees, but don't crouch. That's it." (She thrusts and again he makes no effort to stop her sword)

"I could make a very painful hole in your love life if I wanted to," she giggles.

"That you could," he smiles.

"Still it feels incomplete."

"The next step is to penetrate my flesh. Is that what you would like to try next?"

"I've already done that," she speaks unsteadily. "I'm feeling queasy now." (Lowers her epee, takes his hand and she exits alone stage right).

(Benjamin to audience) "I didn't exactly hound her, but I often brought up the subject. As she resisted, my juices flowed against some obstinate dam. I wanted to marry her. I coveted her image day and night, carrying it around in my head like a bright illumination. I couldn't stand those evenings when, after a movie or dinner with friends, we made love and she made me get up, dress at three, then drive home. She claimed she was concerned about her about-to-be-ex finding us together and using it in the final push to the divorce. Then, just as I thought I might be making progress, that maybe I was breaking through her resistance, she devastated me.

12

The Private Eye Makes Several Phone Calls

"Thanks for giving me Alex's phone," Armand says to Keely.

"It had a bunch of phone numbers on it. I hope it will be useful."

"Checked it out. It has been useful already. Found a few phone calls she made just before she died. I'm following up."

"How about Dr. Goldsmith?"

He chuckles. "Thought you might ask about that. I did call him and, furthermore, I recorded it. Just a sec. He plays the recorder. 'Dr. Goldsmith, he begins, my name is Armand Desqueyroux. Keely Rosen hired me. We re inquiring about Alexandra Rosen and, specifically, anything you might be able to tell us about her unusual death.'"

Pause. 'Yes, Dr. Goldsmith says finally, even softly, 'we were so sorry to hear about Alexandra's passing. She was a valued employee and, from what I hear, a very fine person.'

'So, you did not know her personally'

'I never met the lady,' Dr. Goldsmith says.' I understand that she died from hantavirus. Such a death is most unusual. We have recorded no such deaths here in the past three years other than hers.'

'You were her employer?'

'Yes, but as you can fully understand, this corporation hires hundreds. I may have initially approved her employment, but I would not have been her direct supervisor.'

'And that would be?'

'Give me a second, please while I pull her up on the computer. Yes, she worked under Dr. Farras. If you would like to speak to Farras, that of course can easily be arranged.'

'I would like to speak to him…perhaps at a later time…can you tell me whether you are working on the hantavirus in your firm?'

'We are indeed,' Dr. Goldsmith replies. 'We are working on several series of viruses, hantavirus being one of them.'

'Even though there are so few incidents of the virus here that it can't be worth much to you.'

He laughs in a quick gulp. 'Yes, but in Asia there are literally hundreds, thousands of cases… Eventually, the virus may become extremely important. We are trying to find a vaccination for it or a cure.'

"So that was what Dr. Goldsmith contributed," Armand concludes.

"So, they are studying hantavirus at Pharynx," Keely says. "That means that somewhere close there may be samples of the virus that someone could obtain."

"Possibly."

"And then did you get on to Farras?"

"I did," Armand confirms." And, as is my habit, I recorded that conversation as well. I need to tell you that I thought Dr. Goldsmith considerably more open than Farras. I found Farras defensive."

"Let me hear that conversation."

He starts the recorder. 'Dr. Farras, I was given your name by Dr. Goldsmith. We're looking into the death of Alexandra Rosen.'

Pause. 'Why would you want to do that'" Farras asks in a stilted tone. 'She died a natural death.'

'So, you are aware of how she died.'

'I am'

'And?'

'And what?'

'You have nothing to add about her passing from a hantavirus which, as I understand it, is the area of your expertise...and Alexandra was also working in this area, no?'

'A simple coincidence,' Farras says forcefully. 'Pure coincidence'

'It is my understanding that this virus is almost non-existent in these parts, and here one of your employees dies of the virus, and you call that a coincidence'

'There is no other explanation. I can assure you that no samples of the virus left this lab.'

'How can you be certain?'

'Because we keep tabs on this virus and all others under our control. You can imagine that each sample that leaves our lab is catalogued. There is no record of hantavirus out of our control.'

'Couldn't be smuggled out?'

'Mr. Desqueyroux, now you are truly reaching. Yes, impossible to be smuggled. There are codes that only a few people know to each sample, and there would not have been any motive or reason to move a sample.'

"So," Armand continues, "you see that Dr. Farras did not quite convince me."

"Or me," Keely adds. Good work. I assume you followed up.'

Armand glances up at her. —-I raised the matter with other colleagues of the good doctor."

"What do you do now?"

"I need to find out exactly where the samples are, who has access to them, and go from there," Roger adds.

"So, you believe that this is not an accidental death."

"Don't you?"

"Too strange to be accidental."

"We need to find a motive," Armand says.

"Cut, stop. Stop this scene right now, Jason Fierst yells, just as Keely is about to recite a line. "Look, Armand, you are a detective working on a murder. It isn't the theft of a stick of gum.

"I get that," Armand says trying not to sound defensive.

"But you speak as if this assassination is of little import. To Keely it is everything. This is her sister we are talking about. You need to be more assertive. Remember, you are trying to convince her that your hunt is digging up results, not just endless speculation. And Keely, a little more feeling in your responses won't hurt either. This is your close relative and she has just been fucked over by the Big One never to be seen again."

"Not sure what I can do," Keely says in a terse response. "The lines don't allow much emotional divergence."

"Are you an actor?"

To this Keely has no answer, rouges, and simply slumps into the security of a chair.

13

The Return of Pascal

(We are in Benjamin's living room, stage left. Dali and Miro etchings grace the walls. A blue damask sofa. Two armchairs. A coffee table crammed with papers and piles of books. Benjamin is on the sofa plopping a pillow behind his back, smoking. Pascal turns towards him)

"I haven't seen you since you were working on your book in Paris. Did you complete it? Publish it? You hardly write, you don't call. You're mainly out of sight like our evasive French squirrels."

Benjamin grimaces. "You don't know my life, sweetheart. I'm slaving in the vineyards of higher ed, trying to drum some semblance of the past into my charges. I've given up on the book. Not enough time, not enough tranquility to complete it. But I'm always pleased to see you, Pascal. You came to visit, and this in and of itself is a rarity."

"A couple of months away from the sport of soldiering. Ben, do you recall how we used to talk about our future? In our younger years, everything seemed so clear. A straight and unending carpet was laid out for us to stride over."

"Pascal, your path came about easily, I thought. You craved military life. You wanted to promote France wherever she laid a foothold in the world, and you've managed all of that."

"True," Pascal retorts, "but I've gotten tired of killing. You shoot some guy one day. Tomorrow he turns into your ally, maybe even could have been your friend. But now it's too late to retrieve his body, much less his soul."

"I always thought it was a waste," Benjamin agrees. "Still, you used to take pride in the killing. How you could do it so well, even methodically, I found electrifyingly immoral."

Pascal snarls pleasantly. "Always useful to have somebody judge you who doesn't know shit about it. If the killing had a useful aim, I found morality in it. Nowadays, I've had to re-evaluate. Mind you it's not the taking of a human life that bothers me. Go on, check your atlas, killing is normal everywhere. The more sophisticated societies like ours have elevated it to a normal course of daily life, like eating, breathing and farting. No, we all owe God a death, don't we? It just depends when and where we are called to pay that debt. Put it into context. Some politician decides it's in the best interest of France to fly in troops to some desolate spot in West Africa. Who are the enemy? The ones la France has labeled bad guys. We shoot at them and they return fire. We don't know shit about them, and they haven't figured out why the fuck we bombed them."

"A good soldier doesn't question, we learned, you and I. Rule number 1," Benjamin avers.

(Pensively) "Of course," Pascal concurs. "I react that way most of the time. Only when I stop to clean the blood and guts off my bayonet do I occasionally puzzle about the uses of war. (He snaps out of it) Anyway, that's an enigma I still should resolve. As for you, my friend, you look good. All goes well for you?"

"Don't you remember that I always spruced up when times

were rotten?" Benjamin smiles. "Her name is Marcella."

(The scene shifts. As Benjamin and Pascal remain seated, enter Marcella and Janice Johnson from stage right. Janice is a southern woman in her late thirties, an art instructor at the college and clearly, a good friend of Marcella. There is a table where the two sit).

"Ah, yes. The fuckable female of the moment," Pascal says knowingly.

"They all want you servile and reeking sex, while afterwards they complain that you're boring," Janice says to Marcella. "How could I not be boring if I saw no one for weeks besides my boyfriend? When you and I were growing up," Janice asks, "didn't we have similar expectations? That some sweet prince would ride through our garden and steal us away from our childhood. That was our mission – to wait for Mr. Jackass. Shoot. A funny thing happened while we were waiting. For one thing, we took the time to observe our parents' marriages which didn't look so splendid, even those that survived. So, I joined the woman's movement. Screw the male sex, I thundered! I flowered in the bath of my own worth independent of men. For a few shining moments, anyway."

"And I married Mr. Right," Marcella adds, rubbing her eyes, "when suddenly everything I had been groomed for collapsed around me. Mr. Right wasn't so right at all."

"And I married the same guy," Janice replies ruefully.

"Four times, wasn't it?" Marcella laughs. "It's hard to keep up with you."

"Four is the number," Janice laughs. "In fact, I'm working on bachelor number five. He's into pork bellies and steers," he says.

"The woman I love," Benjamin complains: "I can't get her to commit to me."

"Mistake number one," Pascal avers… "Get her to commit to you? What a silly notion. She either does or she doesn't. Why do you love this woman?"

"Why do you bother marrying them?" Marcella asks Janice.

"I don't know," Janice responds with a guileless look on her face." I guess because they ask me really nicely. I do love them, each of them, but finally, belatedly, I realize I can live without them. I ought to live without any of them. They're like furry little animals. Snuggle up, settle in, and what they want from us is nothing short of everything. It's too damn much. Screw that!"

"Men are an insensitive lot," Marcella snorts.

(Benjamin to Pascal) "You never change. You chat them up, you go to bed with them, but you prefer to engrave notches on your memory rather than in your heart."

"Out for a good lay when they get horny," Janice says contemplatively. "But never before a good meal. They prefer to eat first. Satisfies hunger and stokes up the flames with energy. Mornings, they leave with a cheery injunction: 'Fix up the house, Janice, and while you're painting the bedroom, I'll be bringing home the bacon'. Like that is all a man must do, like he tracked down and slew a moose because he brought home a half pound of ham."

"I'm so conventional," Marcella sighs, "I like a man to bring home bacon. So, what's gnawing at me? Maybe in our thirst for our independence, we went too far, Janice."

"So then convert me," Pascal says.

Benjamin waxing poetic in memory: "She's feminine. She's a woman. She's soft."

(Janice becoming more vehement) "Women's liberation? You mean learning to prosper without men?" I don't think so, but I'm not certain. For a while, I forgot about my needs. I do like having their arms around us from time to time. We do need their arms. Not sure about the rest of them."

"So, what are we supposed to be? Daddy's little girl always catering to daddy? Or out there trying to beat them to the punch, to equal them, to best them, to do a better job, to receive a more equitable division of labor at home?"

"Probably all," Janice replies. "What are you going to do? Be Benjamin's little girl or be your own woman?"

Pascal grins. "And in bed?"

"It makes my mouth water to think of her."

"So far, you're just describing a hottie. What else does she bring you?"

"How's this for contentment," Benjamin says. "You ask her what she wants to do tomorrow night, and she replies: 'Anything you want, as long as I'm with you'. I can take her to a pool hall and even though she clearly doesn't want to play, she has fun. I have fun. She listens to me, she's sympathetic to my worries. She is one of the few women I have met who doesn't talk endlessly about herself. Or simply talk endlessly. She is concerned about my life, my state of being."

Pascal laughs. "You always did like to interpret everything. Maybe she simply has nothing to say. An empty vessel."

The comment startles Benjamin. "Damn, I don't know. I never thought of her that way."

Marcella looks up at Janice wistfully. "I love Benjamin, I think."

Pascal moves in closer. "What do you really know about her, this woman you cherish? What are her darkest fears, those moments in the night when shadows creep over her heart? Which is the fantasy man she thinks of when terror strikes?"

Janice takes Marcella's hand. "I know the feeling. It's like hold me, baby, but give me some breathing room from time to time."

"You can't separate your head from your groin," Pascal insists.

"I need time to think us through," Marcella replies darkly.

"Benjamin," Pascal reiterates, "who is this woman?"

"Well," Janice says supportively, "give yourself time then, lots of it."

"She may not be introspective," Benjamin insists, "but I do know who she is."

"I've got to get away for a while," Marcella says suddenly rising and fidgeting with her hair. "I can't stand it anymore."

"Tell me about Marcella's commitment to you," Pascal continues to probe.

"She isn't committed to me. Not yet. Fuck, I don't really know."

"So, go," Janice encourages her.

"Just give me an hour," Pascal retorts." I'd find out what makes this woman tick."

"He'll be angry," Marcella says, with doubt in her voice.

"Daddy will be angry," Janice mocks. "How about Marcella's needs?"

"I'm making progress in fits and starts," Benjamin says. "I believe she loves me but isn't ready to commit. "

"That should make you angry."

"You're right," Marcella concludes." I have an uncle who lives in Miami. He's always wanted me to spend time with him. Maybe now would be just perfect."

Pascal is whipping himself up into an angry state as he beholds his friend's confusion. Benjamin is on a stool, head in his hands, unsure of who or what he is and what this relationship connotes. "Poor baby," Pascal intones, sardonically." Always ready to change people. You don't accept what is right in front of you. Do you recall the somnambulist you hoped to hypnotize so that he wouldn't stalk around the dormitory at night? You can bet he's still roaming. Women don't change either. Uncertain, fickle, foolish and, like the rest of us, they are totally lost in the swirl of competing needs in their lives. Let it go. If it was meant to happen, it will."

"She's leaving," Benjamin says sadly, "for a couple of weeks. Apparently to get away from me."

"I do need to sort myself out," Marcella says with the beginning of a confident tone in her voice. "I do need time to myself."

"You need to act, baby, but act now," Janice replies (They both get up and exit right)

14

Roger and Denise at the Museum of Art

The massive building, its concrete steps to the entrance, seem even sturdier than he remembered it. Partially cloudy today as they near. Puffed up clouds above lazily drifting southward. He takes Denise's hand to climb the steps.

"Haven't been in here for a good while, Roger remarks. But his face expresses contentment.

"I've never looked at 17th century Dutch paintings," Denise replies. "In fact," she says softly to hide a slight discomfort, "I'm not much of a museum goer."

Unsure whether to believe her or not. Previously, he has heard her talk about public and personal history which makes him believe that the past is of prime importance to her. "Yet even though you may not be an admirer of art, I know you enjoy antiquity."

"I like stories of the past."

"But the paintings leave you cold?"

"I can admire some of them," she avers. "I actually prefer the architectural ones. Large spaces with lots of shadows and little people in the background." She smiles because she realizes she is not really describing much of anything.

"Let's broaden our horizons," Roger suggests. He takes her

arm and they enter a room replete with both small and large paintings. In the middle of a room a soft felt covered, gray bench. They sit in front of a work by Breughel. It is a painting of the crucifixion with the dying Christ on the cross central to the painting. To his left, his mother and to his right, Saint John.

Denise gets up and approaches the painting. "The Christ figure looks so vulnerable here," she sighs. "His death is portrayed with depth, even passion."

"What about his mother?" Roger asks.

"She is not looking at him. Too difficult for her."

"She cannot take the sight of her son dying."

"Yes. But Saint John is looking at the Christ adoringly."

"So, you seem to appreciate this one," Roger says.

"I do," Denise affirms. "The mother watching her son suffering in such a horrible manner is exquisitely sad. The Saint's adoration balances her sorrow. He sees only the death of his Savior, not the son of any woman."

"Yes," Roger agrees. "Quite a painting. Let's look at another. Here's one by Cranach the Elder, of Samson and Delilah." Roger and Denise edge closer.

Denise chuckles. "A bit obvious, Samson's large head resting in the lap of Delilah. The only thing that's missing is clippers to shear off his mane. Or maybe one of those barbershop red, white and blue poles spinning in the background."

"I am taken by her enjoyment of the moment," Roger comments. "Look at her pleased expression. She has her prey and is about to rob him of his strength."

"Hmm," Denise frowns. "Not sure whether I can relate to her expression."

"Quite rapturous that she has the strongman in her grasp, that his strength is so little compared to her cunning."

Denise looks up as if she has had an epiphany. "You think women are like that, don't you? They devise cunning to subdue their prey."

In fact, this is exactly what concerns Roger. When they have spoken together about their past relationships, he has been open about his, but Denise seems to preserve a shadowy past or, at least, one she is unwilling to impart. Her former lovers float unseen in a cloud of unspoken memory. She says that since they no longer exist in the now they serve no purpose. "Women often have a distinct memory loss when it comes to their lovers, their mates," he utters with distaste.

"The women I know, once they grow tired of their man, get up and leave."

"Yes, I know," he replies sadly, a sardonic expression crossing his lips. "Without regret, without reprieve, without discussion, sometimes even without a note."

Denise chuckles again. "Boy, aren't you hard on women! You do have a bias as to what women do. In your mind, they are pretty much all craven, insensitive. You draw from contemporary womanhood a rather distinctly gross generalization. Many women are especially sensitive when it comes to leaving a lover."

Roger turns to Denise with a bit of a snicker. "Really! So, what happens to the love they shared? Remember how they plighted their troth? Where does the fucking troth disappear to? Where does it trundle off to? Often troth is easily replaced by the appeal of another. Is it right that women should dispense with the love they once genuinely felt and to which they swore eternal allegiance? And what then? Once again, to bask in the glow of a new love? Yes, new love is thrilling, I grant you that. Yet, it seems you trade off one for the other. But where is the gain?"

"I can see that you have had rough patches in your past. You make it too complicated," Denise retorts. "Love isn't a gold bar that lodges dead in a safe. It's a bar melted into various shapes, into bracelets, watches, jewelry. The excitement your new lover brings may, over time, cool. Some women attempt to refashion the bar. In other words, gold may be different by altering it. Melted down you may discover that it isn't what you thought at first. But a new love may result in something new, exciting, thrilling even. Sometimes a new love appears this way. It is unknowable a priori. You can't search for it. It simply appears. Sometimes out of dross it appears. From a distance a man approaches, and you feel in your gut that this person may be special alloy, not fool's gold."

"Special is one thing. How do you know? You act on your gut. That's the problem, it seems to me. We react on intuition to a new person. Fine. But we thereby damage intensely the one we leave behind, the one we claimed we loved without reservation."

Drinking in these words, Denise believes that Roger, despite himself, may be revealing the depth of his concern about the two of them. His face is slightly crimson now as if the expelling of the words and the attendant emotions were an effort. "So, is that why you won't connect with me fully?" Denise asks. You're afraid that my love isn't durable, isn't sturdy, isn't focused enough?"

"In a word, yes."

"And all of that from Samson's head in Delilah's lap," she smirks. And yet, as his emotions filter through to her, she feels a tentacle, a connection to his concern. For once, she is holding on to his loneliness.

"Exactly where I don't want to be," he retorts as they leave the room. But they are no longer walking together.

15

A Funeral and A Conversation

The church is out of the way, small, its exterior in red brick, and central to the edifice an enormous white brick steeple in the shape of a cross. The inside is fashioned in a bland stucco. Four pillars mahogany support the roof. Once passed through the main doors, Keely enters a large room held for services. At one side, a pepper and white-flecked, bearded organist is softly playing a toccata by Bach. Denise is dressed in a wide-brimmed black hat and jet-black dress that falls to the ankles. She locates her marked seat in the first pew. No parents, she murmurs to herself. Pity! They are both deceased. Only a handful of cousins remain on the west coast, and they have elected to stay home. There are few mourners, she notices, but she is not surprised. Alexandra was not particularly popular. Looks around. No Talbot. The little shit! Dumbfounded at his absence. He always swore that Alexandra was the cradle of his life. They had lived together for several months, she knew and guessed their life together lacked harmony.

Bearers carry in the polished mahogany coffin, set it down near the front pew. The casket is open. Denise stands, looks down upon her sister's sweet face. They have rubbed rouge onto her cheeks, although Alex never applied rouge to herself. But the lipstick, Keely admires, is close to perfect. Keely kisses her forehead. She does not weep. Then the very absence of emotion troubles her. She does not know why she is not weeping. Alexandra's death has been a shock, yet Keely perennially feared, even expected a dramatic, unusual end for her sister. Alexandra begged for it. From early adulthood, she steadily slipped into the undertow of life. As if she could only find happiness by skating beneath convention into a never-never land.

An autopsy showed that she had marijuana and cocaine in her system. No other drugs.

A priest with a short white beard and metallic glasses is speaking. Now droning. Is it Latin? She understands nothing of what is being pronounced. The priest lifts a chalice. Drinks. Turns and looks evenly at parishioners. To the left, a handful of singers intone a hymn. They sing amazingly well, swelling the hymn at the appropriate moment, although to look at them, several old people in jeans and tattered skirts, you would not have anticipated such aplomb. Incense gathers inside Keely's nostrils. She hates the scent of it, and covers her nose with a handkerchief. Remembers an incident with Alex as a child who, at Keely's birthday, lifted her sister's gift, a blond doll that batted its eyes and nodded, and whose outfits you could easily interchange. Then the little girl disappeared into the afternoon. Later, even when challenged, refused to give it back. Symbolic of their relationship. No doubt Alex loved Keely, but only on her terms. A love encased in narcissism. Still, despite their differences Keely felt close.

The priest speaks now in English. Encomium to Alexandra. What a sweet daughter she was, he says. Sincerely. But, of course, he must rave about all daughters. He never met Alexandra. Had he known her, he would surely have tempered his enthusiasm. Keely wets dry lips with her tongue, discerns an elderly man a few seats to her right staring.

The service is concluding with another hymn. Earlier, a few people took communion, Keely not one of them. Raised Catholic, years ago she abandoned the church. Strangely, despite her flouting of morality, Alexandra remained steadfast Catholic to the end, prettied herself up Sundays to attend services, sporting a clean dress topped with a sweeping round hat with a bow and feather.

Boyfriends lined up. She was pretty, slim, and her common sense never interfered with party-time. Men found her amiable, easy, collected around her. She liked sex, she said, and saw no reason to abstain. Seeking forgiveness Thursdays, she went to confession, relating to the parish priest her latest adventure. After a round of Hail Marys, she felt unleashed once more to roam freely. Keely shakes her head. The bearers are now shouldering the body into a hearse and, from there, it will be transferred to the cemetery. Keely follows in a limo, attends the burial service and there, sheds a single tear, feels a slight body tremor, unsure exactly what has prompted them.

Once the coffin has been lowered into the ground, a bit of crumpled soil dropped onto its cover, several people in black sidle up to her. Keely has brought along a small white and crimson doll, a little porcelain piece made in Austria which she tucks by the inert figure of her sister. Once, little Alex doted on it and will be happy to take it with her into the next life. People, most of whom she does not know, whisper condolences. Keely is wearing a veil, lifts it, breathes deeply, and responds kindly. The air is fresh out here, but instead of fortifying her, the chill sets her nerves on edge. For an instant, she feels adrift, no longer clear as what she must do. Until a gentleman she has never seen before leads her by the arm to her limousine, gazes at her as if they were friends, reaches for the door, and positions her comfortably before taking her hand, kissing it. Could this older man have been another of her sister's admirers? The man has said nothing to her, offered nothing but kindness with the sliver of a smile, and Keely does not address him, a nod sufficing as a measure of thanks for his attentiveness. Her driver is leaning against a nearby elm chatting and smoking with other drivers. He has not seen her enter the limo. Above, a murder of crows cluster, then flutter to a nearby elm tree, shrieking as if they were in acute pain. Their racket becomes deafening. One of them eliminates onto the cap of her driver who begins to swear in Italian while brushing off the mess. Now the driver perceives Keely, slides into the limo, turns as if to apologize but says nothing, and simply starts his car.

As Keely is returning home, Armand is pulling up in front of a small, brick apartment building. Inside the main glass doors, he rings Talbot Asese's number. He waits. Rings again. A voice crackles over the machine. Armand identifies himself.

"What do you want?" the voice demands.

"I'm looking for Talbot Asese," Armand answers.

"Who are you?" the voice croaks suspiciously.

"Keely asked me to look you up."

Pause. "You're here because of Alex?"

"Yes."

"You didn't say what you wanted."

"To talk," Armand says.

"About?"

"You and Alex," he answers.

"Not much there," Talbot responds quickly.

94

"Could I ask you a few questions?"

Pause. "If you think you got to. Come up to the second floor." The buzzer crackles open the front door.

Armand grabs the blackened bannister and quickly mounts a set of steep stairs. A scarred black door opens.

"Talbot?"

"They call me Tal."

"Tal."

"Yeah, that's me," he says, opening the door. A young man dressed in dirty jeans. A brown man bun tied in back. A faded, sallow, yellowing mustache. Barefoot. Toes tinged brown. Armand walks in. A tiny entry space leads to a small living room. The room has painted slogans on it. Some are racist. Pastel portrait of Che Guevara on one wall. Different colors cover somewhat the original now faded beige paint. A brown leather sofa has stuffing puffed out at one end.

Tal points to a purple plastic chair. "Take a load off," he murmurs. He himself continues to stand. Toys with strands of his moustache.

"Thanks for seeing me," Armand begins.

"Cut the crap," Tal says pointedly. He shows an even row of teeth. "Talk what's on your mind."

"Just trying to be polite," Armand smiles.

"Yeah," Tal replies with a sneer. "Cool."

"You knew Alex for a long time?"

"Yeah."

"How long?"

"Couple of months," Tal replies. "Maybe three."

"How'd you meet?"

"Does that matter?"

"Yes. It may."

"What the hell are you here for, mister? The cops got no interest in this case, right?"

"That's right. Should they?"

"So, what's your interest"" Tal says ignoring the question. Pulls out a comb to work on his hair.

"I've been hired. I have a client who is interested."

Tal giggles. Takes a drink from a bottle on the mantle. "Got to be Keely. What's her problem anyway?"

"Her problem is that her very young sister is dead."

"So?" belligerently.

"You don't get that? She doesn't believe it was an accident."

"It was a virus," Tal says. "Everybody says so. The paper says so."

"Yes, that is true. But the unanswered question is how did the virus get into her apartment."

"You're asking me""

"Yes."

"I got no idea about this," Tal replies. "Maybe the virus waltzed in without asking." He smiles at the thought of the virus dancing unbidden into the apartment.

"You think this is funny, Tal?"

"Hell no," he says. "I think it's pretty sad."

"Because the death of a young woman, particularly one who you were friends with should be a very sad thing for you."

"Yeah," Tal says, swigging from his bottle. He turns and opens a window. "So, is that what you wanted to find out? If I was sad about her death?" Twirls his moustache ends.

"Not really."

"Because when I found out about it, I couldn't believe it and shook my head."

"You shook your head?"

"Yeah."

"How did you guys meet?"

Pause. "Met in a club off of Chelsea."

"A club where you could get drugs?"

"Is this where our talk is heading?" he asks suspiciously. To drugs?"

"Just asking."

"There are drugs in lots of places in this town," he replies.

"But there are also drugs in that club, right?" Armand asks.

"Yeah. You know Alex used."

"Dope."

"Yeah."

"Is that all?"

"Cocaine sometimes. I seen her take ecstasy once."

"And you?"

"I'm clean," Tal avers. "Mainly."

"Sure."

He rolls up a sleeve. "No marks," he points.

"Good for you. And you were together for months?"

"Yeah".

"You lived together."

"Yeah."

"Here?"

"Sometimes."

"And other times?"

"Sometimes, Alex got money and rented her own place. She said she liked to be alone sometimes."

"So, she didn't like being with you all the time."

"I just said."

"Yeah," Armand replies. "You did say. Did you hit her from time to time?"

"Hell no," Tal says. "I don't hit chicks."

"So why did she leave?"

"She got edgy," Tal said. "Edgy bitch."

"Nervous edgy, you mean?"

"Digging nails into her arms edgy."

"I see," Roger says. "What kind of a woman was she?"

"You mean looks?"

"All over."

"She was pretty. But the drugs was makin' her face wrinkly. She could see it. She'd get up in the morning and stare in the mirror and start cursing, yelling, stickin' out her tongue."

"At you."

"At herself. She was pissed because she couldn't stop."

"So, she was unhappy."

"Yeah, at the end, she was not a lot of laughs."

"Did you kick her out of the apartment, Tal?"

"Hell no. I'm not that kind a guy." Thinks this over. "Well, maybe once or twice."

"Why?"

"Because she wouldn't stop crying and shouting at herself in the mirror. It got old."

"She was depressed."

Tal looks at Roger and chuckles. "I don't know anybody who ain't depressed."

"Bad depression?"

He shrugs. "How would I know? She wasn't thrilled with stuff. Sometimes she had a bad trip from crapped up drugs. She hated everything and everybody then. Including me."

"Where did she get the money for the drugs?"

"She worked," you know.

"And you?"

"I can't find work. I been to jail and people know that."

"So, she was supporting you and your drug habit too."

"Yeah, pretty much. Occasionally, I'd find a day job where I loaded pallets onto a truck, but usually, Alex paid. She said she loved me. That's why she paid."

"You loved her?"

"Sure. She was great until she started the shouting and crying."

"Did you kill her?"

Tal laughs through a cough. "Why would I do that? I just threw her out when she got too much for me. I didn't need to do nuthin' else."

"So, who did?"

Pause. "You askin' the wrong guy. I can't help you no more."

"Well," Jason Fierst cries out, intervening, and moving dramatically onto the set. "This is ok. Sort of ok. But Roger, without screwing up the blocking, given what a shithead Tal is, couldn't you hover closer and be darkly ominous? You are probing him with the right questions, but you need to exercise more physical authority behind it. Remember you're a private dick, a tough guy when you need to be."

"You mean I should carry a gat," he laughs.

"Make your tone of voice into a revolver and point it at Tal. Yeah, that's the issue. I think your tone is what bothers me. When we run the scene again, maybe you could be starker, edgier. Make this craphead believe that you are gonna break his kneecaps if he doesn't answer your questions. And as for you, Tal, I think you played this scene well, but remember you are a druggy, and even if you aren't using this moment, you are probably hurting in some way. Wanting or suffering. You might portray a bit more of the suffering. Your body can show us how you need drugs, how it's painful to be without them, craving them. Can your body writhe for us, Tal?"

"I'll do my best to be tortured.?

"Truly, Tal, that's all I ask. Give me your suffering. So, pick it up from your last line, Tal."

Tal recites: 'You askin' the wrong guy. I can't help you no more.'

"So, what exactly are you telling me about you and Alex? She apparently was not living with you when she died." He draws nearer to Tal, too near.

Tal backs off a foot, stops to roll a joint between his fingers. "No, she wasn't here."

"When did you see her last then?"

Tal moistens the joint with his tongue and sticks it in his pocket. "Not for a couple of weeks."

"Hmm," Armand muses. "So, there was something definitely wrong."

"Not specially. No reason for her to want to see me no more."

"What do you mean?"

"I dumped her, get it? So, after that I didn't see her."

"You didn't tell me you dumped her."

"No? Must not have come up…"

"When did you break up?"

"Let's see. Couple of weeks ago."

"And she didn't come by?"

"No."

"Did she call you? Text you?"

"No."

"Why did you dump her, Tal?" Armand asks, his tone metallic.

"She was makin' a lot of noise which pissed me off. I thought the drugs was makin' her crazy, but it went beyond that…something was bothering her. Maybe about us. She never said."

"So, you didn't love this girl, did you?" Armand asks with scorn.

"Never said I did. For a time, I got from her what I wanted. That's like love, ain't it? But when she got rowdy, it was too much for me."

"No other girl in the picture?"

"I didn't say that either", Tal replies, grinning.

"Which Alex knew about."

"Yeah. I mean she kinda caught us doin' it, you know."

"Kinda?"

"Well, she was standin' there with groceries in her arms starin' at my bare bottom. Under me was this girl, Jesteba, Nice name, Jesteba. Black girls got great names, you know."

"And that was your last contact with Alex?"

"She dropped the groceries where she was standin', never said another word and slammed the door behind her. She didn't even say adios."

"Did she ever talk about getting drugs from the workplace?"

"Wrong kind of drugs," Tal replied, shaking a finger. "We didn't need drugs that cure epilepsy or stupid stuff like that."

"So, you didn't kill Alexandra," Armand repeats, getting up.

Tal chuckled. "I got rid of the girl. I didn't need to do anything else to get her out of my life. But who knows about where she worked? She didn't talk much about those guys. Maybe one of them had reason to cancel her."

16

Pascal and Marcella Meet Unhappily

(Pascal leads Benjamin to the window) "Look out here. Winter is fighting its last breath, spring is stirring. This is what's going on outside. (He pats Benjamin's chest) This is what's happening inside. Come out, wherever you are!"

"You're a jackass, Pascal," Benjamin says, smiling. "I suppose you are also in love."

"I am also in love," Pascal confesses. "But I can't take it seriously. I'm enamored with both a woman and her husband. She is randy and he is beautiful. He is sensitive to me and she has power. When we make love, she tosses me about like some tumbleweed and he, the Britisher, is sensual and warm. So, what am I to do?"

"About what?" Benjamin asks. "Sounds as if you've got the situation well in hand."

"I want to be with both of them. I love both of them for different reason, but I don't know whether they can handle my equal love."

"I don't really understand."

"Now," Pascal says, "they want me to choose between them. Of course, at first, it was a lark, but I have changed. Still, I hate change. I wanted us to be as it always was. How can I choose between them? They complement one another. Separately they offer only pieces. They complete my life only as an entity."

"You can't be serious," Benjamin scoffs. "It's hard enough to love one person."

"Separately, they would hardly hold my interest."

"And here I thought I had problems with Marcella. You want too much, Pascal."

"Don't we all? But I hope you understand that I don't take this sentimental stuff to heart. You do know that."

(Marcella enters from stage left reading a paper). "Hello, Benjamin," she says looking up.

"Is that your plane ticket?" Benjamin asks.

"I was just checking it," Marcella affirms.

"I'd like you to meet my friend, Pascal. I've told you about him. My oldest friend in the world."

"Marcella, Benjamin described you perfectly. You are a lovely woman, Pascal beams."

"Why thank you," she says gazing up at him. "Are you here for a visit?"

"An unexpected, if short reprieve from my work."

"You're a soldier," Benjamin has told me. "My father was also in the military."

"A dentist," Benjamin adds.

(Feisty, Pascal chuckling) "A curious state for the military. I can guess at his weapon of choice. Did he drill the enemy to death?"

"Benjamin," Marcella laughs, "I'm not sure I appreciate your friend. My father had his place in the army."

"Pascal is being playful rather than charming, aren't you?"

"I leave all the charm to Marcella. And trust that she, in turn, will sprinkle you with it," he adds sarcastically.

"As I do," Marcella affirms. "Pascal is on the verge of being irritating," she adds.

"Maybe I don't like to see my best friend inflicted with pain," Pascal says caustically.

(Marcella, to Benjamin) "Maybe it would be best if your friend stayed out of my affairs." (She exits quickly)

(Benjamin scratches his head) "Good work, Pascal. You've not only advanced my cause but made a friend for life."

(Pascal smiles) "Don't you have an expression about too much heat in the dentist's office?"

"The kitchen," Benjamin corrects him. "If there's too much heat in the kitchen..."

(Seriously, puts his arm around Benjamin) "Watch yourself with this one," Pascal confides to Benjamin. "You're not seeing the obvious. Her eyes move beyond you. She speaks to you but she does not truly see." (Exits right).

(Benjamin strikes his fist against a wall, addresses audience) "Damn! Two weeks went by without an email. Not even a telephone call. When she left for the airport, she refused to let me drive her. I was watching our bond disintegrate, and I was feeling anxious, even nauseous."

(The phone rings)

"Janice! I'm glad you called back. Do you know when Marcella is flying home?

(Pause, demurring) Let me take responsibility for that, please."

(He writes down some numbers on a pad, pockets his phone, addresses audience again) "I thought it would be a nice surprise for her. Who am I kidding? I was desperate to see her. All the more because Janice said she preferred not to see anyone when she came home. That burned. So of course, I ignored it. She came out of the gate, and I was hiding because I wanted to see what she looked like without any warning of my coming,

whether she was troubled or happy, or…with somebody else."
(Marcella enters from the left).

"Marcella!"

(Puts down a bag. Looks stunned) "Oh, Benjamin. I didn't
expect you." (They hug in a perfunctory way).

(Benjamin watches Marcella exit, speaks to audience) "She
looked the same and yet was different. I was sore that when we
hugged, she didn't kiss me. I was sore at myself that I didn't kiss
her. I was playing it safe, waiting for her to come to me, engage
me, and when she did not, I played it safe. She went downstairs
to pick up a suitcase at baggage claim. I could have gone with
her but I was embarrassed. For once, I had nothing to say.

I had everything to say. How I missed her! How I wondered
what was in the recesses of her mind. Whether she had lost
feelings for me. Whether she had met somebody at her uncle's. I
said nothing. What could account for her not calling? She must
have met somebody else." (Exits right)

(Marcella enters from left. Speaks to audience) "They seem
to have misplaced my case. Wasn't I clear? And then, I ask
for one thing, one little thing. Didn't Benjamin know better
than to meet me? When a person wants a little privacy, can't
she have it without having to beg for it? (Crosses to a living
room setting, sits gently onto a sofa). Here's what happened in
Miami. I drank a lot. I don't drink much, but for some reason,
it felt excellent to be high, buzzed much of the afternoon and
evening. I lay out on the beach with my uncle. We went to
fine restaurants and talked about sailing and marlin. I know
nothing about sailing and marlin, but the talk was refreshing.
No matters of the goddamned heart came up. What a relief. I
forgot everything. If I saw a couple arguing, I drank another
vodka martini. Benjamin was an intrusion in my time away…I

couldn't stop myself from thinking about him from time to time, but to tell the truth, a brief intrusion. I hope nobody opens that valise. I have all my dirty underwear in it."

(She files her nails on the sofa. Janine enters from left with a bemused look, to audience). "Shoot, it's not over. Old Benjamin texting me every day as if I had the key to Marcella's heart. A sincere man, but he resembles a possum that got stomped on by a pony.

Why doesn't he let Marcella swim out of the river by herself? He thinks he's a friggin' life preserver, and he doesn't understand that this woman isn't in peril. She's doing what all women do when they're confused: she takes out her check book and works at balancing the credits against the debits. I don't mean like a callous person. I told Benjamin that. I said: lookee here, let her do her 'rithmatic, the calculus of the heart. See! Men are so logical, so rational, they miss the essentials. So, Benjamin says to me..."

(Benjamin entering from right) "I love her. She loves me. Ergo, we should be together. If we are not together, it must mean that somebody else is in her life or, for some other incomprehensible reason, she is distancing herself."

"Benjamin, to his credit, is a romantic. So why doesn't he think with his guts? Why does he want to box her up into some little rational cubicle? Do I have to understand Chagall to adore the son of a bitch? Hell, no! I just have to dig the lines."

"I couldn't believe what followed," Benjamin says. "Marcella and I continued to see one another sporadically. I spent a good bit of time at her house. But we were no longer making love. Nor would she talk. She claimed she could not shed light on anything. I went through a process of concern, anger, fury, and then without any ammunition left, decided to let nature take its course." (He heads for a wing but stops short of exiting)

(Janice watches Marcella enter from left) "Back one week and still moping, I see."

"It's Benjamin's fault," Marcella says. "He's sulking. He wants all the answers right now."

"And what do you want?" Janice asks.

(Laughing) "Damned if I know. Change, I guess."

"Did you ever get your case back?"

"Yes," Marcella responds. "The airline sent it via Guatemala, but I did get it back."

17

Roger and Denise On Holiday

"We're taking a ten-day break for Christmas and New Year's," Jason Fierst announces to the assembled crew. "Take some rest. Eat and drink until you burst for five days, fast for the next five, and be ready to come back to work with pride, enthusiasm, and no unwanted fat. Anybody who returns more than five pounds overweight will be fined an ice cream cone. Am I clear? Now get the fuck outta here and enjoy yourselves. You deserve it".

"Why Baden Baden?" Denise asks Roger. You know somebody there?"

"Yes," Roger says. "But I have other reasons to go ... there is a casino there, a very old casino."

"I don't gamble."

"But I enjoy a bit of sport," he replies.

She looks at him and the corner of her mouth arches upwards. "Do you now? I would never have thought it. I see you as somebody who plays safe. You actually gamble?"

"Not always," he replies. "Certainly not with you." Said with tongue in cheek, she is not sure whether he is ribbing her or not.

"I don't want to spend a week sitting in a casino playing

blackjack."

"I play roulette," he says.

"Whatever. Sounds both dangerous and boring at the same time."

"You can be reading a paper in the antechamber while I'm playing. Or buy yourself a cup of coffee."

"Exciting," she exclaims. "Are you sure you want to do this? I don't even like Germany. Can't say I trust that country. You haven't forgotten I'm Jewish."

"Ever been?"

"No," she replies. Hesitates. "But I don't like it anyway. I hear the name of the country and my nostrils fill with the stench of death camps. I had relatives who lived there and died there prematurely."

"Your ancestors may have had bad experiences…but the country is new. And you are new to the country. Treat the place as if you are seeing at it for the first time. You will be, you know. You shouldn't judge what you cannot know."

"Ok," she relents reluctantly. "Baden Baden it is. You have a place to stay?"

"Yes. I have a friend there who says she has space for us in her house….in a small village."

"A woman?"

"Not what you think," he replies. "She is both married and, I hear, pregnant. But she is also quite wealthy, has a beautiful house I am told, and won't be offended if we want to explore the countryside on our own."

"Ok," Denise replies. "I'm game. Are we bringing scripts along to work on?"

He is thinking: "Why would we bring work on our vacation? Jason would be furious. "But if you insist, I'll leave that up to you."

"We better," Denise replies. "I have a feeling I'm going to be wringing my hands in some little village in Germany wondering what people are saying about me. I don't have a clue about the language."

Roger shrugs. "Work on your German. We leave in four days."

Five mornings later, they arrive by plane in Frankfurt, in quite a brisk, frigid Frankfurt, switch to a heated train and, in a few hours, find themselves in the Baden Baden rail station. When they disembark from the train, Denise immediately searches for a rest room. There is a sign before the restaurant attached to the station. They trundle their bags inside the front door. "Where is the rest room?" Denise asks. A waiter dressed in a white shirt and black bow tie responds in a reasonable English tainted by a sharp Germanic accent. "You must sit down and order something," he shakes a finger.

"I don't want to sit," she responds impatiently. "Just want to use the bathroom."

The waiter is unsmiling. "You will have to go elsewhere for that. We reserve our bathroom for customers."

"Not very civilized," Denise says angrily.

"It is our way," the waiter insists.

"Let's go," Roger prods.

But Denise turns to him and whispers. "I have a pressing female thing." So, instead of leaving, they slide into a booth and order coffee. Now, she is invited to use the bathroom.

"I knew I would hate this country," Denise says, returning to the booth and lifting the coffee cup to her lips.

"Give it a chance," Roger replies. "You've been here about ten minutes."

Outside, beyond the circular driveway, they spy a taxi station to the left, and hail a cab. The taxi drives languorously from the train station through Buhl, Haft and finally to Lauf where it mounts a slow and long ascent into the mountain. They are now in the Black Forest. Several hundred yards up the hill, the taxi slows before a large wooden domicile. Roger rings the bell. One minute, then two transpire. He rings again. There is a heavy steel knocker on the door which he now raps, the echo resounding around them. From inside they can hear the muffled voice of someone asking them to be patient. Another minute passes before the door opens. A young woman in a bathrobe peers out. "Roger," she says smiling. "I was hoping it would be you." Her English is fluent and accent free. They embrace as Roger introduces Denise to her. Her name is Lydia.

"How long before you expel your baby?" he asks. "Or maybe the right term is 'usher in your baby'."

"Couple of months," she answers. "But I have had complications and the doctor is recommending almost complete bed rest. It's really a form of German torture," she complains, "and a way for them to work on another client." They think if you stay in bed day after day, month after month, that eventually you will go stark raving mad, and the doctors then have an entirely new patient to deal with."

"I don't think I will ever get pregnant," Denise offers with a shiver. "It sounds all too horrible".

"It's not really that crazy," Lydia says. "You go nuts with bed rest, you gain weight at an alarming weight and your body stretches out like some haywire balloon. You start with morning sickness and end up eating your weight every evening. Could be worse," she adds, with a wan smile.

"No help in the house?" Roger asks.

"Not right now. Our valet, butler, nursemaid and cook all

rolled into one, Jacob, is off to a tennis tournament for a couple of weeks in Paris. My feckless husband, Bedrich, is in the Ukraine personally sucking out the oil from the ground. He says with a straw," she chuckles. "He promises to come home before the birth, but I don't believe him. Anyway, after a trip like this, he stinks of oil and oily residue for a week. I couldn't take that now. I told him to stay where he is until I call for him." She smiles broadly. "But I am so pleased to see you and your friend. You must tell me everything. Your acting career, I hear is improving and, judging from present company, even your taste in women."

Roger cautions her: "We are not dating," he says to Lydia. "Denise and I work together and decided to get away while keeping one another company."

"Is this true?" she asks Denise, not quite believing Roger.

"An alternate truth," Denise smiles ruefully.

"We are best of friends," Roger concludes firmly, pinching Denise's arm.

With this, Lydia haltingly leads the way up a flight of worn marble stairs to the second floor. An ebony, carved and quite old bannister provides security. The house itself, Denise notices, is replete with antiques, perhaps an antiquity itself, dead quiet, even ominously dark. "My room is at one end," Lydia says out of breath, holding onto the bannister. "Opposite yours. If something happens, you will not be able to hear me. The finest carpenters crafted the house. They have soundproofed the house and every room in it. The house could withstand the fiercest hurricane. Still, Roger, I do have your phone number, she adds, in case I get desperate."

"And if we were not available?" Roger asks.

"I would be calling the police in town. They are quite prompt and responsive."

Their room is encased in heavy mahogany paneling. Large, almost massive. The feel is heavy, but the large picture window looking out to the mountains, towards a panoply of pine trees and pastures teeming with goats lends tranquility to the afternoon. There is one large bed with a heavy quilt. In a cupboard, blankets, sheets, pillowcases, and the like.

"Yes," Lydia points, "if you look out this window, you can see the ancient Schloss up the hill. Further up, there are minor settlements. A few people elected to trek the entire mile or so up to the top of the mountain and build there. I have no idea what kind of life they have. There are streams for fishing, trout mainly, clear streams, if you can believe it. And there is hunting up there as well. Deer abound. Small game as well. If you hear shots it's always from the top of the mountain in the forest somewhere. Don't be concerned by it. By the way, I've put you in one room. I mean one bed. Is that going to be a problem for you? If so, I have plenty of space elsewhere."

"No problem for me," Denise responds.

The two women peer over at Roger. Hesitates. "Fine for me," he assents steadily without changing the expression on his face.

"Sure?" Lydia asks him. "No problem for me to make up another room."

"Sure," he affirms.

Lydia then leaves slowly for her room holding the edge of her bathrobe up in one hand. Stops and turns. "Dinner around 7," she says. "We'll eat and chat. And I promise to spruce up. I used to look like a young, energetic woman at one time. And for dinner, I've invited one of the ladies from down the hill to come up and cook for us while Jacob is away. You won't starve, promise."

Napping on the bed, Denise curls up facing Roger's direction. His eyes are closed. He can hear Denise's breathing, labored breathing. Turns, stretches, and opens his eyes.

"Nice bed", he says.

"Too firm for me," she responds. "But I can feel the curvature of my spine extending."

"Were you napping?" he asks.

"Yes. You"

"Not really. Just dozing off and on."

Props up on an elbow. "We could snuggle, Denise says, softly fluttering.

Shrugs his shoulders. "Look, Denise, "he replies pointedly, "let's review the ground rules. We are going share one room for several days, but not as intimates. Just friends. If that isn't ok, then I will take up Lydia's offer to move."

"You're no fun," she pouts.

"I've been told that."

"Don't you find me attractive in the least?" Denise complains.

"Of course, I do. I've told you that."

"So!"

"But I also told you I don't want to get involved with you on any level other than the platonic. Can't you live with that?"

"It might be hard if we are in the same bed together night after night."

He sits up. "Your choice."

"I give," she says abandoning her posture and sighing.

Later, they descend the long, curved marble staircase, to the ground floor and make their way to the dining room. Lydia is ensconced at the head of the table. Chairs are complemented in an old leather stretched over and around ebonized wood. "They are 18th century," she says. "I think they originally came from Austria." The mahogany dining room table itself has been polished to a high gloss. "Let's repair to one of the salons," Lydia says. "That way, we chat more comfortably."

The temporary cook brings in a bottle of red wine in one hand, white wine in the other, pours, then fetches plates of venison with green beans and potatoes.

"If I remember correctly," Roger says to Lydia, "you were brought up near Buffalo. True?"

"Yes."

"Away from the center of town?"

"Not so far. I considered myself a city girl. I worked abroad as an accountant for a local oil company. That is where I met…."

"And he spirited you to Germany."

"Well, no. We met in the Seychelles. Quite a while later, he induced me to fly to Germany."

"Not too bored here?"

"Sometimes. But I've gotten to know some of the people in the village. Once a week they have a luncheon, about a dozen of them, called a Stammtisch where all we do is eat, drink and talk. No subject is too sensitive to be off the table. None considered too indelicate. There's a former admiral in the German navy, a retired butcher, several married women closer to my age. So, it's quite a group."

"All of this in German?"

"Yes," Denise responds. "I don't catch everything. Sometimes I ask somebody to repeat what they just said. But my German after a year and a half has improved dramatically. I get along pretty well now."

Liqueurs are served in the library. They sit around an enormous marble, sculptured chimney, faces of eyeless stone gargoyles jutting out on both sides. Fire burns softly, whistling through the tinder, biting into logs. "I'm done now", Lydia says after a time. "I'm off to bed. Treat the house as if it were yours," she adds, rising. She kisses both on the cheek before retiring.

"I'm for bed too," Denise says. She and Roger leave together for the bedroom. "I like your friend," Denise says. She's open, honest, aboveboard.

"Yes," Roger assents. "That's why I dote on her as well. And see how a girl from Buffalo, NY, easily fits into a village in the Black Forest without complaint. She looks for opportunities to improve herself as well as to find entertainment."

Out on the balcony, their eyes rise into the mountain and, above, to a spectacular starry sky. Shooting stars abound. Roger locates the Pleiades. The stars themselves provide extraordinary light, a filtered white light that hovers over the ground below blending into the snow.

"Wish I had a cigarette," Denise said.

"Can you live without one?"

"Yes. I'll forget about it once in bed." When Denise returns from the bathroom, she is wearing green and white pajamas adorned with a pattern of frolicking bears. Slips into the sheets, sighs.

Roger slips in as well in his shorts. Night table lamp turned off. On his back, looking up into the ceiling, beams of wood interspersed with stucco. After a moment, he starts to doze. Denise, however, is having trouble sleeping. She edges closer to Roger, her right hand on his chest, her head towards him, kisses him lightly on the lips. He continues to doze. Now she presses her entire body against him. In an instant, his eyes shoot open, his head still fixed on the pillow. Next to him a burning log is pressing into his side.

"My God," he remarks to her, "you are virtually steaming. I

can see passion clouds rising from your body."

"I'm going insane," she blurts out, backing off. "Totally insane!"

Roger pulls the light chain. "Listen," he says....

But before he can speak, she is already fidgeting, words tumbling out of her mouth in rapid succession. "What's wrong with me? You claim you find me attractive, but you don't want me. What the hell is wrong with you? Are you secretly gay?"

"I am not gay."

"Goddamn you," she roars, "then what is it?"

Sits up. "All right. Impossible for you not to know," he grunts. "Two years ago, I met a girl named Tammy. I fell for her hard. We were intimate almost immediately."

"Lucky girl," Denise sighs.

"Don't interrupt," he cautions her. "You're being rude and I am trying to explain myself."

"Sorry," Denise grumbles but sits back and crosses her legs.

"After a couple of months, Tammy had fallen in love with me. She confided her feelings. In fact, she sat down one day and wrote a letter describing me as the love of her life, the only completely satisfying connection she had ever experienced. She even contacted my sister whom she had briefly met at dinner one night. She drove to my sister's place and personally handed this letter to her and her husband and said:

'I just wanted you to know that I've never felt this powerfully about anyone. Roger is everything to me.' My sister read the letter: it verbalized in print what she had just indicated to me out loud, that I was the moon to Tammy's sun.

My sister finished reading and, somewhat bewildered, said to Tammy: "This is fine, but why did you bring this to me?"

"Because," Tammy replied sincerely, "because I wanted you to know the extent of my feeling for your brother. He has often said to me that you have been among the harshest critics of the women in his life. I simply wanted to express my feelings about him."

As soon as Tammy left, my sister called me and said: "Something wrong with this one. She then described the scene in which Tammy delivered the letter followed by an avowal of her complete attachment to me. "I still don't get why she brought it to me," sis said. "It was unnecessary. I have nothing to do with her or with the women in your life."

"I guess she just wanted to negate any nervous feelings you might have had."

"I had no feelings one way or the other."

"Ok," Roger continues, "after I heard this I was certain this was in fact the girl of my dreams. Totally connected to me, Tammy could not even look at any object in the universe without reference to me. I was floored, and totally enamored of her."

"Why do you stop?" Denise asked him.

"Not quite sure how to convey this part," Roger retorted. "Well, I guess the best way is to jump off the plank. After Tammy had visited my sister, I thought we would be seeing one another pretty much non-stop. Instead, it took her three days to get in touch with me."

"Three days?"

"Yes, I found it strange too. She called my cell and said that something had happened which I needed to learn about. I immediately said: just tell me on the phone. No, she replied. Too important. We must see one another face to face. So that afternoon we met at a Barnes and Noble. I could see her pull in with her Jeep, jump out sprightly, thin, athletic, enter the store, and then spy me sitting at a little table. She came towards me, her face wrinkling as if in deep contemplation, and immediately suggested she order coffees for both of us. I said fine, but was somewhat hurt that she hadn't kissed me. But given her obvious distress this could have been a small oversight on her part, so I thought no more about it."

She brought over the coffees, stirred cream in hers. "So, something happened the other day which affects us," she began.

"Go on," I said.

"You know the condominium complex where I live."

"Of course."

"There is a manager of the complex whose name is Andrew."

"I may have met him," Roger said, impatiently.

"Yes. Well, he and I have been friendly for several years. The other day, I had an outage. My refrigerator stopped working and Andrew came over to fix it. We weren't sure at first whether it was a short or something more serious in the refrigerator itself. So, he came and attended to the problem.

"Great."

"And then he grabbed me by the waist and kissed me." Pause. "I didn't ask for that. I was completely surprised and vulnerable. We kissed for some time."

"What?" Stunned. As if a mini-explosion had ignited in my brain.

"The next thing I knew we were in the bedroom making love. It was as if I had lost all control of my thoughts or emotions. I had ceded everything to Andrew."

Roger turns towards Denise, his face reddening. "I was going crazy at this point. I couldn't believe what I was hearing. I jumped up unsure whether to slap her face, scream bloody murder or simply leave."

"And then," Tammy continued unabated, "Andrew confided that he loves me, has always loved me, but knew that I was in a relationship and feared intruding."

"Fucking you was his way of not intruding?" I yelled harshly. "Half the customers stopped their conversation as they overheard my rant, and began to titter."

"He said he could not help himself," Tammy replied. "He had to have me. Entirely. He had thought about me in this way from the first moment he leased the condo to me. I was moved to tears. For the first time, I understood romance. I realized in that moment that I in fact am, that I have been, also in love with him, so I have come to this coffee shop today to inform you that Andrew and I plan to move in together."

"I was speechless, floored," Roger says to Denise, his face reddening as he is speaking. "At first, I felt dizzy. My whole world was revolving upside down in a few moments of talk. Then I started to rage. I asked her what the fuck was the business with the letter she had written, the letter she felt she needed to share with my sister who, frankly, because she was suspicious of Tammy, was the only sane one in this story. Tammy simply shrugged, got up stone-faced, her lips drooping, said she was sorry, and departed slowly without finishing her coffee."

"So that is why you have resisted me?" Denise asks.

"Yes."

"Bu this has nothing to do with us. Ours is not the same thing at all," Denise counters. "I am not offering you love, marriage, a shared home or anything of the like. I just thought we might enjoy being together physically. I like sex and I thought it would be fun with you."

"So, you don't love me?" Roger asks somewhat sheepishly.

"Not in a blue moon," Denise replies.

Roger sits up straighter and takes account of the situation with a pause. Clears his throat. "Well, that makes me feel better. So, if we made love, it would not necessarily bring us closer together? I am talking entrapment, you understand."

"Exactly."

Roger breathes a long breath of relief. He seeks to explain himself clearly for Denise to understand his point of view perfectly. "As long as you don't love me," he ventures slowly but now more confidently, "I'd make love with you…anytime," he begins. "But if this ever were to change," he goes on, "and should you make the huge mistake of falling for me, you promise to let me know so that we can re-assess the situation."

"Not likely, but you'd be the first to know," Denise responds with a delicate smile.

18

A Proctologist Enters

(Benjamin to audience) "I once met an elderly, Jewish Hungarian woman in the south of France. Married for ten days, the Nazis arrested her husband, and she never saw him again. They were sent to two separate camps. She herself survived Auschwitz. After liberation, she went on to London, became a librarian, but could never shake from her mind the passing of her young husband. She never re-married. She never dated again. In her mind, her fidelity remained, entombed as it were, with her husband. She didn't have much use for American women. She used to say: 'American women change men like underwear'. What's the point? Isn't old underwear softer to the touch?"

(Janice entering with Marcella) "His name is Matt something, a proctologist from St, Louis."

"A proctologist?" Marcella asks idly.

"Rich, not bad-looking, a messenger from God if you ask me."

"Not sure if I believe in messengers from God, she scoffs."

"I know he's interested in you," Janice goes on.

"Did you give him my number?"

"Just awaiting clearance from the tower."

"What is the point?" Benjamin interjects. "Isn't old underwear softer to the touch?"

"I'm ready to have him land," Marcella replies.

"Good for you," Janice says, delighted.

"You have to break in new underwear," Benjamin continues musing. "And once it's broken in, doesn't it become like the other? Doesn't it get soiled? Then you have to think about changing it."

"You need this," Janice affirms.

"I don't know what I need, but I have to break out of my rut."

"Magda, my Hungarian friend, said she kept underwear until it shredded."

"Did you ever meet Benjamin's friend, Pascal?" Janice asks.

"Yes, he was antagonistic towards me. Benjamin must have given him an earful."

(Benjamin musing) "Magda lived on the seventh floor of an apartment building in Nice. It had a balcony and the pigeons would swoop down onto it. One of them, she called him Loupie, flew in one day and she adopted him. Can you imagine?" A pigeon that pooped all over her hardwood floors. But Magda housed that bird until it died." (Crosses to sofa)

"What's Pascal like?" Janice inquires.

"He's cute as can be," Marcella responds, "but he's got a mouth on him that could start a fire." (Janice exits left. Marcella sits on sofa)

(Benjamin to audience) "Marcella dated the proctologist. Certain evenings she would call and we spent time in front of a late winter fire in her den. So as not to talk, we watched television. And then, one evening without warning, it began."

"I think we ought to stop seeing one another for a while," Marcella says edgily.

(Benjamin nods acidly) "Are we having dinner first or do you want me to leave now?"

"I'll put your pork roast back into the freezer," Marcella says.

"This doctor, what's his name again?"

"Matt."

(Speaks slowly at first, then picks up speed). "Matt! What do you and Matt discuss "Ass-ignations" When he comes to the house, does he enter by the back door? Is he intelligent or as-inine? When he ass-ays your body, do you ass-ent to an ass-ault on your ass-ets? Or do you ass-ert yourself? Why do you ass-ociate with him anyway? As-ylum from me? Does he ass-ume that he's ass-uring his as-cendency over you?"

"You're hopeless, Benjamin," but she does not refrain from smiling.

"Seriously. What do you talk about? Does he know his sigmoid from his elbow? I bet he was an officer in the military...how about rear admiral? Allow me to sketch his personality for you. His favorite toast: bottoms up! His favorite movie: Rear Window, naturally. When he goes to a topless club, is he disappointed? Does he consider intestinal fortitude to be a gourmet meal?"

"You're outrageously jealous, Benjamin," she says giggling.

(Benjamin pacing) "If he asks you to dance cheek to cheek, do you know which way he wants you to face? His favorite baseball position: umpire behind the plate. For Matt, is black bottom a dance or a source of income? Let's check the good doctor's verbal intelligence. When his secretary asks whether his dictation requires a period or a colon, does he drop pants to look? Does he pray that people will greet him with 'up yours'? Can you seriously date a man who confuses hurricanes with breaking wind?"

"Stop it," Benjamin. "Matt is a kind and gentle man."

(Suddenly becalmed, Benjamin stops) "So that's it, then?"

"Don't be upset with me, please." (She puts her arms around him)

(Benjamin breaks away) "Why would I be upset? Just because the woman I love has just dumped me for a buggering doctor?"

"We'll see one another from time to time. I'll call you."

"To tell me which end is up."

"We need to spend time away from each other."

"Yes, you've said that before."

"That doesn't mean it's over," Marcella continues to speak with gravity." I need to see other people to get a good grasp on us."

19

Armand Meets Apepi

They are huddled together in a booth at Hamburger Heaven devouring burgers and fries. Their waitress refreshes their waters.

"No startling developments then?" Keely asks with slight annoyance in her voice. She takes off her sunglasses, peers outside. On the other side of the plate glass window, a teeming avenue filled with yellow cabs, buses, throngs of walkers, couriers on bikes.

"Not yet," Armand replies. "Anything on your end?"

"Not really. But I remembered something which should have been forefront in my mind as well as yours," she adds, "and somehow in all the rush to bury my sister and launch the investigation, I hadn't given much thought. Alexandra had a dog. His name was Apepi.

"Apepi? Kind of unusual."

"The name of an Egyptian pharaoh. The dog is a pharaoh hound. I only saw him a couple of times. A handsome animal, kind of orange, with large ears and a regal disposition and posture. The pharaohs are the ones who had them for centuries. And they still exist."

Four teen-agers push the swiveling glass door hard to enter

the diner, laughing and cavorting.

"Interesting," Armand remarks. "What happened to this dog?"

"When Alex's body was discovered, he was taken to the pound. I decided right away I didn't need a dog in my life."

"Hmm, Armand says. "Maybe I should follow up on this?"

"Would there be any connection to my sister's death? Anyway, as a private detective, you should follow every lead, don't you? Why would you even hesitate?"

Armand thinks about that for an instant. "I'm going to track down Apepi, if he is among the living. As for the rest, I still believe pay dirt will be found in the workplace. It's the only place where anyone could have obtained samples of the hantavirus. When the cops went through her apartment, they noticed mouse droppings in several areas, samples which they analyzed and which were contaminated. Now how could infected mouse crap be littering an apartment without some exterior mouse carrying it in, eh?"

"I believe you. But it is entirely possible that Alex herself brought in the samples into her own apartment."

"That is what I am trying to understand. Still, I was told that there is no record of her being in the lab where the samples were stored."

"I'm not telling you how to do your job," Keely remarks acidly, "but I'm surprised that you didn't learn about Apepi, and so search for him earlier. That dog could be vital to the investigation." Armand has no response but a slight lifting of an eyebrow.

Later that day, a pensive Armand drives down to the pound. He is greeted by Luke, an employee of the pound, fortyish, blond with tattoos on his temples. Wears a t-shirt inscribed: 'Cats rule.'

"I keep stringent records," Luke assures Armand. He pulls out a

127

pad from his overalls, opens the notebook in which he lists each dog's arrival, his adoption or, failing that, his demise. "I recall the dog. He had an ethereal look about him. He whimpered a lot like some animals who are depressed because their lives are so dramatically changed. But a few days before we were going to euthanize this impressive boy, someone came by and adopted him."

"You have the man's name?"

"Yes."

"And he is?"

Luke looks up from his notebook and shook his head with a vague smile. "I couldn't tell you that. We're supposed to keep these things confidential."

"It's important," Armand insists.

"Sorry," Luke replies firmly, closing the notebook. Slowly.

From his wallet, Luke takes out a twenty-dollar bill and hands it to Luke. "Would this jog your memory?"

"I do remember his first name. He looks through the notebook. "Earl, I think. Yes, it is Earl. I probably have his last name around here somewhere. Hope I haven't misplaced it."

Armand hands him another twenty. "Does this help?"

"Could be," Luke cracks a smile, re-opening the notebook. "The man's name is Earl Standers. I have his address also. He lives on the west side near the ports. I remember this because he said there are parks along the Hudson where he could walk Apepi for miles."

"Did Earl look at any other dogs to adopt?"

"No," Luke replies. "He specially asked whether we had any pharaoh dogs. I didn't know that Apepi was such a dog at first but after he described him, I took Earl to his crate at once."

"Tell me, did Apepi recognize this man?"

Luke shrugged. "Impossible to know. The dog stopped whining, even looked up. He was a docile dog. He allowed Earl to lay a leash on him and after filling out papers and paying a fee, Earl walked him out with no problem. Some dogs put up a fuss, but you'd think they would be thrilled to be out of this place."

Now Armand drives to the west side of town. The street features a row of stucco townhomes. Alongside each home, rows of ferns. In front, young elm trees supported by stakes. Four steps up to a landing. Rings a doorbell. No answer, but he does hear the sustained bark of a dog. Earl is probably at work, Roger believes. I'll come back later in the afternoon.

He returns to see Earl driving into his one-car garage. In a moment, before Roger has time to ring the doorbell, Earl is already exiting the garage with Apepi. The man has a handlebar moustache, bright brown receding eyes, fading, blondish hair. As Armand approaches, Apepi leaps up, Earl yanking him back hard. "Quiet now, Apepi," he yells. The dog cowers.

"You seem to have a good handle on this animal," Armand says. "I was looking for you earlier in the day. I wanted to ask you about him."

"The dog? What about him?" Earl asks quietly. The words issue as if they are whistled.

"I know you fetched him from the pound."

"He's not for sale."

"I don't want to buy him. I want to know whether you knew his owner."

"Who are you?" Earl asks.

Armand identifies himself, handing a card to Earl. Earl scans it briefly, places it in his pocket. "I am making inquiries on behalf of Alexandra Rosen's sister."

"I worked with Alex," Earl says clearing his throat and speaking with some sadness. "I was one of her supervisors. She was a fine woman, a good worker and what happened to her was unconscionable."

"How do you mean?"

"Clearly, the virus that killed her came from our lab. We didn't have adequate control over the it. Her death is really our fault."

"But the virus didn't walk into Alex's house by itself," Armand protests. "Somebody brought it to her."

"Walk with me," Earl says. "There's a park nearby and I can see that Apepi has to go."

They walk together quietly for a half block. Now Armand sees a green area in front of him. There is a fenced-in dog park. Earl lets Apepi loose to cavort with other dogs. Two smaller mutts begin to play with him.

"You don't have to worry about him in there with dogs he doesn't know?"

"No," Earl smiles for the first time. "He gets along with everybody. Funny for a guard dog. You would think he would be more selective in his friends."

"So, tell me how the virus got out."

Early frowns. "I have no idea. Either Alex herself managed to open the enclosed part of the lab and pull out some of the mouse feces in a vial, or somebody else did it. Brent would know since he keeps records of whatever leaves the lab."

"Brent?"

"Brent Sadowski. But there are so many others who may have needed to work with hantavirus. Since we have a fair number of employees who work in that area, impossible to know. We do know that it would not have been easy for anyone including Alex to simply grab a vial and walk out undiscovered."

"Did you know about the dog before Alex died?" Armand asks.

"Wait a sec," Earl says. From his pocket, he pulls out a rawhide bone and throws it to Apepi. "That will keep him occupied for a bit. Yes, Alex talked about him a good deal. I only saw them together once by chance but I admired the dog right away. And when I learned he had been sent to the pound, I assumed Alex's sister did not want him, and I was determined to fetch him for myself."

"And when you did, how was he?"

"Apepi? Beautiful, as you can see," he responds proudly.

"Yes, I do see. But was he completely healthy?"

"Aaah, I see where you are going with this. True, the guard said that the dog was recovering from an infection in the lungs."

"Who made this analysis?"

"A vet who comes by from time to time, I was told. But the vet said that he thought the infection would heal quite quickly with antibiotics, and by the time I picked up Apepi, he was basically healed."

"The infection was diagnosed?"

"You mean as to what specific infection it was?"

"Yes."

"Not as far as I know. You might ask the vet, but with so many dogs, it's doubtful whether he did the usual tests on this dog. It's not as if he was being paid big bucks by a client who cared about his pet."

"I am wondering whether the dog also was infected with the hantavirus which killed his owner," Armand said quietly.

Earl's head shot up. "My God, I hadn't thought about that. It is entirely possible. Hanta would not have done much to a dog, but is fatal to human beings. This opens up some avenue of thought, doesn't it?"

131

20

Roger Gets Closer to Denise

Arm in arm on a bench on a very chilly morning overlooking an ice skating rink below. Huddled together in their overcoats, Denise is covering her face with a scarf. Roger puts his arm around her and pulls her in close. "You are trembling," he says to her, cuddling her.

She looks up at him. "Damn cold here," she responds with a crick in her throat.

"We can leave."

Shakes her head negatively. "Not just yet. I'm watching the girls down there arabesque, twirling around in skating costumes as if they are totally unaffected by the cold. They are astonishing."

Takes her gloved hands in his and rubs them softly.

"You are a very good man," Denise purrs. "You take care of me, don't you?"

For some reason, her comment stops him rubbing. He leans back against the icy wooden frame of the bench.

"Did I say something wrong?" she asks.

"No," he says with his face muffled as he speaks into her coat. "It's just that when we became lovers, we were clear that this was no romance. It was only as advertised, a roll in the hay. Good for you, good for me, good for our morale."

"I agree," she responds, visible words issuing from her throat. "But when you are nice to me, I want to say something about that. Am I not allowed?"

Sighs. "I'm just over sensitive. Forget I said anything. But you enjoy the lovemaking?" he asks quickly.

"Can't you tell?"

"Not always. I know you orgasm, that much I know. I think I know," he adds, thinking that some women feign pleasure for their man. "But your emotions have a moat in front of them," Roger adds.

"I am having a whale of a time with you in bed," she says smiling, her eyes bright and wide open. "Is that what you needed to hear? That we fit together nicely. I have a release or two, sometimes three every time we are together. You do care to know that you satisfy me, right? We do fit together like a hand in glove. A fine jigsaw," she adds laughing. "But," she adds, why do we stop there? If we are congruent in other ways, isn't it all right to explore?"

He looks uncomfortable, his eyes away from Denise and onto the rink. "They are spectacular, aren't they?" he points to a group of three girls in gossamer skirts pirouetting gracefully one after the other.

"You'd rather not talk about us."

"I'd rather not," he replies. "We're good together as it is. I don't want more. I don't expect more. I don't need more. And you?" He continues with a small rasp in his tone.

"I'm fine with things as they are," she lies.

"Great. So, this is what I want to talk about," he continues. "The script, our roles."

"Sure," she says.

Above, a propeller plane is circling lazily in the sky. Beneath them on the rink, laughter as a slew of skaters tumble into one another, one after the other. Young people with dogs are running along a path into the woods. Squirrels chasing one another up trees.

"Tell me what you think of it."

"The script? It's all right. Sometimes, it feels just on. Other times, I'm not so sure."

"You think it's flowing in the wrong direction?"

"No," Denise answers. "It has to follow your character from one clue to the next. This is how it goes."

"And the words we're using to express that progression?"

"Maybe not as creative as I might like," she says.

"Yes," he agrees, "but that is what you get in the soap. You really don't want philosophy or three syllable words. You want an occasional jolt of emotion, as well as some movement of plot and character. Still I think your role isn't fleshed out enough."

"Really?" She looks up suddenly interested.

"You seem more a sounding board for the private eye than an actual flesh and blood person."

She laughs quickly. "I agree with you. I wish I had a larger presence. But the focus must be on you. Aren't you the one who unveils the secret of Alexandra's demise?"

"I'm hoping that the writers are going to put more meat on the bone."

"For your sake?" she asks

"Partially. I'd like to interact with more than a stick."

"Heah, I'm no stick," she grins.

He prods her gently in her ribs. "I know that, miss. I do know that better than most."

She chuckles. "I am getting frozen bound to the bench. Not

sure if I can get up." He yanks at her and they stand together laughing, shaking off snow pellets. They begin to walk back towards fifth avenue and towards central park south.

"Good coffee place on the corner," he advises her.

The walk through the light snow easily and without concern. But in Denise's heart, the emotion she experienced previously, she now seeks to stamp out. It is a feeling about Roger, about the delicacy of his yellow hair and how it feels in her hands when they are touching. Beyond that, she is finding a lyricism in the depth of her recesses expressing a larger feeling for Roger than she has admitted to herself. God forbid, she can never show a hint of it to him! It is an emotional surge of love, she is thinking as they now crisply cross the street where neighing horses and covered carts were once stationed. These were once a symbol of romance for couples who clip clopped their way through and around the park, she remembers fondly. She dare not speak of it. She dare not let any feeling or even the suggestion of her feelings slip. It would mark the end of their fragile bond. Nor does Denise dare to consider what may develop between them in the future. She does concede that eventually their love-making will be less dramatic, less frequent. If nothing else takes its place, say a more mature desire for togetherness, surely their bond will crack, and only the sterility of their bond as actors would remain. Her bones cry out against such an ending. Yet, she keeps tenaciously quiet. Nor does her face reveal anything but a reaction to the frost of the late morning. Roger is pushing open the door to the little café-bakery, moves quickly to the counter to order coffee and raspberry croissants, spinning around to Denise and wondering why her expression appears suspended in some alien, if neutral place, attributing her distance to the wind-whipped frost they have left behind. Takes off her coat.

135

"You'll warm up quicker," he explains.

"Yes," she says. "I will." The coffee is lusciously warm flowing down her throat, but her core feels empty, her sense of herself collapsing within her despite or because of the presence of her lover. As she turns to see him shake out his yellow mane and position himself comfortably into a chair opposite her, his legs jutting out into the lane, the trembling she experiences is not a remnant of the cold but of an opaque future.

21

Benjamin and Marcella Jousting

(Benjamin to audience) "We did see one another on Sundays. We had been fencing for several months when we joined the Middle Ages Jousting Club. A group of men and women who dressed up in papier-mache replica outfits of the dark ages, and ventured out every Sunday morning with wooden shields and swords to whack the shit out of each other. It was the last time I was to see her before we broke up." (Exits right)

(Marcella enters masked with helmet, sword and shield) "I'm a woman after all. I'm supposed to be holding out for a yellow and black scarf to drape around my champion's neck as he fights for me. What am I doing in this get-up?"

(Benjamin enters with costume) "The rules are simple. I hit at you and you hit back at me until one of us cries uncle. No swiping below the belt. Ready? En garde!" (He advances towards her with his sword and strikes her gingerly, but she parries)

(Marcella swinging at him and missing) "You're a professor, for God's sakes. (She swings again and hits his shield) What are we doing with these loonies?"

"We're fighting in a controlled way. This combat even has rules. A hell of a lot better than uncontrolled verbal abuse."

(Marcella swinging again, this time hitting him) "Well, take this controlled swipe. I hit you!" she chortles. "I made you fall!" (Delighted, she swings at him again, but he parries).

"Can't you even wait until I get up, bitch?" he cries out angrily.

"You never said anything about waiting." (She lunges again and hits him).

"That was a low blow."

"What do you intend to do about it, Sir Knight?"

(On the ground) "You've caused me plenty of distress," he says nursing a small cut. "I think you drew blood."

"Come on, you coward. Get on your feet."

(Gets up and knocks her down) "Who are you calling coward? Ready to cry uncle?"

(Dusts herself off) "Hell, no."

"Well, get up then so I can beat you to a pulp."

"I'm out of breath. Give a damsel a moment."

"No pre-menstrual excuses. Get up and fight."

"You're bigger, heavier. It's not fair."

"And I am a professor, a male and I have genitals unlike yours and I have a history of success."

(Marcella getting up with a roar, knocks him down with repeated blows) "Success, my ass."

(Marcella continues to beat him) "Wait. Stop. Uncle," he cries out.

"Say it again, you twirp."

"Uncle." (Gets up slowly, sheepishly) "Do you love me?"

"I won!"

"You hurt me, he avows." (Dusts off)

"You're the one always talking about taking risks."

"I asked you a question? (Takes off his helmet, mask and armor) Be honest."

"I am. I didn't answer you." (She divests herself of her mask and armor).

(Benjamin to audience, undressing) "Maybe she was. I just couldn't fathom the whole thing. I did know that her attitude was big trouble, bigger than I had expected, and when I resisted, called her, hoping to see her again, she turned me down. I couldn't stand it. The more I complained, the more she resisted. I stopped calling her. A week elapsed and we had not talked. My friends urged me to give her up, just shunt her aside. Not so easy to do. I launched into work as hard as I could, and learned that week that my book would be published by a scholarly press. But that mattered little compared to how I felt when the phone rang. I would jump out of my seat and try to breath normally when I answered it.

I heard through the grapevine that Marcella had been offered the position of special assistant to President Jager, and that she had accepted it. I knew he had always been fond of her, the letch! He liked her energy and creativity, or so he said. Deep down, he simply liked having her around. She was to do community relations, a bit of fund raising and trouble-shooting for him. Hearing nothing day after day, I began to despair." (Exits right).

(Janice enters from left with Marcella) "So what did you say?"

"I wasn't sure what to write," Marcella answers.

"What did you write? You sure made a 180 degree turn here. First you made it almost impossible for him to contact you. Now you're opening the door again. So, your text to him must have been super cool."

(Blushing) "I wrote Benjamin that he had left his pork roast in my freezer and that he might consider retrieving it before it spoiled."

"What a great piece of prose!" Janice roars. "Shakespeare must be turning green with envy in his grave."

"He should have found my text this morning."

"What else?"

"Nothing else."

"No notation to call you back about the friggin' pork roast?"

"I just wanted to get in touch. I missed him."

"Well that might be the most romantic, if senseless notion under God's sun. But you never told me what happened between you and Matt," Janice asks with anticipation.

"It just didn't work out," Marcella confesses.

"Tell me."

"He doesn't have soft lips like Benjamin. He's not sensual like Benjamin. He endlessly describes night shifts at the hospital, and seems to have an unusual fondness for hemorrhoids."

"I can see that you are more repelled than attracted. You better be getting home girl," Janice chuckles. "There just might be a message for you."

(Benjamin enters from right, spies Marcella and walks towards her. Holds out phone) "What's this supposed to mean?"

(Stammers) "Pork roast spoiling in freezer. Not clear enough for you?"

"I think I'll leave you fools alone," Janice says, exiting left.

(Points towards sofa) "Sit down over here and tell me whether my pork roast is still edible."

"I'm convinced it is."

"I paid $14.98 at the butchers for it, you know," Benjamin growls.

"I noticed the cut is lean."

"And what happens if someday I appear at your house to fetch it?"

"Maybe we could cook the roast. Then, what else do you do with such a thing but eat it."

"You and Matt and I? Two sparring partners and an assman…."

"Just the two of us."

"If you put it that way, lady," Benjamin smiles, "you've got a deal." (He shakes her hand)

(Marcella crying) "I missed you to pieces."

"You almost blew this one, Marcella," he says ruefully.

"Silly me. Still I had to do it this way. Bring your face over here." (He complies and they kiss) I've got to go. I was on my way to the President's office."

"What time shall we eat?"

"Come when you can and don't bring pajamas." (She exits left)

(Benjamin to audience, shaking his head slowly) "Well, what do you know about that?"

End of Act One

22

Practicing Passion

Denise and Roger are lounging in the second row of the theatre with their feet propped up when Jason Fierst swoops down upon them. Birdlike indeed, thinks Roger, his eyes darting upwards. He has never before been able to describe the resemblance between Jason and a heron, but now it strikes him full in the face. Jason is balancing on one slender leg looking through his script.

"Nice to see you," he begins, not looking at them. "Here, let me place myself between both of you." Denise shifts one seat and Jason moves in. "I've been looking through the dailies, recent stuff as well." He turns to Denise. "Your dresses are too matronly for this role," he begins. "To be blunt, they suck."

"I don't choose my dresses," Denise counters.

"Well, I'm here to tell you that we need to streamline your outfits, make them more a apropos, more modern to today's woman. In other words, I don't want you to be perceived as just the grieving sister. True, your lovely half, Alexandra, has died a tragic and mysterious death, but after an appropriate time lag you should be terminating grief-time and molting into little pink blossoms, a woman evolving into a sexy little number."

Denise smiles. "I rather like the change."

"Thought you might. "The role is shifting. Roger, the P.I. is your employee, of course, but is it possible that he could represent more to you in your tender young life? Regard your pitiful existence. Your sister is dead under less than auspicious circumstances. You have nobody else to lean on. You've hired this tall, heroic stud to sift through the clues. The two of you enmeshed in torrid embraces! That is what I want the viewers twittering about, pondering. But who the fuck can think about the two of you in clinches if you look like an Italian matron in war-torn Sicily?"

"So, is that the plan? Are we going to be in romantic clinches?" Roger asks.

Jason laughs, bats his eyes mysteriously. "You know I ain't no Cassandra, I can't reveal the future. I just consider and reflect what our viewers are tweeting and texting us. They deem the two of you ideal for hanky panky. It is also true, however, that the screenwriters may be preparing a different set of outcomes."

"So, I'll be getting better, prettier outfits," Denise coos. "I approve."

"Yes," Jason continues, his bird-head down, "but you must also step up your game. More seductive, less distant, please. You can't be totally pre-occupied with the death of your sister. You are also a young woman with hormones gushing through your veins, perhaps even running amuck from time to time."

"Running amuck for Roger?"

Jason grins and sits back, raising his nose back into an upright position.

"I don't think Jason is gonna reveal squat," Roger says, smiling.

"It's time for me to shut my trap. This is one of them. But I also have a quarrel with you as well, Roger. You are playing the detective as if you were a cool, level-headed cop who spends

143

his time sifting clues from a computer. I don't want that. Our audience doesn't want that. We need you to step up to the plate and become rakish."

"Rakish?"

"Jaunty. You're not only a smart P.I. You're also a man working with Keely day after day, and this proximity intrudes on your calculations. Sometimes, even, you may experience urgings in your nether regions."

Roger giggles. "Nether regions? You mean like a boner?"

Jason slaps him on the back. "Ultimate expression of approval," he roars. "A boner never lies. Not for public consumption of course, but your acting will make the audience believe that you are not impervious to this lovely girl's charms. She is not only a wounded damsel in distress, but a girl with round lips, great tits, and a sterling behind. In other words, a whale of a package."

"Got it," Roger says. "I'll make a note to be more randy on set."

"You might try it off set too, just for practice, of course," Jason says his lips working as if he were nibbling on a cracker.

Roger and Denise glance at one another. "I see you may have beaten me to the punch on this one," Jason quips observantly. "Bring it all back to Babylon. We shoot tomorrow and I'd like to see you both dripping with pheromones, shedding them like some wet robin drying herself."

Late that afternoon, as Denise is catching a vintage flick on TV, popcorn in hand, her door bell sounds.

"Roger," she says surprised. "I thought you were going home to practice jaunty and rakish."

"I don't need to practice that," he responds. "I believe I have mastered it. And that's why I came here. Are you going to let me in?"

"Sure," she says. "Something you could get here which you

144

couldn't find at home, perhaps?"

He grabs her waist, Denise clearly accepting, draws her near and kisses her. "Could be," he says." I'll only know if I find it."

"Let me know if you do," she says, smoothing her lips together. She is beginning to undress him. He stands there almost idly. "Not feeling it yet," he says, sniffing the air as if the answer were in the ether, as his shirt comes undone. Belt buckle is loosened and his pants drop. Her hands are in his shorts exploring. "Yes," he says." I should have brought a pen to take notes for our director. I am, however, noticing something stirring. And it ain't soup."

"Did you want to stand there naked all by yourself?" she pouts guilelessly.

"Hmm, let me consider…actually, it would be more scientific if you also divested yourself of your garments. That way, we might compare notes when the other is also standing naked."

"True," she agrees. She undoes her blouse, strips off her bra.

"Allow me to touch those nipples of yours to see whether this interaction will generate emotion in either of us…" He massages them with his fingers. "I do feel something. Can't quite get whether this is what Jason was reaching for."

She closes the gap between them, reaches up and kisses him on the mouth, a hand on the nape of his neck. Backs off for an instant. "Could this qualify as seductive in his lexicon?" she asks demurely.

"I believe so," Roger replies. "At any rate, you're on the right track. I'll make a mental note of what is going on in this moment." Now, he lifts her up and anchors her on the dining room table.

"But Roger," Denise demurs innocently, "this is a place where we often take dinner."

Scowling, Roger enters her slowly but convincingly. "Rakish

enough for you?"

She shakes her head negatively. "You could still be a bit jauntier," she suggests. "I hardly find myself titillated."

"And this?" he asks as he continues to probe within her.

"Grab my hair."

"Good thinking," he says. "He yanks at her hair."

"Ouch," she cries. "Roguish is one thing. Being Tarzan another."

"Too hard?"

"Too hard up there, not enough down there."

"Is this better?" Roger says pounding into her.

Scarcely able to breathe, Denise smiles. "I think you're on to something. Maybe your jauntiness is becoming more apparent."

"I hope so", he says breathing with difficulty, "because I wouldn't want Jason to be disappointed."

"This seems like just the thing," she whispers. "But how am I doing? Giving off the right vibes?"

"Hmmm. Just about," responding breathlessly. "But maybe if you got on your knees, that would strike a better tone."

She descends onto her knees and takes him in her hands, looks up at him. "Let me know if this does anything for you."

"You're nearing something special here," he responds thoughtfully. "I truly believe Jason would be proud of us. Tomorrow let's enact this entire scene in front of him to prove it."

23

Denise Has A Visitor

When the doorbell rings, Keely hastens to buzz the door. Looks in her viewer. Disappointed. It is not Armand. Through her peephole, she discerns the frame and face of a stranger.

"My name is Brent Sadowski," the lips say. He is dislodging a set of red earphones.

"And who is that?" Keely asks cautiously.

"A friend of Alex," he replies.

She opens the door for him. Brent Sadowski is a large man with a pronounced belly. A round face with a short, crew haircut, lackluster brown eyes, lips which after speaking, slip. Eyes are large, somewhat distended. As a child, Brent could hardly see. Waffled through most of elementary school without glasses, his teachers certain the boy was retarded, if not simply a dunce. With glasses, he ultimately muddled through school. Only later did he undergo surgery which partially cured his vision. But it left behind a residue which he would bear for the remainder of his life. He saw people and objects with auras. Were he to examine a face, the aura would surround the entire globe. A car? It carried vibrating about its frame a kind of a glossy sheen. As time went on, Brent was able to modify the glow. For objects or people of which he approved, he perceived them with auras of differing hues. So, as he looked at Alexandra, he saw her face cradled, bathed even, in a golden tint. He never again pictured her in any other fashion.

"You knew my sister?"

"Very well," Brent says. He offers Keely a bouquet of flowers, chrysanthemums. Denise brings out a vase from the cupboard and arranges the flowers. "We worked together. Didn't Alex ever mention me to you?" Now he takes off a black woolen coat and lays it on a chair.

"Please don't do that," Keely says, irritated. "Put it in the closet. I hate to have clothing lying around."

Brent picks up the coat and places the coat on a hanger. "She never mentioned me to you?" he asks with disappointment.

"Not that I recall."

"Hmm," Brent says, his lips drooping. "I thought I meant more."

"She often didn't tell me about her friends," Keely responds quickly.

"But she told me a great deal about you. She said that you were a lovely flower," he continues without self-consciousness, "and I wholly agree."

"Really!" Keely lilts melodiously. "A flower!"

"And," Brent continues with the same tone, "I own a little dog. His name is Fernando. I call him Fer for short."

"So, you have a dog…" Keely says, perplexed, unable to follow the train of thought.

"Yes, he is a poodle and some other tiny dog mix. He sits up when I ask him to."

"And you are mentioning Fernando for some special reason?"

"Naturally," Brent replies, taking long sips from a glass of water. "He used to play with Apepi."

"Ah, Alex's dog."

"Yes. They played hide and go seek."

"Really!" Keely says, sitting down demurely. "How did they do that?"

"Fernando would disappear and Apepi would sniff the apartment until he found him. Then there would be playful barking to celebrate their reunion."

"And did Apepi ever hide from Fernando?"

Brent looks at Keely as if the question were outre. "Well no," he retorts with virtual dismay. "That's not how the game is played."

"I don't have Apepi," Keely says as if that dog's presence would satisfy the reason for Brent's visit.

"Pity."

"Because the two of them could play together," Keely prompts.

"Yes, Fernando is having Apepi withdrawal. He is hardly eating these days because he does not run and jump with his pharaoh friend."

"But I believe I know where Apepi is," Keely offers.

"Me too," Brent replies, "but the owner refuses to allow the dog to see mine. It is both unkind and perhaps even bigoted. Don't you agree?"

"Aah, well…." Keely murmurs tongue-tied.

"I mean they were the fastest of friends. They played together twice a week, sometimes more if Alex got sick."

"Oh…did Alex get sick often?"

"Hardly ever."

"So, Brent, if I may call you by your first name…. was there some reason you came here today?"

"I almost forgot," Brent chortles, his belly protruding and jiggling. "I'm here to offer my condolences. I could not come to the funeral because Fer was not up to it." he continues to chortle.

"I see," Keely says, not seeing at all. Pause. "Maybe you could elaborate a bit."

"I mean he was throwing up and didn't want me to leave," he continues with a slight giggle.

"Of course. Brent! May I call you Brent? You don't quite get to the point. Is there a point to all of this?"

"So, I am here now to tell you how sorry I am that Alex was poisoned to death."

"Excuse me!"

"You do know she died, right?" he asks tentatively.

"Of course," Keely exhales, "but you think she was poisoned"

"That was the cause of death, no? Poison."

"But not administered by anyone else. Are you claiming…."

"I have my own theory about that," Brent says crossing his legs.

"Which is?"

He uncrosses them. "I believe," he hesitates.

"Go on, Brent." Keely is now irritated by Brent's uneven speech patterns. "This is conversation, Brent. I speak and you answer. Sometimes it works the other way around."

"Keely, I hate to speculate. That's why I am hesitating."

"Brent, you have my full attention, Please."

"Well then," he says crossing his legs, "I think she may have taken the wrong bottle with her home."

"What bottle are we talking about?"

"In my cabinet at work there are drugs, one of which she may have brought home. Some of them are extremely virulent. I mean they contain poisons. Harmful to humans, I truly mean. Many of them look alike because the vials are pretty much identical."

"What sort of drugs?"

Brent shifts uncomfortably in his seat. "I wouldn't know about that."

"But I think you do," she probes. "At the very least, make a guess."

"In fact, there may have been some cocaine there," he relents at last.

"Why would there be cocaine in your cabinet?"

"For medicinal use, I suppose. It's sometimes prescribed as an anesthetic. I wouldn't know exactly. But everyone was clear that Alex was imbibing drugs now and then."

Keely stands. "Tell me about that. I understand drugs were found in her system when she died."

"I really don't know too much. I asked her out once."

"You did?" Once again, Keely is having difficulty following Brent's narrative.

"Yes."

"Well, go on."

"Well," she said right away as if she were waiting for me to ask her all her life, sure. Let's grab a bite to eat at the Lonely Kitchen which is a food truck near her apartment. And we'll carry food home and we can catch some TV."

"So, you had a date with my sister."

"No. I had dinner with her," he says his lips declining.

"I see. Not a date, then. And?"

"So, we bought junior tacos at the Lonely Truck and stopped at the liquor store for a bottle of Chilean red wine. I paid. Almost let the bottle drop as we were walking. I sometimes talk with my hands, you see," he explains. "Then we went upstairs to her apartment and ate. It was quite nice. I didn't have to do dishes. Alex said so. Apepi showed up. A neighbor brought him by after ten minutes. Brent hastened to explain. She had an arrangement with a neighbor for the dog. The dog seemed to like me and jumped up to lick my nose."

"And the drugs? Can you get back to the drugs?"

Brent licks his lips. "Well after dinner, she said let's repair to the living room. So, we did. We repaired there with a glass of wine. And when we finished the wine, she said she had rolled a joint, and would I join her in lighting the joint. So, I immediately agreed, although I want to say in my defense I had rarely smoked an illegal drug before. I found your sister amiable, you see."

"So, you smoked a joint together."

"Yes. Then, when we had finished the joint, Alex said she had a turbulent headache, that the room was spinning around, and she needed to take a pill. So, she went to the bathroom. After a few seconds, she called me. She said: Brent. Come to the bathroom. So, I did. Then she said. 'Could you help me find the right pill? My headache is so stinging I can't see.' So, I looked through the cabinet and found a box entitled cola. I opened it up and there were sachets of white powder. She took one, opened it up, carefully lined powder on the counter of the sink, and sniffed it up. Then she turned to me with a smile and asked whether I would like to do the same. I said sure although I had never done this before. So, she set out another line and I sniffed it up. It felt like a hot iron in my brain and spun me around. The next thing I knew is that we were back on the couch together and she was talking about you and saying what a great sister you were although she rarely saw you, you were so busy she opined, and how lovely a flower you are and how smart, and the next thing she was sobbing in my arms. Dried her tears I did. With a handkerchief I had in my pocket, a clean, cotton handkerchief. A white, embroidered one," he adds. "Cleansed her of the sobbing. Next thing she put her face close to mine and applied lips to my earlobe. I thought this unusual but I wasn't complaining at all. Just thought it somewhat unprecedented. I hadn't had anybody plant two lips on my earlobe since I was two." Brent now looked up and smiled. "I've said too much, haven't I?"

"I'm fascinated," Keely replies, her face agape with amazement. "Go on."

"Well, then, I stood up to go home figuring that Alex looked exhausted and her crying had stopped for the moment, but she clung to me and begged me not to go. She said she was lonely. And I said: just like the lonely truck, but she did not laugh at this joke. The joke was a good one, though. She just curled up in my lap and began to sob a bit more. Then she fell asleep."

"So, what did you do?"

"Well, I couldn't move. Because if I moved, she would have awakened."

"So, you didn't move?"

"I just stayed there with Alex's head on my lap. Then I turned out the light."

"You couldn't move her head out of the way?"

"Oh no," Brent said loudly, jowls drooping as they moved, "that would have been ever so impolite. I waited until she herself woke up around two in the morning to go to the bathroom, and then I waited until she had flushed before leaving. After she rubbed her eyes with her fingers, she shook hands with me. When I left, I remembered I had to go too, so I stopped in a bar."

"That's quite a story. Did you date again?"

"Yes, several times," Brent said.

"And you never met one of her boyfriends, a guy named Tal."

"Once she told me Tal had broken up with her," Brent replied slowly. "That's all I knew about him."

Keely hands Brent a cup of hot chocolate which he accepts

153

with a wan smile. "You went out with her afterwards?"

"Yes. Not as her boyfriend though," he hastens to add.

"Then what?"

"As her friend. She told me I was fast not becoming her boyfriend, but fast becoming her friend."

"And what did you do together?"

"We cooked meals, sometimes at my place, watched TV. Occasionally, we went out to a movie. Once, we took a hike."

"So, you saw a good bit of Alex."

"I did," he says proudly.

"And how did she appear to you?"

"I have to say," Brent continues, his lips depressing, "that she seemed more down each time we met. By down, I mean she was concerned."

"About what?"

"She didn't like to talk about this, but once she mentioned she had real trouble with Tal. She said she would throw him out of her life soon if he didn't shape up."

"Interesting. Because I heard that Tal threw her out."

"Oh no," Brent erupts, a lock of hair curling upwards. "Oh definitely no. She found him increasingly disagreeable, even violent when they argued, and they argued quite frequently. She said he hit her. But I never saw marks on her face. I said this to her. In the stomach, she pointed, then took my hand to the spot where it occurred, with his fist. This way he hurt her without visible marks. Have you met Tal?"

"No."

"He's a brute," Brent gushes. "An ugly creepy brute who lives off others." Now he takes a sip of the hot chocolate. "Say, this is quite good, but it is awfully sweet."

"I may have dropped in too many sweeteners," Keely confesses.

154

"I like it very sweet."

"But it is awfully good," Brent replies, holding the cup as if it were a testament to goodness.

24

Benjamin and the Ring

Act Two

(The set is unchanged with one exception. A display counter, as if from a jewelry store, stage right. There is a phone on the counter. A bed stage left. Next to the bed, a nightstand with a statue)

(Curtain rises to reveal Benjamin center stage) "I own a bronze statue of Arora, the goddess of dawn (He walks to the nightstand, picks up the statue and caresses it) "In that miserable ten-day period I waited for Marcella to call, I would rub it like some Aladdin's lamp, and pray for her to return to me. Now we all know that in real life these things don't happen.

(Pensive) My existence hasn't been superior, but I've never wanted for basics, certainly not food, shelter, clothing. Happiness, whatever that is, contentment, well, that's another story. I learned about the yin and the yang. When you're emotionally up, some force reminds you that ongoing contentment is friggin' elusive. It also works the other way. Distraught, I always foolishly yearned for change, but if it flowered, I couldn't accept the bouquet. I was suspicious. Steeled myself for the worst. Wasn't it just a matter of time before Marcella withdrew entirely? I lost weight, smoked furiously despite the fact I had sworn to quit months before. That is, promised myself to quit. Uncertain of events, suddenly I got a note from her. I couldn't interpret it at first. Even when I met her for dinner that night, I was too dense to understand either her or the situation.

And yet, when I began to believe in Marcella's conversion, I caved into the wonderment of it. Is there anything more miraculous than to experience a cherished love withering when, suddenly, out of nowhere, without expectation, hope dashed, it blooms once more. Like a perfect blossom rising before you very eyes. Enthralled, imbued with love.

(Marcella enters from left into living room. She has brought cleaning materials with her. Both begin to clean throughout the following exchange.) "That was a feast. You cooked up a storm, Benjamin."

(looking up at her) "Do you want to tell me what's happened?"

"It was a temporary confusion, she responds shrugging, which I have now sorted out. I've been shortsighted. There was something holding me back, silly promises unfulfilled. I thought I needed to see other men, but all I needed was to experience a single woeful experience. Once was enough."

"Was it?" Benjamin asks suspiciously.

"When Matt and I were together," she speaks intimately, "he'd be telling me a joke or maybe a story when I realized that I was hardly listening. Instead, I was lost in a hug with you."

"Did you sleep with him?" Benjamin asks roughly.

"Does it matter?"

"Yes, it matters", Benjamin cries out. "Of course, it matters."

"I couldn't stand him touching me," Marcella affirms with a

slight tremor.

"Ok, that was Matt," he says, his tone yielding. "What else do you need? More of a basis of comparison? Is that what you're after? Then maybe one proctologist isn't the end of your research."

"I thought about you, only you," she responds. "Isn't that enough?"

"Yes, I guess so," he replies, sighing.

Marcella stops cleaning, turns to him without a smile, a lock of hair falling over one eye. "I want us to make love."

"So, do I," he says, still wielding a brush over a dish, "but for some reason, I don't think it is possible."

Marcella looks up at him. "So, you don't believe me, then."

"I just can't swing up and down like that," he replies animatedly. "And it's not because I find you any the less attractive. Just the opposite. I love you like some thirsty, lost nomad who has stumbled onto a desert oasis."

"You don't know what you're missing," she laughs. "I just had a jacuzzi put in my oasis last week."

"Slowly, Marcella, slowly", he affirms shaking his head. (Stops working. To audience) "We did make love. Not that night, but the following night, and it felt incredible. Within a week, I was soaring with Marcella within me, my mouth forming words I couldn't possibly have been ready to say." (Goes to Marcella on sofa).

"Don't you think we ought to go in the direction...permanency is...don't you want to marry me?"

"Yes."

"You do?" his mouth fumbling the words.

"Yes."

"That's the wisest decision you've ever made." (he touches her cheek, now turns to audience, recites the following as if it were poetry). "Charm of love: resist all you like but once you abandon yourself, it is a blinding sun that sets itself burning indelibly into the brain. I was out of my mind. Insane with expectation. I forgot everything, the hurt I had experienced, the unsettledness of this woman, her problems in communicating, her reluctance to know herself, traits which I treasured and found essential in any woman. I shunted all aside, my mind engorged with the riot of her scent, her essence. My question had been retiring as if I fully expected her to turn me down, but when she agreed, something surged inside me, and it hasn't stopped skyrocketing."

"Yes! Yes!" Marcella croons. "Yes!"

(Kisses her. She exits stage left. Benjamin goes to the jewelry counter. A young woman, Heather, entering from stage right, waiting on him) "I know you, don't I?"

"Yes, Dr. Perls", Heather replies.

"Heather! I haven't seen you since graduation two years ago. What are you doing here?"

"I work here."

"What happened to teaching, to graduate school?"

(Embarrassed tone) "I got involved with a townie and now we're living together. I took the job at this store because we needed the money. How can I help you?"

"Heather, I'm engaged. I'm here to find a ring for my fiancée."

"I'm happy for you," Heather says without appearing happy. "Who is she? I guess it doesn't matter. I'm out of that loop forever. Let me show you what we have." (She takes out several rings from the case, holds one up). "This is a classical, fine ring, full, clear carat, mounted on 18 karat gold. (He examines it) "If you prefer something less expensive…"

"No," Benjamin says. "I'll take it. (To audience) I paid a small fortune for this little number. I wanted desperately to make Marcella happy, to give back a percentage of what she was giving me these days. She told me what when she and her ex got engaged, he offered her a puny ring, because at the time, he couldn't afford anything else, and how disappointed she was. (Marcella returns to the stage, sits on sofa. He goes to her and presents her with the ring. She looks at it, lifts her head, smiles, hugs him) I believed her happy. A while later, as we were completing a list of people for the engagement party that President Jager had proposed, I learned how wrong I had been."

(Marcella holds up the ring) "Benjamin," she begins, "this gesture was wonderful."

"I thought you would like it."

"I love it," she gushes. "Lots. You were so thoughtful... (Takes his had affectionately) But to be honest, this ring just is not me. It's so conventional. Have you ever even looked at my jewelry? It's different from what you ordinarily see in stores. Local stores, I mean," she adds thoughtfully.

"I never gave it much thought."

"Before the party, we need to find something more suitable. I'd be embarrassed wearing this ring."

"Just tell me what you want me to do," Benjamin says grimly, his face crimsoning.

"Take the ring back."

"Exchange it?"

"No, get the money. I've seen a more beautiful ring elsewhere which wouldn't cost much more."

(To audience, Benjamin turns slowly) "Talk about embarrassment. How do you take back an engagement ring without looking like a total loser? But it had to be done! (To Marcella) "Let's do it now. I'll get a refund and then we'll buy the ring you want. (They approach the counter) How am I going to pull this off? Do jewelry stores return monies on engagement rings? They may only credit me on another ring."

"Tell them I turned you down," Marcella responds firmly, "and then there will be no question about it."

(At counter, as Marcella waits at a discrete distance. Heather comes forward. Benjamin gives her the ring. She exits stage right with it (To audience) "I could hear them tittering in the back, Heather and her female manager. I saw several other employees back there, their noses pressed against the glass to get the best possible look at this year's number one loser."

(Heather returns from stage right) "My manager says we can credit back your card. I'm really sorry for you, Dr. Perls. What happened?" she asks innocently. Clearly, Heather is relishing this situation.

"I must have misread the cues," Benjamin responds, his teeth baring slightly.

"Did the lady reject you outright?" she asks, but does not look up. "Or is this situation temporary?"

"I gave her the ring," Benjamin says almost snarling, "and she refused to accept it."

"You always did have trouble reading women, didn't you, Dr. Perls?" Now, her smile is broad and insidious.

(Accepting a receipt from Heather, turns to audience) "Little shit. She got her own back over my supposed misery. Now what have I learned from all of this? That the best intentions aren't enough. And yet, after I left the store, I felt as if I had pulled off a heist, and my spirits soared."

(To Marcella) "I got the refund. You should have seen them in there, all those cackling women. Lord, I hope I never meet any of them again."

(Arm around Benjamin) "I'm so proud of you." (The exit right together)

25

An Audition

The air in Quebec is cold, and many passageways are icy. Snow covered streets have been swept clean, but the sidewalks are largely impassable. Denise, in a fake mottled fur huddled up to her cheeks, a tufted woolen hat covering her hair, has taken Roger's arm as they tread lightly on the glaring white pavement. Occasional traffic has them edge over, but generally, due to the wind-whipped snow the night before, there are few cars. Above, smokestacks are smoking out wafts of hot air into little clouds that glide aimlessly above the town.

They have been talking about their role on Babylon Revisited. Roger declares that the role will soon be exhausted, to which Denise quickly asks what will happen to her.

"Of course, the mystery of Alex's death will need to be resolved," he hastens to add. "But after that, not clear what follows, if anything. They may elect to keep us, maybe not. I've been on for several years, but I fear, as I age, that my capacity to interest this audience is waning. As for you, you seem to have done well for yourself. I think you are getting as much fan mail as I am. Maybe more."

"Is that some standard?" Denise asks, the speech from her

mouth exiting in frosty, tiny clouds. And aren't I aging too?"

Roger pulls up his coat around his neck. "Should have brought a scarf," he says.

"Well don't leave me hanging," Denise prompts. "Tell me what you think."

"Frankly," Roger replies, "I have no answer. They could keep either of us, possibly both, and start a whole new vein of activity, an entirely new storyline, but it also possible that we both will vanish. And I am beginning to think the latter is more and more likely."

"Excuse me! You have some information?"

"Yes and no," Roger says. "I know that after all these years Jason Fierst is finally leaving Babylon."

"Really! To do what?"

"He is producing a new play by a young Czech writer, Arnost Geryk. Possible he may decide to direct it as well. His reputation is so assured that he can pretty much do whatever he wants."

"Fine for him…but what about the rest of us?" she asks with some irritation.

"So, next month there will be auditions." Jason has strongly recommended that the two of us vie for the major roles of Benjamin and Marcella. The play is called *Wars of Independence*."

"Wars."

"Figurative wars," Roger says. "The battle of the sexes, my dear." They are now at the steps of the Chateau Frontenac. A doorman bids them enter. The warmth inside is almost staggering. They both ingest a long breath. "Come on, Denise, I'll spot you a cup of coffee."

Denise has the cup in her hands, warming them. Occasionally, she sips. "What's this play about?"

"It's really a romance sometimes gone right, often gone awry.

I haven't read it. There is no script available outside of partials. But I do understand that there are issues of passion and revenge."

Denise grins. "Right up my alley."

"Jason thought you would be right for the part of Marcella. She's pretty, seductive, intelligent in a certain way, dipsy in others, clearly enamored of the opposite sex. Loving and seducing seem to be her major occupations."

"Sounds rife with opportunity."

"As for Benjamin, he's a college professor who begins a relationship with Marcella. Yes, she is his student, but an older student, one about to divorce as they meet. He falls madly in love with her. There is a fair bit of conflict in this bond. That's about all I know to this point."

"You're auditioning?"

"Of course. If the play is good, why not move forward with it, do something different after all these years on the soap? If successful, and I fit the part, then my career might take a turn for the better."

"And mine. I need to build up my resume. What a great opportunity."

"Besides, since we are in good with Jason, we have the inside track. Nothing guaranteed, of course."

"Should we talk to him about it when we get back to New York?"

"I wouldn't. I'll get the exact date, and you and I can run lines together if you wish."

"I do wish," Denise says. "I think I'll take a scone with the coffee, if they have a lemon one."

Roger gets up and goes to the counter. In a minute, he returns with a strawberry scone. "Not exactly what you wanted," he says.

"Good enough. The hike in the snow made me hungry."

"Hmm," Roger says softly. "It kinda made me hungry for you."

She looks up with the sliver of a smile crossing her lips. "We might be able to do something about that."

They walk up the staircase to the second floor, each one with an arm around the other's waist. At the door of their room, as Roger is shifting the electronic key up and down, Denise says. "There is something that concerns me." Their door clicks open.

"Are you sure you want to discuss concerns right now?" Roger asks.

"Yes," she insists firmly. "Yes."

"Go on."

"You do agree that you and I have pretty much equal billing on Babylon these days."

"I suppose so," Roger says, his forehead wrinkling. Is billing a problem for you?"

"No", Denise replies. She is taking off her coat, now slips off her boots and sits on the bed. "I've been in my role for the better part of six months and I still haven't seen much of a bump in pay."

"Oh," Roger smiles, "it's about money."

"Yes," she smirks, "as if you don't care about money".

"All right. Get on with it. He sits across from her in an armchair, takes out a cigarette and begins to smoke."

"This is a no smoking hotel," she remarks.

"I won't tell if you don't," he replies, puffing.

"So, tell me how much you make?"

Hesitates. Pause. "I don't think that's any of your business," he answers brusquely.

Smiling, she lifts her head, her fingers at the corner of her locks. "I think it is. I bet that I don't make half of what you do."

"I wouldn't know."

"I would if you told me how much you make."

"Look, only somebody like Jason or our accounting people dispense that information. If he wants to share it with you…."

"You know damn well he would never do that."

"Exactly," Roger remarks pointedly.

"But since we are close," she says almost snarling the word, "you would be the right person, in fact the only person, to clarify this."

"But my dear," he says to her, "we are not married. We aren't engaged. We are in, what did we call it? A physical arrangement. My salary doesn't fall into that parameter unless you want us to fuck under a shower of dollar bills."

"Come on, Roger. It's important to me."

"And if I don't?"

She crosses her legs.

"I see," he responds. "If I want to get snuggly, I have to reveal numbers."

"You get the picture," she replies smugly.

"All right," he says impatiently. "During shooting, I am making seven thousand each round."

Denise whistles. "Knew it," she says, leaning back on the bed, her legs cavorting into the air. "Knew it."

"You are earning less, I suppose."

"A shitload less," she replies. "Not half of what you make."

"And the moral of this story is…."

"I should be better rewarded."

"I agree. Take it up with the people who can do something about it".

"Well then," Denise replies, "as soon as we get back to NY, I'll talk to Jason about it."

Roger laughs, arises looking for an ashtray, finds a drinking cup and douses the cigarette in it. "I wouldn't do that. Not now."

"What's sacred about now?"

"You are about to audition for a new role, and just before you compete, you plan to argue money with the guy who can potentially make that role a reality."

Denise slumps onto the bed, holding her knees against her chest. "I guess you're right," she agrees, "there's always some reason we women can never get a raise."

"You could take up a new profession," he smiles. "How about dolphin trainer? Doesn't pay much, but it's in the sun and swimming is a bene."

She looks at him before slowly lowering her head.

26

Brent Sadowski

As a teen-ager, Brent Sadowski labored summers at odd jobs. When he turned 17, he found work at a diner busing tables. He did not enjoy this work because he was rarely tipped. He also found patrons infernally rude. In fact, due to his lowly position and the unusually large, red earphones which he permanently affixed about his ears, customers often scorned him. The following summer he served as a waiter in another diner. There he was constrained to wear a paper blue and white hat. It had the word 'Winnie's Diner' imprinted on it. An apron was tied about his waist, and he was not allowed his usual white socks with black tennis shoes. In those years, Brent was an enigmatic young man. In class, he rarely spoke up, but if called upon, invariably provided the right answer. "I'm shy," he explained to his teachers. Instead, they found him perplexing. Before attending college, as a summer job he joined the elevator operator's union to become an operator in an east side hotel. For this job, he was provided a uniform, a tan suit with a white shirt and black bow tie. He was also issued white gloves. He was, however, informed that he could not wear earphones on the job. Brent did not appreciate this rule. His earphones helped to shut out the rest of the world. This job, then, meant that he would have to let people into his realm. Of course, he could manage this, but he resented it and, furthermore, thought it unfair of management to impose restrictions.

And yet, Brent found harmony here. Work started at ten in the evening and ended at six in the morning. He scarcely minded the people, sometimes sober, sometimes tipsy, who crowded next to him in the elevator and asked him, their blubbery, weaving, smiling lips awfully close to his face, whether he enjoyed his ups and downs. This is the way people are: this is the way people curiously speak, he said to himself. They believe they are amusing. Most things said in life are not amusing. Even the very attempt to be funny. After all is said and done, these crude attempts are mainly clichés. People hardly ever held back stupid statements or questions. And rarely posed important questions. In that entire summer, nobody asked him whether he was happy. Had anyone done so, he would have replied, 'yes I am', lying to them, because, in fact, Brent was mainly dour. To the degree that he could not tell you what constituted happy. "Are you content?" his mom would ask him. And he would answer that he was, but he had no idea what that word meant. Did it mean that he wanted for nothing? If so, then he wasn't content. Maybe it meant that he had eaten and drunk well. Or napped easily? That could be, but it could never describe the Brent Sadowski throughout an entire twenty-four-hour cycle. Too much happened every day, much of it boring, mainly filled with passengers shouting out their floor numbers, or people asking him whether he was going down when in fact they wanted to go up. All of this was confusing, but it taught him the indisputable fact that people often did not know their ups from their downs.

One evening, as an early group of people had left the hotel for dinner, as he was reading a novel by Ramsey Samurt, a young woman entered his elevator. Turned to her and got up from his stool. "13, she said. She said it with a tiny smile, her lips curling in all the right places, he considered. A young woman, in fact quite young, he judged, perhaps no older than twenty.

"Ha," he exclaimed, laughing broadly, "we have no thirteenth floor."

The girl examined her key. Handed it to Brent. "Could you read this for me" I can't read the print very well without my reading glasses. "31st floor," he responded, pocketing his own glasses. "But you don't do very well without glasses either," she continued.

"I can see," Brent boasted.

"How old are you?"

"19, he replied.

"Going to school?"

"Not now," he replied, lifting the elevator.

"But in the autumn?"

"Yes," he replied. "I am studying biology, the sciences. I want to be an astro-physicist."

"That's exciting," the girl gushed.

He slowed the elevator to line it up with the floor. "31, he announced."

"Yes," she replied. "My name is Gerta."

"Brent," he confided. "I'm clear I am allowed to tell you my name."

"And Brent," she asked, standing half in the elevator, half on the floor. "Do they allow you guests to visit?"

"Oh no," he grimaced. "That is forbidden."

"Unless a guest asks, right? You cannot a guest who demands you anything turn her down."

He scratched his head and let out his stomach. "Could be."

"When do you from work have time?" she asked.

"Six."

"When you finish, come to my door and ring my bell. I don't know this town and some questions to ask you I have on my tongue."

"I shall be with you at six," he answered. "Thank you for asking. I rarely get to speak to anyone night after night."

"You are perfectly welcome," she replied with her slight German accent. "I shall expect you later."

"I can bring hot chocolate," he said suddenly without thinking.

"Better still," she laughed. "Wunderbar!"

Now he watched as she ambled down the hall, long blondish hair cascading down her back, hips moving rhythmically. Then she turned and waved. Brent self-consciously closed the door and descended.

A bit after six, he ascended with two cups of hot chocolate in Styrofoam cups. Knocked on her door. She peered through the tiny aperture. Her eye backed off. Opened the door. Still maintaining the chain.

"Oh," she smiled slightly, "it's you. Come in," she added, sliding the chain off.

"I brought chocolate," he said.

"I never drink chocolate after four," she replied. "I cannot with this thing stimulating me with anxiety sleep."

"I'm sorry," he replied, with anguish starting in his voice. "Terribly sorry. I thought…"

"It is sometimes better not to think," she replied. Then her voice altered and took on a more strident tone. "Take off your jacket."

"What?" he questioned, surprised.

"Your jacket. It's warm in here, nichtwahr?" You shall try and be so comfortable, yes?"

He took off his jacket.

"Now loosen your tie."

"Easy, he said," stripping it from his neck. "I can do that easily."

"Sit now on the bed next to me."

He sat next to her, descending his body slowly so as not to jostle her.

"You're a funny boy," she chortled. "I think I like you." Paused. Yet, she said, appraising him, "you are not handsome."

He sighed. "No. I am not."

"But you have a nicely round body and you are good-spirited."

"Thank you, Gerta."

"My name is not Gerta," she pouted. "It is Angela."

He grimaced. "Where did I get the idea that your name was Gerta?"

"I should not know this," she said. "Call me Angel for short."

"Sure," he said. He now noticed that she had put a pudgy hand on his thigh.

She looked over at him in a glance he could only describe as concerned. "You have never before with a woman been, is this so?"

"Partially," he replied, his hands trying to communicate the undertone of his words.

"You mean you never pushed in, yes?" Her pelvis moved in and out to underline the thought.

"Oh no," he replied. "I have never pushed," he replied, alarmed.

"Well then," she smiled, loosening the bonds around her hair and shaking out the curls. "Would you like to try such a thing? Pushing in can be entertaining, you know."

Pause. Brent needed to think this through. In fact, it was not that he was lacking arousal. But what his body was speaking mainly, palpably, was fear. Fear of what was demanded of himself. Naturally, he knew what to do. At least, he thought so. He had seen the order in magazines, in porn on the internet, so the expected actions were clear enough. First in the order of things, you grab a hand. He did this quickly, perhaps a bit too forcibly.

"Relax," she whispered, patting his wrist.

"Sure," he said. Then, following the second item in the order of things, he leaned in, and put his mouth on Angel's. For a moment, this contact was quite heavenly. But when she prompted her tongue to enter and probe his mouth, Brent became anxious. Never had he read about a tongue entering between teeth. So, he thought she was probing for food particles.

"Hungry?" he asked her as he pulled his mouth away.

"Not now," she replied in a huff. Then she looked in his eyes. "You can't be serious."

He knew, recalling the next step, that he was required to grab a breast. He reached out with his right palm. Once he had it in his hand, he would roll it like a pizza. This made women squeal with pleasure, he had read. Hence, he grabbed Angel's boob and began to roll it as flat as he could.

"No, no," she recoiled. "Too much," she cried out.

Pulled his hand back.

"Look," she said," I can see that you are a new boy to the sex. Do you want me the ropes to show you?"

"The ropes?" Brent asked.

"This is an American expression, nichtwahr?"

"Sure. The ropes. Show them."

"She carefully took off her blouse, and then asked him to reach behind her to unhook her bra. He did so with the focus of a man on a scientific mission. Every bit of it was to be remembered, analyzed, stored in memory, less as a pleasurable series of moments, but as an exploration which contained new, unusual, elements, some them possibly enjoyable. "You find these pleasure places?" she asked, showing him ample boobs.

"Very entertaining," he replied, his lips terse.

"You may touch them. In addition, even kiss them. Kiss the nipple. It is quite tender. I mean sensitive. My English is not always fantastic." He did so. "Ach, this is much better," she replied. "Do you want to go around the next corner?"

"Sure," he said.

"But you don't seem very embraceable...or aroused," she said craning over his body, then up to his face. In another instant, she had placed her fingers between his legs. But for an instant, she rubbed gently.

"Not sure what is happening to me," he gasped. Out of control, his beating heart spoke first. Then his brain began to tighten as if it were bound with pretty colors. Suddenly, he felt a bodily sensation unlike anything he had ever known, and then noticed as his eyes turned white into the heavens that his pants were flooding with some viscous solution.

She looked at him with disdain. "You came," she alerted him.

He said nothing. She raised both of her arms towards the ceiling. "I don't think, my friend, that this is a marriage made in heaven."

Aghast, he stammered. "Marriage?"

"One of your American dictums I learned in the Gymnasium," she responded acidly. "I think you better leave now."

He looked at her with gratitude, because he was unclear whether there was another corner or more to go around, but if there were, nothing in his ken suggested ways to get there. He rose shaking himself to his full height. She stood in front of him like some prey to be seized, but when he moved forward, he simply said: "Thank you so very much." Took her hand, shaking it. "It was so nice to meet you." The following morning, Angela returned to Germany.

Up to that moment, this had been Brent's first "and only" sexual experience. In fact, for the next decade, shy, fearful of rejection, Brent could not communicate with women with any modicum of confidence. Women did not relate to him, a timid, rotund, progressively overweight male. He went through college quietly, studiously, earning a degree with honors in the sciences, and almost at once found a job handling and containing viruses for the Pharynx Corporation. And there he remained, year after year, cataloguing the medicines and viruses that crossed his space. Careful, he made no mistakes and, as a result, earned increases in pay over the years. Yet no real advancement with regards to a career. Bosses thought him too introverted. Nobody understood him. If he spoke, he spoke too straightforwardly, often without guile, and this failure to communicate normally caused tension in his colleagues.

And then he met Alex. She was ten to twelve years younger than he when he first spied her bubbling towards him at the corporation. Pretty, outgoing, yet ready to espouse the same culture as her fellow workers, he thought her the right person to help him mend his social skills, and thus promote his career.

Almost a half year later, mustering his courage in a heroic moment, holding his breath throughout, he walked towards her cubicle intercepting her as she tread towards her tiny office. He blurted 'hi'. To which she replied in kind and walked by him. Following her into her area, sweating profusely with trepidation. Nonetheless, summoning up elements of courage he never knew within him, he continued by telling her his name.

"Brent," she repeated quietly looking up at him.

"Yes, Brent.: He stuck out his hand. She took it and shook.

"Alex," she replied. "You work with the viruses, don't you? I think I've seen you in the virus room." She needed to go in there occasionally, she said, and he replied what a marvelous coincidence this was.

With these words, Alex had bestowed meaning to this moment, this hour. This day, perhaps this entire week, for she may have already noticed him.

"Yes," he said. "I work there." Continued in a boastful voice. "I've been employed here for many years."

"Well maybe you can show me around," she replied. "I'm still relatively new."

"Aah, the ropes! I know the ropes," he responded.

For weeks thereafter, when they passed one another in the corridor, they would smile and wave, occasionally stop to chat for a moment, then go on. Each encounter was invariably followed by a lighter step in Brent's walk. Evenings, he thought about her. Daytimes, he daydreamed about her. Once, he snuck a photo of her without her knowledge, blew it up and pasted it to the wall above his desk at home. He could look at this photo admiringly for a half hour at a time imagining scintillating conversations they might conduct about viruses. And after a time, he began to converse animatedly with the photo, taking both his role as well as hers.

"Looking lovely today," he would say to Alex.

"You're not looking so bad yourself, Brent," she would reply. Once, he asked her to whistle at him the way men whistle at attractive girls. Then he chortled to tell her what good taste she had in men. She, of course assented, and asked whether he wouldn't like to squire her to the movies. He agreed at once.

On 42nd street, a double feature which included the Bad and Beautiful and The Killers with Burt Lancaster. There, in this imaginary paradise, he was free to play with her hand, share popcorn with her, put his arm around her shoulder, and at one moment as Burt lay incapacitated, take her in his arms and kiss her on the lips. Thankfully, she did not place her tongue inside his mouth, the notion of which he thought both weird, unsanitary, and not an attractive feature for any girl. Instead, she hugged him, leaned over to put her head on his chest which he supported easily with his protruding belly. She complimented his belly then for its soft support. Months elapsed in this fashion. But at a certain moment, Alex as photo began to make demands on Brent. She suggested that they take a weekend together at the Waldorf Astoria.

"I don't have that kind of money," he replied sadly to her likeness. "Otherwise I would be pleased to spend time with you there."

"This is no way a suitor treats a girl," Alex complained. "If you want to win me, then you have to court me properly."

"Ok, ok," he relented. "Of course, I'll spend the weekend with you at the Waldorf."

So, they went to their weekend at the Waldorf, and high up in the hotel, in the executive section, in a suite which cost a bloody fortune, Brent nonetheless controlled the girl of his dreams. He noticed in the room that there was only one bed and asked whether Alex thought he should have them arrange a cot for himself. "Silly you," she said flirtingly. "This bed is big enough for two."

So that evening, after a sumptuous dinner in a restaurant around the corner, they returned to the 17th floor fatigued. And undressed. "I'm going to make love to you," Alex said to the astonished Brent.

"Please do," he coughed.

"Do you need some water?"

"No," he said, coughing. "Just give me a second. Lots of phlegm, you know."

"Of course, sweetie," she replied. And then in seventh heaven because this spectacular woman had called him 'sweetie,' he undressed to his shorts and slipped in between plaid green sheets. In a moment, she was propped up against him, and he began to bathe in her body heat. And then something happened which he had not considered. They made love, she still facing away from him, he fastening onto her as if she were a lifeboat.

Before Brent could claim total satisfaction, the image faded away, and he was left with the photo and his disappearing fantasy. The next time he saw Alex in the hallway, he was hard pressed not to be more intimately vocal with her. The lines between his office time and his photo time were beginning to blur.

27

The Audition Takes Place

In a theatre on 47th street, Roger and Denise are sitting on the stage in jeans, legs dangling. Denise nervously ties a rose ribbon around her hair. Roger is eyeing a chorus girl in the third row who is all legs. Jason Fierst arrives bounding down the center aisle and leaps onto the stage.

"Sorry I'm a bit late," he says to one and all. "Never happened before, never happen again (Speaks to the two actors) Look, I realize this audition is called on somewhat short notice, but do your best. I think the two of you click, and that is essential to the velvetiness of this play. We witnessed your chemistry in gobs on Babylon, so just ship the hormones over to *Wars of Independence*. Now, before you begin, let's be sure we understand what these wars are about. There is no armed conflict. There is no shooting. But there is warlike activity, enmity, sneaking around, arguing, betrayal, conflict, and the like. Between two people who say they are in love, you wonder that they don't massacre the other. Well, maybe they will. Anyway, not for the moment. So, Roger, take up Benjamin's role on page 38. He has just discovered that his love, Marcella, is dating someone else, and in this instance, and Benjamin cannot escape deriding the competition. It is a proctologist."

(Looking suddenly becalmed) "So that's it then," Roger begins, then clears his throat.

"Sadder, please, Roger," Jason says, scampering up to him, "the girl is dating a guy who puts his finger up your ass. Who knows what he's doing to hers! So, you are sadly, angrily bereft. Play bereft, please!"

"So that's it, then," Benjamin says reflectively, his eyes wide open.

"Don't be upset with me, please," Marcella responds. She stretches an arm around him

"One more time, please, Marcella," Jason interrupts. "You do after all care for this poor son of a bitch, and you don't want to lose him. What happens if the date with the good doctor does not produce sparks? Eh? You may want to rope that old stud, Benjamin, and bring him back to your stable."

"Don't be upset with me, please," Marcella whines, drying a tear from her eye and cradling her arm around him.

(Breaking away) "Why should I be upset?" Benjamin says with an angry sneer. "Just because the woman I love has dumped me in favor of a buggering proctologist."

"We'll see one another from time to time," she coos. "I'll call you. Promise."

"To tell me which end is up? I know when our ends have been reached, Marcella."

"The line," Jason interrupts again, pensively, is "'I know where your end is, Marcella,' but I think I like yours better, Roger. Let's keep it."

"We need time away from each other."

"You've said that before," Roger speaks sternly.

"This doesn't mean it's over. I need to see other people to get a better grasp on us." (She begins to exit).

"I'm feeling the pathos," Jason exclaims, applauding. "Feeling it in the gut," he adds, pointing to his abdomen. "She claims she needs to see other people to uncover her true feelings about you, Benjamin. Oh shit, what lovely, adorable self-deception. How you must be burning inside, Benjamin. Aren't you ready to puke this woman out of your life? What do you think?"

"She led me to believe that she loved me, and now out of nowhere she is fucking me over. I'm pissed to the gills."

"Of course, you are, poor sap," Jason crows. "You realize that love demands trust as its main element. And if you can no longer have confidence in the one you love, it stings to the core."

"You sound as if you have had personal experience with this," Denise comments.

"I'm no virgin living in a convent," Jason responds. "No sirree. We all get screwed by life now and then. But Denise, your Marcella, what a piece of work. On the one hand, true, she needs to turn herself inside out to uncover what her true feelings are for Benjamin. Apparently interacting one on one with the guy is not enough. She must create a distance between the two of them to see whether her love is strong enough to bridge the gap. But what a piece of work she is. To find out about her love for him, she'll date another guy. Not very courageous of her, is it? Kind of an easy solution to a complex problem. So, Denise, you have to demonstrate a component of cowardice in your role, perhaps a somewhat hidden component in the role, but it exists. This woman flees when confronted by uncertainty. Roger's character, however, tends to thrust right through the mist and into the heart of darkness. Doesn't mean he'll be protected because of this action, however. Roger, your character is burning between love, despair, and incipient hatred. Yes, I am convinced you feel this as strongly as I do. OK, now let's push on to later dialogue.

Here Marcella has learned that the ass doctor is no panacea for what ails her. Catch this: her way of showing Benjamin that she still has feelings for him is to remind him that he still has a pork roast in the back of her freezer. Freud is rolling over in his fucking grave. From this, apparently, Benjamin is to deduce the depth of her emotion for him. So, Roger drives over to pick up his meat. Sorry about the language. I couldn't resist. Go for it!"

Benjamin says "We made love. Not that night, but the following night, and it was incredible. Within a week, I was bursting with her being and my mouth was forming words I couldn't have been ready to say…. (Goes to Marcella on a sofa) Don't you think we ought to go in the direction…permanency is…don't you want to marry me?"

"Two things are happening here," Jason intrudes quickly. "You love the bitch, true. But you are afraid, even as you broach the subject of togetherness, that she may reject you again, thereby chucking you into the lower circles of hell. Remember, trust isn't simply regained with a roll or two in the hay. Take it again from your proposal."

"Don't you want to marry me?"

"Yes."

"Perfect, Marcella, perfect. Simple. No bullshit. Straight to the heart of the matter. Yes, yes, yes! Who cares at this moment whether we believe her or not?"

"You do?"

"Just as I told you, Benjamin. You're not really sure she is in this as deeply as you are."

"Of course," Marcella responds.

"'Of course,' is the cavalier way of saying yes," Jason comments, striding about the stage. "Lacks real assurance, don't you know. Gives her a bit of distance from the emotion of the moment.

She doesn't like you questioning her commitment."

"That's the wisest decision you've ever made," Benjamin says, exhaling, and touching her cheek.

"Yes," Jason says. "Such a wise decision. But is it really? Now, Roger, you go rushing right into your romantic soliloquy. Give it miles and miles of heart!"

(Benjamin turns to the audience) "Charm of love! Resist all you like, but once you abandon yourself, it pulls you in like some inexorable, fiery sun that burns itself indelibly into your brain. I was out of my mind, I went blank, my life disappeared. All that remained was the aura, the glow, of Marcella. As for the hurt, the unsettledness of the woman, her problem in communicating and in understanding herself, I shunted all of it aside. My mind was ablaze with a riot of her colors. My proposal had been timid as if I fully expected her to turn me down, but when she said yes, something leaped inside me and it hasn't stopped leaping yet."

"Yes, Roger. I see you know about abandonment," Jason analyses. "You drop all of life, all functions, all color, all hunger and thirst, everything, and place the naked bundle of yourself on her altar. You haven't forgotten what a shit she is, how adept she can be at betraying you, how she has essential gaps in her make-up, but you, poor dunce of a love-soaked man, are so titillated with the girl you have stopped brain activity altogether. You can see nothing, nobody else on this earth."

"Yes, yes," Marcella echoes.

"While you, little target of our ardor, Jason continues, you keep on affirming your love for this benighted son of a bitch whom you have wounded to the core. Hope it lasts, I truly do.

Folks," Jason intervenes before the next dialogue," I am liking the way you interact. I know you can master these roles. Mr.

Geryk will be proud to have you two delivering his yin and yang lines. Several months from now, I expect this play to be rocking and rolling off-Broadway and, if it ignites, we'll take it to one of the yummy up-town theatres, the big time, my fellow thespians, the sunniest time there is in theatre. We will start rehearsals right after the last taping of Babylon Revisited."

28

Armand Interviews Brent Sadowski

In the doorway, Brent Sadowski. His figure is large. It looms. He is a bit over six feet tall, and must weigh close to three hundred pounds. The weight rolls mainly about the belly.

"Good of you to come to my office," Armand says, shaking hands with Brent and closing the door behind him.

With one hand, Brent lifts an earphone off his ear. "It was on my way home," he replies pleasantly.

"As you can see, I am a private investigator. I am looking into the death of your co-worker. I gather Alexandra was your friend."

Brent suddenly gulps in a great bit of air.

"Are you all right?"

"Yes," Brent replies, settling his breathing, now wiping his nose with a kerchief. "I am so glad you are investigating her passing," he remarks at last.

"Why is that, Mr. Sadowski?"

"Brent. Call me Brent, please."

"Brent."

"Thank you. I like it when people call me Brent."

The dialogue is already weird. Armand hesitates an instant. "Ok. Brent it is."

"Yes."

Silence.

Armand can see that more work is demanded from him in this interview. "I was asking you why you were glad that I am investigating Alex's passing."

"Because," Brent says, leaning forward conspiratorially, "because I believe that something untoward occurred."

"Like?"

"Yes." Pause. "Oh, you mean, what I am thinking?"

"Yes. Tell me," Armand's tone flows with the question, his eyes probing Brent's placid face.

"She may have taken home the wrong vial from the lab. I knew she liked using cocaine from time to time, and we store a bit of that in the lab. This is no secret, is it? I mean no harm will come to her…what am I saying? Ha! ha! No harm can come to her anymore, isn't that so? The cocaine is what concerned me the most when I heard she had died."

"No vial was found in her home."

"She must have disposed of it before she passed," Brent conjectures.

"That's one theory. Could be. Would you like a smoke?"

"A smoke? Oh no. I don't smoke. I have never smoked."

"But you've used cocaine."

Hesitantly. "Once. Only once."

"Glass of water?"

"Not thirsty for the moment," Brent says with a wan smile. "I would like to help you crack this case," he continues. "I've often thought that I could manage researching clues."

"Thank you." Armand lights up a cigarette.

"You're entirely welcome. You know I worked with Alex."

"Yes, I knew this."

"And that outside of work we were also friends."

"But not romantic entwined?"

"Hardly," Brent said. "Hardly!"

"You would have liked that though?"

Brent shuffles in his seat. "Yes. I think I would have enjoyed a tryst with Alex."

"Not a relationship?"

"I've never had one of those," Brent says.

"But you've had trysts?"

"No."

Pause.

"So, Brent, you didn't kill this girl, did you?"

"That is a matter of opinion, Brent says breathing out the words with some difficulty. "From time to time, I do feel a twinge of guilt. I do however realize that death is not a matter of opinion. But feeling guilt as I do...."

"How so?" Armand inquires leaning forward intently.

"Because it is my job to keep the vial room intact, and somehow Alex must have managed to enter and retrieve drugs for which she did not sign. How could I miss that?"

"I see. So, your guilt is not associated with your behavior."

"Anyway," she died from a hantavirus, Brent replies, avoiding Armand's statement. "There is no way I or anybody else could have killed her," he adds with satisfaction.

"Unless the drug was administered to the girl."

Brent smiles. "Unlikely, because the person administering the drug would contaminate himself."

"Not if he knew enough to protect himself against infection," Armand counters. "Somebody in the know could have done it. Somebody like you, Brent."

"True," Brent breathes carefully as if he were sniffing the air.

"True."

"Anybody else in the corporation who might have wanted to harm this young woman?"

"Certainly not."

"You seem quite sure about that."

"Because she was a lovely woman. Everybody's friend. No one would have had a motive to snuff out her life."

"Well let's conjecture for a moment. You, for example, wanted a closer relationship with Alex, or so you just said. But if she were not willing to give that to you, because, for example, she already had an ongoing bond with some other guy, this might have given you a motive to kill her."

"But I cared for her," Brent protests.

"Killing her out of jealousy," Armand insists.

"We were never together in that way," Brent replies sadly. "Never, never." His face brightens up suddenly. "But I was fond of her dog, Apepi."

"Were you? Yes, her dog that was put away. Yet, you could have claimed that dog at the pound. Why didn't you?"

"Because I have my own dog," he replies defensively.

"Not because Apepi would be a constant reminder of the bad thing you did to his mistress?"

"You're fishing, Mr. Desqueyroux," Brent says with a wry smile.

Sighing, Armand agrees. "Just pushing the envelope a bit."

With that, Brent rises, pulls out earphones from his pocket and adjusts them around his head.

"Anything I can do to help," he says, opening the door. "Please feel free."

29

An Engagement

(Alberto enters downstage left with Gabriella as the engagement party is about to begin) "I told you it wasn't too early" (Festive noises in the background)

"We're among the first," Gabriella insists. "Straighten your tie, Alberto. (Points into the distance) Who's that gentleman over there talking with Marcella?"

"Our host, the President. I've seen his pictures in the papers."

"He has class to lay out this party for our Marcella and Benjamin. But look at the suit he's wearing. It's polyester. A good wife would have chosen something more elegant. Isn't he married?"

"Not so loud, Gabriella. I don't know whether he's married."

"It's a scandal to dress like that at an engagement party."

"Can't we be happy he's doing this for our girl?"

(Pascal enters from right) "Good afternoon."

"Pascal," Gabrielle says with pleasure. "Good to see you again. Benjamin wasn't sure you could make it."

"I've been ill off and on with bronchitis, even a touch of pneumonia. As soon as I get over one illness, the next one begins. I've spent a good part of the last month in bed."

"You need loving care and chicken soup. Haven't you snared

yourself a wife yet?"

"I prefer freedom to chicken soup," Pascal laughs.

"Still the playboy," Gabriella says chucking him playfully. "You do look gaunt. I'd put some flesh on you, Pascal. You come to my house and I'll make you a pasta dinner your bones are not likely to shed."

"It's true that my appetite has not been so lively lately," Pascal says. "Maybe pasta is just what I need."

"I heard you quit the Foreign Legion," Alberto says.

"Once my health deteriorated," Pascal confessed, "I couldn't do the drill anymore, so I moved to San Francisco and opened a cleaning business."

(Janice enters from left) "Hello. Where's the happy couple?"

"I haven't seen Benjamin yet," Alberto answers, "but Marcella is over there chatting with the President."

"And you must be Pascal?" Janice gushes. "Don't deny it. I've seen pictures of you."

"Then I won't deny it."

"Benjamin must be so pleased that you could be here."

(Marcella entering from right) "Have you seen Benjamin?"

"Probably reconsidering whether he wants to attend," Janice says. "He must know that everyone in the room is going to inspect him closely, from tie to zipper."

"Don't be silly, Janice. I bought him a new suit which he's picking up from the department store this morning."

"You look lovely, Marcella," Gabriella says, "in blues and golds."

"Mother, I want you to circulate. We're expecting about forty-five people to show up today, and I want all of them to get to know you and dad. And daddy, please don't ask them to open wide, please?"

"But that's how I make friends," Alberto smiles. "Like dogs

that sniff each other's genitals."

"Go on," Janice sniffs (She and Marcella's folks exit)

(Pascal and Marcella conversing) "Marcella," he says, waving his hand in front of her face, "aren't I made of flesh and blood? You're looking right through me."

"I was hoping you were a ghost and that the wind might blow you away."

"Still harboring ill feelings over our first meeting. Can't really blame you. Let me apologize to you. I was out of line and this party shouldn't be spoiled because of a few, thoughtless words."

"Apology accepted."

(Shakes hands with her. Holds her hand an instant to long. She retracts it quickly) "Maybe we can start over. You realize I was concerned about you and Benjamin. I thought your behavior was, well, let's just say erratic. Benjamin is my oldest, dearest friend, and I couldn't stand to see him hurt."

"You have nothing to fear," she protests.

"Look, I'm not the sort of guy who beats around the bush. You're an attractive woman. Still I don't quite get the appeal. You're not especially gorgeous, but you are pretty and men clearly flock to you. Maybe that's it. As if you were asking all of us to try you on. An expensive Chanel suit. I felt it at once. You say to every man you meet: look at my silks and imagine what's underneath.

"Pretty fanciful, Pascal," Marcella says, annoyed again.

"I was attracted to you," he intones softly.

"You were?" her tone now changes.

"As soon as I met you, and that's why I made the point of making sure there would be distance between us. You frighten us mortals, you know. Who are you anyway? Some mythical creature, Circe? Lorelei?"

"Just a woman in love," she says quietly.

"But with whom?"

"You are a bore. With Benjamin, naturally."

(Pascal spies Benjamin entering from left) "Speak of the devil."

"Sorry to be late," Benjamin says. "The cuffs weren't quite right."

"You look stunning," Pascal says.

(Holding Marcella) "And my bride to be?"

"Ravishing. When do you…. excuse me if I have trouble repeating the horrific expression…. tie the knot?"

"We haven't set a date yet," Marcella says.

"Soon, my friend, soon."

"I don't want you gabbing with Pascal when everyone here is dying to get to know you better," Marcella says, prodding him.

"I do feel chatty," Benjamin laughs.

"Good. Walk around and chat everybody up. Particularly Jager. I'm not so sure he's sold on you." (She leaves stage right to join her parents' group off-stage).

"Are you certain you're up for this?" Pascal asks.

"I'm ready," Benjamin says.

"You do look awfully happy. It's unlike you. And it makes me want to hug you and fart at the same time."

"I wish you had worn your uniform," Benjamin says. "I can't get used to your civilian persona."

"The damned uniform doesn't fit anymore. I've lost too much weight. Decades of bad army grub have decimated me. But now that I'm about to become a rich American, all that will change. Benjamin, you're hardly listening to me."

(Benjamin to audience) "Revolution has a way of clearing the air, compressing pent up emotions of an entire people into a nucleus of fury. Once launched, the ball destroys, but out of

193

destruction emerges change, a new day. Isn't that what we all live for, the unknown moment of triumph around the corner? That moment of exultation when Marcella responds YES, of course, YES, and all the years of struggle, all painful episodes are sublimated to one moment of acceptance."

(Marcella brings him a drink) "Talk to my dad. He'd like that."

(Benjamin still to audience) "Pascal looks ill. Out of that illness a whole new way of life, it seems. Illness has middle-classed him. Next thing you know, he'll be announcing his own engagement."

(Gabriella and Alberto enter stage left) "I'm totally opposed to it," she says. "Totally." (They walk to center stage)

"Look out the window," Alberto exclaims. "There's a man puking into the fountain."

(Benjamin, still to audience) "Once, when I was walking with my dog, we came across an early spring dandelion, and the two of us sat down motionless before it on the lawn. Its buds swayed to and fro in a slight morning breeze. I don't know how long we were there. But after a time, I felt as if I too were swaying with the flower, and after a few more moments, that I had subsumed the identity of the flower. I felt enchanted!"

(Pascal to Alberto center stage) "Guns have the distinct disadvantage of taking life at a distance. A bayonet, however, is the honest tool for a solder whose job it is to kill. Open the chest and turn the blade inside. Locate the heart, turn the metal again, stare into the eyes of the opponent, watch his mouth slide open, the mix of blood and spittle at the corners, as his eyes give up their light."

(Gabriella to Pascal) "Rather than death, let's talk about birth today. Pascal looks at her as if she were totally out of step with her era."

(Marcella with Janice at stage right) "I bought a new blouse."
"That red and gray one?" How much was it?" It's perfect on you."

(Benjamin to audience) "I feel like dawn itself, vibrant and important, creative, generous."

(To Alberto) "There is no question about it," Gabriella says caustically.

"Under thirty dollars," Marcella announces. "But you have to search carefully for your size. The sizes are all mixed together."

(To Alberto) "We are at a moment of rebirth. Life exists at the moment of conception," Gabriella says.

(Alberto turning to look out of the window) "He's puking again!"

"Every Friday at the end of the month," Marcella says.

(Pascal to audience) "Could it be that we serve as a counter-weight to one another?" Benjamin has joy, I feel the loss of mission…. where did I lose it? In the uniform I no longer wear? Is that Benjamin's place in my life these days? To remind me how low I've sunk. God, I've felt better."

(Benjamin in an aside to audience) "Pascal looks wretched."

"Have the baby," Gabriella says adamantly. " Give birth, that's what I say."

"Pascal looks sick," Alberto confides (He and Gabriella exit stage left)

"Has Pascal lost weight?" Marcella asks.

"How would I know?" Janice responds. "I've never seen him before."

30

Roger Is Smitten

The retooled Babylon Revisited has been running for several months, Roger as Armand in hot pursuit of the truth with regards to the death of Alexandra. Must be more than the halfway point, he considers, so that the death of this girl will shortly be explained. The writers give away nothing. No inducement obliges them to tell the future. He himself is somewhat buffaloed. Could be the girl died of natural causes, he ponders. Failing that, perhaps the kind of error that Brent Sadowski suggests in which Alexandra inadvertently brings home the wrong vial, opens it unwittingly and suffers the consequences. Finally, there could be a murderer, but so far, nobody is revealing a good motive for doing the girl in. The writers surely have a tight grip on the script. Patience, patience, he repeats to himself.

On 49th street and Second avenue, there is a club for actors. You have to show your actor's card to enter. Or lacking the card, good connections. Roger has both. It is Wednesday afternoon, the sun warming considerably, a fairly strong breeze from the west blowing pollution out to sea so that one can breathe easily. Imbued by the warmth of the day, Roger's body feels lithe yet sturdy. He has little understanding of the joyful feeling until an epiphany smacks him in the gut: it is good to be alive today, he smiles. Sits at a table by himself. He is thinking about Denise. He is fond of her. But not so fond that he cares to cultivate their link further. Instead, he is satisfied that they see one another as their needs dictate, rip one off, then revert to their professional stance. Until this moment, this pattern has suited him fine. But now, something is missing. He cannot fathom it. Recalling the last time they fucked. Staring into her eyes as he probed her, not finding whatever he was looking for. Shocked him. He did finish, but without elan, without fireworks, with only a simple, if marginally satisfactory jolt. So, he is convinced that he need do nothing further in her instance. To continue in this fashion may be the best he can hope for unless he breaks the bond permanently, and this he is loath to do. Usually, he enjoys their sex, especially if they are in the shower or he has her strapped over a kitchen table. As for Denise, she gravitates to their games, but has rarely tested the limits of their bond. She has asked for nothing else. Certainly, nothing more.

The warmth of the afternoon has dissipated. In its place, an annoyance. Roger considers the tension and wonders what in hell is gnawing at him. Gets up and orders a cappuccino. A boy carries it to the pick-up at the end of the counter. Roger adds a bit of synthetic sugar, juggles the burning cup between his hands and quickly sets it on his table. To his left, three men and a woman chatting. He knows one of the men, a bit actor who has played a hundred stunt roles, mainly those in which he is burned alive, shot to death, or irretrievably mangled by cars flipping into one another. The man makes a decent living, he overhears. The two others he does not know. The woman he does not know either. But there is something about her. Once he locks onto her, his eyes cannot quit her face. Listens to her.

She is speaking about her mini-role in an off-Broadway play in which she plays a seamstress lesbian. Charming this calmly creative manner in which she discusses her role. Her face is splendid, symmetrical, lips almost perfectly paired, a hint of lipstick, a dash of rouge on her cheeks, eyes that look green in one light and, when she turns, virtually black in the other. Red hair cut short patterned along the curve of her head. She speaks with a British accent. He does not believe the accent is fake. Nowadays, the girls who practice accents are so gifted, you often can't tell. But this girl's mellifluous tone seems spot on. Even her laugh. Downs his drink. She has not glanced at him once. Unsmiling, she speaks to the three men. Roger searches their faces. At least one has the glint. The other two might as well be doing crossword puzzles for all their personal interest in the girl.

Ten minutes later, two of the men get up and leave. The one with the glint remains. Moves closer. Huddles with the girl. He calls her Marina. Puts a hand on her arm. The girl removes it. The glinted man continues probing, but the girl leans backwards as if she were a general looking for a fallback position. Her chair is tilting. The guy is practically off his seat, balancing himself on tippy toes. Then the girl arises swiftly, speaks monosyllabically, waves to the glinter and disappears towards the lady's room. The glinting man sits back, straightens himself, particularly his hair which has fallen over his face like a mop. Now he swears under his breath, arises and leaves. His cup remains on the table steaming. In a moment, Marina exits the lady's room, glances around, air in her lungs. The jerk has left. Breathes normally. Grins slightly. Roger notices how small she is. Couldn't be more than 5'2", he judges. Marina leaves, more upper body than short legs. She has never seen Roger.

Now Roger steps up to the counter. The barista looks up. "The girl who was at this table. Do you know her"

"Yes, the barista replies. "She comes in three or four times a week. Sometimes alone, sometimes with others.

"Her name"

"Marina. Marina Benson.

"Do you know where she lives"

The barista grimaces. "I don't, but even if I did, I wouldn't give out that information. There are a lot of nutty people in this town.

"Just interested, Roger says and pulls his Iphone out of his pocket. He has the right app, searches it, and finds both an address, telephone number and even an email for Marina Benson. He goes home. He will not call her. That would be stupid, he thinks. But he can send her an email. He needs to think carefully about this communication, this correspondence, because if he does it incorrectly, if he frightens the girl into believing he is some kind of perv, she will surely bolt. He walks to the park, sits on a bench. Intrigued by soccer players shouting in Spanish to one while another running in a dozen directions at once. The day waxes to its close. The players are packing up their equipment and locking the fenced-in field.

Finally, he has thought through what he needs to convey, and he flies home to his computer.

Dear Marina, he writes.

You don't know me, even though we are both actors. I know this about you because I accidentally overheard a conversation today between you and three gentlemen in Starbucks. I did not wish to intrude and, in fact, the words I am writing you now I could not have said then. I would have been the object of scorn, ridicule or perhaps a merited horse whipping.

I don't even know whether you are available to encounter someone new in your life. You can undo me if you wish by not responding, but I hope this will not be necessary. I am no stalker. I saw you, overheard your voice, observed you for a bit, and became besotted. I webbed a fantasy about you. I imagined you an ice cream cone, and I a simple tongue which might lick you into delicious bliss. Not that this should scare you. I am considerably more than a tongue, witness this mail. I have a creative brain and two slender hands with all ten fingers, and beyond that an ineffable curiosity about you. Would you email me back and tell me either that I am deranged and should leave you forever, in which case I will scurry to the nearest bar and try to assuage my sorrow" Or, if you are so inclined and willing to take a chance on a total stranger, perhaps indicate how your admirer might meet you for a coffee, a drink or a hike through the park. He signs this simply, Roger, and leaves a telephone number and email address.

For an hour, he awaits a reply. There is none. Then two, three hours pass. Night descends. He has no hunger and skips dinner. Denise calls him but he pleads gastric distress and will not speak to her. Throughout a sleepless night, he awakens periodically to check his mail and, finding none, returns to a toss-filled bed. Nor is there a response the following day…or, for God's sake, the following week. After ten days have passed without reply, he concludes that Marina has in fact labelled him a creepy fool and will not respond.

He and Denise spend a rather lackluster weekend together. Sex is hurried, passionless, thus forgettable. But he cannot forget the little redhead in the cafe. Denise senses trouble. She questions him about his lackluster demeanor, but he has no answers. He claims fatigue. Blessed fatigue! It is usually good enough in a relationship to carry one through a week or two without complaint or reprisals.

Suddenly, unexpectedly, Marina replies. She writes that she has mulled over the email for the better part of a fortnight, uncertain whether to reply at all. In fact, she has discussed it with two girlfriends who have advised her to seek safer ground and not tempt fate. But curiosity, a driving force in Marina, brings her to her computer.

"This may be stupid of me, she writes. As you request, I will meet you for a coffee at the local Starbucks on 48th street. 3PM on Wednesday, if that is agreeable. I will be wearing a red carnation…no I won't…. You know how I look. But you will have to introduce yourself, Roger. If you are wearing a clown outfit, you will excuse me if I run out the door. Marina.

Nervously, that Wednesday at 3, Roger enters Starbucks. Looks for her but does not see her. Orders a cafe americano, a tall one. Fixes it to his liking. Sits at a table idly watching patrons. There are some dozen customers chatting with one another. A couple of false alarms. First a trio of chattering teen-ager girls, followed by an older man wearing a Marine uniform. Then the door swings open again and she enters. Even smaller than he remembers her. But that may be because he only saw her standing for an instant, he gauges. Pretty, the red, coiffed hair descending onto the fringe of a pink shawl, a black, trim, velours coat. Lips painted in a light reddish mauve. She is not wearing heels. He watches her order coffee and when she reaches the end of the counter, he intercepts her and introduces himself.

"Roger, he says, with a thin smile. "Marina, she responds firmly, and shakes his hand, picks up her coffee gingerly, and they repair to his table.

"You have a lot of nerve, is her first shot. "You could be a serial rapist, killer, stalker. I have no idea what I'm doing here with you.

"What are you doing here" he asks gently.

"Judging the situation.

"And your assessment is"

"Whoa, boy, you're still moving way too fast for me.

"Sorry.

"What happened the day you saw me? What the hell happened to you? Whatever happened, should it really have motivated you to contact me?" she prods him forcefully.

Taken aback by her strength. He has assumed her more delicate, a dandelion, not a steel rod. "I saw you, he blurts out, and at once is abashed by his failure to communicate more effectively. "And was taken by you.

She giggles. "That's a sorry statement!

He hangs his head. "I realize I am a sod.

"You said you were an actor, she probes. "I don't recognize you from anything.

"Babylon Revisited.

"The soap"

"Yes, for several years, he admits.

She shakes her head. "Never caught it. As for me, I've been doing a minor role in a play for two years as well as an occasional gig on a sitcom. Just enough to keep me in bread and water…. but alas, no chocolates.

"I can get you chocolates, he says seriously.

"No need, she laughs, I'm on a diet this week.

Their patter is circular, one moving around the other to determine whether there are sparks that warrant them closing their circle. She finishes her coffee quickly.

"All right, she says, thoughtfully. I think I can take you mano a mano if you get out of line. She stands with a smile, so if you want to continue your assault, let's try dinner.

"Sure, he smiles. Although I kinda like the mano a mano image.

"Sure you do, she says smacking her lips together. Bet you do! Let's go to Vino di Firenze, say seven o'clock this weekend. Saturday ok"

"I'll make sure it is. Shall I pick you up" he asks.

"Not necessary. I'll meet you at the resto. Bring lots of dough. It ain't cheap. If it turns out we don't connect, at least I'll get a good dinner out of it.

"Sounds about right, he concedes. Fair enough!

Now Roger is thinking quickly as to how he can beg off Denise Saturday night while courting Marina.

"I'm going to mother's for dinner, he will say to her. But then she will counter with: Suppose I come along. No, that won't do, he furthers his imaginary conversation, because mom wants to talk to me about legacy matters. I mean what happens when she passes. "Of course, Denise would reply. "Then you must go alone. I'll just sit alone, starving, and cataloguing my cheap jewelry, dying of tedium while you learn how rich you are about to become.

Dresses well for the occasion. A jacket. No tie, of course, but an expensive long-sleeved shirt from Boss. Leather jacket. Shoes that match. He meets Marina at the restaurant, no longer nervous. He has won the first round, perhaps even two, he assures himself. Their table is reserved. A waiter in a bow-tie and white apron appears and prompts them towards a bottle of wine apparently from the era of the Medicis. "Couldn't cost more than a grand, Marina giggles. Instead, they each decide to order a glass of a Marques de Caceres.

"Tell me about your name.

"My mother was an avid movie fan, but not only American films. She loved the French ones. When she was pregnant with me, she happened to see a couple of French films with Marina Vlady, an eastern European actress who was beautiful and sexy, and she thought that a great name for her daughter.

"It is a fine name. Reminds one of water. Marina, you know.

"I have heard that one before, she says archly.

"I'm not often entertaining, he grimaces.

"I don't need to be entertained, she says. She reaches over and takes his hand in hers. "Relax. The evening is young and we have a lot more we can screw up before the evening is over.

"I was afraid of that, he responds with a laugh.

But the chatter is easy-going, fluid, on-going. Neither of them overwhelms the other, a sure sign of nervousness or boredom, he thinks. Reading the dessert menu in front of them.

"Think I'll pass, Marina says. I've eaten enough pasta to fill my belly twice.

"Ok with me, Roger responds. He calls for the check, pays with a card. He helps her with her coat. "I'll walk you home, he offers.

"Better still, she says, "you may take me at home.

"Then let's hurry, he whispers agreeably.

Giggling, they are cruising down the street. Two blocks later, they spy her brownstone. "I have the upstairs apartment. I share it with a girlfriend who, as luck would have, is out of town.

"Sure, it's luck" he asks suspiciously. "You didn't have a hand in this lucky coincidence"

She laughs. "I am a believer in planning my own destiny.

Now upstairs, settling into an over-stuffed armchair, he thinks he would like a drink to settle the butterflies.

"You have your choice, she says almost gravely. "A drink or me, but not both.

"That's an easy one, he replies. Got any rye" But before she can complain, he lifts her by her armpits and pins her against the wall, kissing her.

"I do have rye, she says, her voice muffled against his arm.

"Forget the booze, he says. In an instant, they are flailing about on the bed, trading places as they turn. But Marina, unlike women Roger has known, is not acceding to his will. She won't be pinned underneath him. Instead, she signals to him clearly that she wants to ride on top. Not only on top but facing away from him.

"Sure, he says, kissing her again, after a bit of foreplay.

"Fuck foreplay, she responds. "Better yet, she adds as if the idea were original, fuck me instead.

"Happy to oblige, he chuckles. But in an instant, he realizes something odd is occurring. In an instant, he is inside her. They are connected by his penis, but in no other way. Facing away from him, riding him up and down, she might as well be masturbating, he is thinking. There is something vital lacking: intimacy. He waits patiently until she has climaxed. But he himself does not follow, and she turns towards him inquiringly. "Something I need to do" she asks.

"Yes, he says. Get closer.

"Oh, she responds tentatively. Is that what you need" But Marina seems unsure how she can narrow the distance. Finally, she spoons against his body, still facing away. He is holding her and asking whether she will turn towards him. She nods negatively.

Now he flips her around and sits her up against the railing of the bed. "I don't like to fuck just to fuck, he admits. "I need to connect to what I'm screwing, he forges on blatantly.

"Very romantic of you, she says crisply. I don't need any of that. You did for me what I need.

"And for me"

"You are a big boy, she answers, and need to provide for yourself.

"As you said, he retorts. "Not very romantic.

She shrugs and slips off the bed into a bathrobe lying on the floor. "I don't like men who make demands, she says her lips screwing into an antagonistic way. "Especially the first time. Maybe if you hook me into this relationship, we can give it a try later.

"Not asking for all that much, he smiles.

"I think you are.

Now they are looking steely-eyed at one another.

"We're getting off the wrong foot, he says quietly.

"Tell me what you need, then. A blow job" A hand job" Just tell me.

"None of the above…at least not right now…I would like to hold you and even to be held by you.

"Much too soon for that sort of funny stuff, she guffaws.

Roger rises from the bed, finds his shorts, gets dressed quickly. In the interim, Marina has slipped into the bed under the sheets. "Good night, he says to her evenly.

"Good night, Roger, she calls out as he reaches the front door. Behind him, the lights go out.

31

Brent Sadowski's Testimony

Periodically, Alex would appear in Brent's little office, often to suggest that this or that evening she had nothing to do and, since she was free, would Brent enjoy spending some time with her. "I enjoy spending time," he said to her. "With you, I mean, of course," he added with a stammer.

"Good," she would say, "so let's go to the corner pizza after work and later, we can play trivial pursuits there against other customers."

"I would like that," Brent said, "but you should know I do not think quickly."

"But I'm sure you think very well indeed," she countered with a smile.

So, they went to the corner pizza and indulged in a large sausage and pepperoni pizza, each of them adding a small salad and a bottle of sparkling water. Brent enjoyed watching Alex eat. Once she had separated a piece of pizza, she took it by its crust and hoisted it into her mouth making the slice disappear, not without some effort.

"You do that so well," he marveled.

"Try it," she laughed. "Stuff the whole thing in."

He tried it and choked.

She laughed again. "Not very ladylike," she said, pulling another piece apart and preparing to heave it into her mouth, "but this is the way I enjoy eating pizza. Does it take anything away from me as a woman?" she asked suddenly alarmed.

"You look quite lovely," Brent replied," even with slabs of sausage caked on the corners of your lips."

"That obvious," she muttered. "I better learn to do this in a different way."

"Please don't," he countered. "I think you look like a print I saw in a magazine once. It was of a raptor swallowing a small pig whole. I never forget this print, it was so different."

"So, she replied pouting, you think I look like a raptor?"

"Quite a lovely raptor," he hastened to reassure her.

"You do say the nicest things," she cooed in mock sarcasm.

Then they sat down two by two to play trivial pursuits. The first question they encountered had to do with the largest country in the world. Alex thought it was China, but Brent put his hand over her mouth before she could verbalize the answer. "It's Russia," he said.

"You sure?"

"Yup. And I'm sorry for shutting you up," he added.

They did not win the contest, placing third among six couples. But Brent felt good. He thought he had made a real connection with Alex as woman. Somehow, he was able to dissociate her real persona from the imaginary one generated by the photo. Perhaps because when he kissed the photo, it did not kiss him back. That evening, as he was about to leave Alex, she reached over and pecked him on the cheek, applauding a great partner he was.

As a result, Brent was now convinced that Alex had fallen in love with him. Kisses and compliments were hardly the staples of his life, so that when he received them from this vibrant young woman, he felt enchanted. He also realized that considerable time had passed since he and Alex had become friends and that, surely, she was expecting him, shy though he may have been, to initiate the series of physical maneuvers he had read about and which he had once before begun to unfold with Angel so many years ago.

That weekend, he suggested she come to his apartment where he would have a meal catered followed by watching one of her favorite films, Doctor Zhivago. Alex agreed at once. She appeared in a paisley skirt and white blouse, carrying a bottle of red wine from the Saumur region. Brent had called a local Italian restaurant to send over a dinner of veal rigatoni, salads, and cannelloni.

After dinner, he started up Doctor Zhivago, the two of them lounging on his red velour sofa. For an hour as the film progressed, he watched none of it, instead listening to Alex's breathing, her modulations as Zhivago became hunted or when he succeeded after braving a blizzard in finding his love.

"It's so beautiful," Alex cooed. "So, lovely."

It was at that moment, that Brent mustered up his courage and reached his right hand to place the pinky next to, just lightly touching the pinky of this extraordinary woman. Engrossed in the film, Alex did not move. Or react. As a result, Brent was now perplexed. What am I supposed to do next?" he wondered. He felt as if he had achieved the first base of the progression, a seizing of the hand which, even though he had embraced but a pinky, seemed to meet the demands of the first move. Perhaps before seizing one of her breasts recalling the hurt in Angel's voice when he manipulated one of hers, he could simply move his arm around Alex's waist. Yes, an intermediate step, he prided himself. Somewhere between step and step two in the progression of love. When he put his arm around her, she straightened her back slightly but otherwise did not protest. The lady does not protest! Brent reflected. Consequently, she must be congruent with my moves. They are, in fact, quite well-oiled, practiced. Like the conductor of an orchestra, he planned the next series of moves, placing his body stealthily against hers even as Alec Guinness was steadily berating Zhivago.

Suddenly, Alex became fully aware of the touching which had now been achieved from her pinky to her back and arm. She turned to Brent. "Seriously," she said gently to Brent, her tone dropping. "I thought we were friends."

"We are friends," he stammered.

"But then what are you doing with your body against mine?" she asked. "That is not the mark of friendship."

"What is it" he asked timidly.

"The mark of affection a woman permits to the man she loves."

"Yes," he replied hopefully. "Yes."

"But we don't love one another," she stated firmly. "We are simply friends."

"We don't love each other," he repeated woefully. "At least one of us does, he added, clearly correcting Alex.

"Oh, she said, now springing up. "Oh!"

"Did I not do the order correctly?" he asked her, still sitting.

"What order?"

"The order of physical intimacy," he replied earnestly. "Before we make love, I take your hand, then I grab your breast, perhaps both. And then, as we undress, I go the next step."

Alex giggled. "You're putting me on."

"So, I didn't do this correctly?"

"No," she said, her laugh quieting. "No, you did not. There

must be assent from the other person. Get that? I have to agree to allow you to touch."

"I thought you did."

"When?"

"When I touched your hand, you did not pull it away."

"Because I wasn't aware of it," she replied, "I was engrossed in the movie."

"Oh, I see," he replied uncomfortably. "You're angry with me."

"Not really," she said sitting down next to him." But you should learn to read the clues better," she admonished him gently.

"I don't know how to do that," he said.

She shrugged. "I see that. I'm sorry, but I'm not the woman for you."

"Forever?"

She looked at him with wide open eyes.

"Well, yes," she exhaled, having thought about it an instant too long. "Yes. But now I see you are hurt."

"I have been hurt often," he said bringing the feeling up deep from his gut.

"I am so sorry," Alex said.

"But," he responded, "you can't deny you gave me the indications which I was looking for. I was about to feel you up, you know."

"Indications?"

"Yes. I have a manual."

"Oh boy," she burst out. "I really am sorry. I have made a grave mistake here. We need to stop seeing one another."

"Really?" But nothing has changed, has it?"

"Yes. It is entirely my fault. I gave off the wrong signals. I liked you. Like a puppy dog," she added. "I thought you were harmless company when I couldn't get together with my boyfriend," she added. "Tal is his name. You do know I have a boyfriend."

"Yes," Brent answered, his face hanging." I did know this, but I thought I could…."

"It just doesn't work that way. I can't quite explain how it works, but both of us have to be on the same wavelength. Now it's clear we are on completely different beams. I think I'll leave now and I will suggest that outside of work we don't see one another again."

"Maybe if I re-read the manual? he said brightly. "I probably didn't read it properly."

"Good night, Brent," she said, beating a hasty departure.

32

A Marriage

(Benjamin to audience as he moves to center stage) "Charm of love! Waves cascading warm on the body. I had forgotten how wonderful it is to wake up with my hand cupping a woman's breast. Damn, how I've missed that.

Several months passed with us together and we had not set a date. But it didn't matter. These were months of bliss. We lived together and touched and made love and, mornings, after an early run, I would come home and nuzzle in Marcella's warmth. Despite the sweat…she craved me sweaty. I had never known happiness like that. Sure, my past included nights of pleasure, even moments of transcendence, but what happened in this period was beyond my ken. Had I to describe what constitutes earthly paradise, I now had a yardstick. Marcella!

So, this is where it ends. Bring down the curtain. The play is over. It must be over! (Benjamin leaps into the air as if to force the curtain down) Just once, damn you, curtain.

(To audience) Isn't that the way we were meant to be? Loving and uncaring of anything but the joy of awakening next to the person whose heart beats with yours. How did the movies of the thirties and forties end? With a long kiss, hosannas, two riders together on one stallion setting out after the struggle was resolved. So, bring the curtain down.

(Sadly) In our time, our plays end differently. There are no exiting stallions, hearts beating in tandem, not at the final moment."

"Tomorrow, I'll take a lovely bath in my whirlpool with a new plastic pillow for my head," Marcella says, exiting left briefly.

(Benjamin facing audience, moving to the left) "The party ended. It always does, and the aftermath fired up. For a time, we were all in unison until a breech occurred in President Jager's office. He wanted to can a young woman in my department. Louise was her name. On the grounds that we didn't have enough students to keep her on. That wasn't factually true. He simply disliked her honesty. Too direct at faculty meetings. She scolded the administration. Anyway, I resisted her firing. Marcella, Jager and I had a meeting about her in which, strangely, Marcella took his side. The bastard then fired Louise."

(Marcella entering from left) "That was a rough meeting." She hands Benjamin a drink

"You were wrong to support him," Benjamin cries out angrily. "I had all the facts. Louise has worked with more history students than anyone else in the department."

"Let it go," Benjamin, Marcella says.

"Easy for you to say. You're not the one who has to tell Louise. Why did you take Jager's side against me?"

Marcella shrugs. "Jager would have fired her anyway. As for you, all you accomplished was to make a bad impression."

"But it wasn't right," Benjamin says, pacing. "She's the only person we have in Chinese history, and the future of the department is probably in Asian studies."

"It's her own fault. She wouldn't submit to student evaluations."

"So, she's a bit eccentric, but a fine teacher. Come on, Marcella, you were afraid to disagree with your boss. Maybe he'd think less of you if you took Louise's side. Maybe he'd even wonder if he hadn't picked the wrong hatchet woman. But you know I was right."

(Drily) "You have your own perspective on this, Ben, but I don't share it. Why must you always believe that your approach to an issue is the only one that has merit?"

(Benjamin to audience) "We didn't speak for a couple of days. Marcella hated confrontation so we rarely argued. I expected her to relent and tell me she was sorry. Whatever the strength of her position, she knew how I felt. Loyalty is everything, particularly when truth is at stake. But when she didn't broach the subject after days and I began to miss our closeness, I took the initiative and told her to forget this little spat. Tried to smooth things over. But for some reason we were never quite the same. An edge of charm had broken off. It is called trust.

Just about that time, I received a wonderful piece of news. (To Marcella, reading) Sweetie, look at this, you'll never believe it. I've been awarded a Fulbright Grant to France to write my book."

(Genuinely pleased) "That's terrific, Benjamin."

"Better still, I can do this in Nice. Think about it, sweetie, the Riviera, the two of us for a year."

"I couldn't be happier," Marcella says. (Pause)" But I'm not sure I'll be able to go with you."

"Of course, you're coming with me."

"I've only just settled in as Jager's assistant."

"Surely, he'll understand and let you go under these circumstances."

"And if he doesn't?"

"Then we'll quit", Benjamin says. "With this Fulbright followed by the publication of my book, I'll be able to write my own ticket."

"I couldn't be happier for you, Ben, but there are two of us in this relationship. You've not paid any attention to what this might mean to my career."

(To audience) "She was right," Benjamin says sadly. "I was so carried away with good news, as well as the fantasy that Marcella and I would have an extended period to ourselves in one of the most romantic of places, I didn't truly consider what she might have to give up."

"I'll need to talk to Jager," Marcella says.

"Of course," Benjamin replies, "but he'll let you go. You do want to, don't you?"

"Of course, I do." (Turns her back to him)

(Benjamin to audience) "Did she? I wasn't present at her interview with the president. It all depended, didn't it, on how she made her case. As an opportunity for the college to make a new international connection, for example? A growth opportunity for both of us which would accrue to the college on our return. How did she present it to him?"

(Marcella turning back to Benjamin) "He simply refused. He says he needs me here. We are undertaking a large capital campaign, and he wants me to be part of it."

"And you said?"

"What could I say?" Marcella replied with a pleading face. "My refusal would have been the end of my work here. I see a future in this job. Fund raising is fun. I like people, I like the small talk, and using my connections to raise cash."

"So, I'm to go over alone," Benjamin says sullenly.

"Not quite," she replies. "He will allow me to be with you for a week, and I'll even be able to visit you later. It won't be lonely for you…. you'll have your work to keep you busy. Anyhow, what would I be doing over there while you were in the library all day?"

"How about the celebrated beach?" Museums?" Learning French. Skiing in the mountains."

(To audience) "What kind of case did she make to Jager?"

(Turns to her) "Haven't you forgotten one small item?"

"What would that be?"

"Our wedding?" Marcella stifles an aura of surprise. "We'll postpone it a while until you've completed your project."

Benjamin now moves closer to her, baffled and angry. "Let's formalize us before I leave."

"That's silly," Marcella laughs. "We wouldn't be together." (She turns her back on him once more)

33

Roger and Marina

He picks up his iphone and, with a heavy heart, dials Denise's number. He is standing with his back to a wall.

"I've been waiting for you to call," she complains. What is happening to you? I hardly hear from you."

"That's why I'm calling," Roger responds, his tone a bit higher than she is used to hearing.

"You're breathing funny. Are you all right? I would have called you, but I know you don't like me to initiate contact outside of work."

"I never said that," he speaks through virtually clenched teeth. "Just a bit out of breath. Been running," he lies.

"Sure, we shouldn't have this chat face to face? Maybe at my place? she asks tentatively.

"Look," Denise, he intones. "I never wanted to hurt…"

"Oh my God," she interrupts. "It's like that, is it?"

"I've met somebody else," he continues quickly.

"Oh," she responds, her voice quivering. Lowers her voice and speaks cautiously. "Want to tell me about her?"

"Not really. Just that we are seeing one another."

Pause. "I thought you…" Denise responds, her voice trailing

off. "Cared for me deeply, in fact. Maybe it isn't the love that we could imagine, but it sure felt real to me. I thought you wanted me," she repeats.

"I have. I do," he responds quickly. "But you know that we haven't clicked together. I don't know why this is. Maybe we were simply not meant for each other."

"Roger," she replies, "you are seeing only from one perspective. I thought there was an endless future for us together. All that was required, I thought, was that you ramp up an iota from the emotional status between us. I waited for you patiently. My heart was open to you. And yet, I made no demands on you, did I?" When you wanted to have sex with me, even when it seemed as if you were using me, I never complained."

"True."

"I thought that over time, despite your dramatic sense of distance, that we would be brought together by the sheer fact of who we were. Two actors in the same soap working together every day, working well together, I should add. Isn't that so?"

"You're trying to be rational about something which has nothing to do with reason," he reminds her.

"So true," she admits, exhaling. "Yes. Still, I want you to know something, Roger. You may not have loved me, but that is not the way I felt, the way I feel, about you. When you leave me, my heart will cascade, a large part of my life will dissolve into a void."

Pause. "I didn't know that you felt so strongly."

"I think you did, but you were so intent on keeping distant… is that what you are doing with the new girl?"

"Marina."

"With Marina?"

"Yes. No. I don't know. We are in a different stage of being

219

together."

"I just wanted to know whether you intend to remove yourself emotionally from all women…or was it just me?"

"Don't be angry," he says. "Please."

"Not angry. Crushed".

"Oh," he says. "Look, I'm expected," he continues. "I should go."

"Just one moment," she comes back shrilly. "One moment. I want you to know that I love you, and that if this relationship of yours fails, I may still be here for you. I cannot guarantee this, of course. I say this based on how I feel right now."

"You are sweet."

"And what happens to us in the workplace?" she inquires.

"Just as we always were. I do care for you, Denise. That will never change. And work is and has always been separate from our lives, isn't that so?"

"Yes."

"Time for me to hang up. It's been a great… time. Goodbye, Denise."

"Really?" Goodbye?"

He clicks off his phone and sits down. A few minutes later, Marina enters.

"My word," she says, "you look like a beaten puppy dog."

He sighs. "I broke up with Denise."

"Oh," she says pleasantly. "That's what this is about? You'll have to take all your concerns, all that unspent caring and love, and aim them in my direction."

"I hope you mean that," Roger says.

"Don't be grumpy. You did the honest thing."

"I should have spoken to her in person."

"Ha! She would have grabbed your chest in mid-sentence and

torn your heart out. No, you did the best you could. Got to hold them off with pitchforks," she adds, "otherwise they advance and seize your cojones".

"It's not like that," he replies resigned.

"Tell me how it is," she prods, her legs dangling over his body.

He sits on his sofa, curls his legs up. His face is screwed up as if insects had been attacking his eyes.

"I care for this girl," he says simply.

"Of course, you do", Marina replies. I wouldn't want you to feel any the less."

"She has been an anchor now for many, many months."

"You sound," Marina says lowering her eyes and pouring herself a drink, "as if you regretted breaking off with her."

"I think I did this badly," he says too quickly.

"How so?"

"I needed to tell her…."

"How much you really felt about her?" Marina prompts. "Out of that welter of words, maybe you would also find one that told her how much you really loved her, and seizing on that word, on that feeling even if the feeling were only for the moment, you might have relented. But tomorrow morning, when the sun comes up, would you have felt right?"

"Something was just off kilter for us," he avers.

"Yes," Marina, says. "Clearly."

"Wish you wouldn't take so much pleasure in this," he complains.

She puts her hand around his neck and pulls him close to her, then kisses him on the neck. "I do take pleasure in this. I have you all to myself now," she purrs.

"Thank God," he murmurs, placing his head on her chest.

34

Armand Questions Brent's Colleague

He is playing with his suspenders, snapping them as he waits. In few moments, Dr. Gregory appears. The doctor is a short, rotund man with a beard and sparse flaxen hair, now graying at the temples. "I have those as well," he says to Armand, pointing at the suspenders.

"Belts are too restrictive for me," Armand replies. He stands up his six feet two inches towering over the diminutive scientist, and holds out his hand.

Gregory leads him into an office strewn with discs. Two computers seemingly operating diligently are lighting up a corner of the room. "Stats," he says pleasantly. "I deal with stats here."

"Yes. You said on the phone that you know Brent Sadowski."

"Indeed, I do. Would you enjoy a coffee?"

"Yes. Black, please."

Gregory calls for two coffees black. In a moment, a young woman enters bearing a tray with coffee and gingerbread cookies.

"Tell me about Brent," Armand says sitting back.

"Sure," Gregory answers, slipping synthetic sugar into his coffee. "A nice guy, somewhat simple I think, but he always does his job to our satisfaction."

"He is responsible for the room with the vials."

Gregory laughs. "Yes, we call it the Vialroom. Get it" He chortles. "Vialroom. Because most drugs are indeed vile."

"Nice," Armand assents with a half-hearted grin. "He does his work well," you were suggesting.

"Indeed. He comes early, stays late, and watches the room like a hawk. He has a little desk and a computer which allows him to catalogue everyone who comes and goes, as well as any drug which is taken in or out of the room."

"Just Brent?"

"Yes."

"He never goes to lunch?"

"Naturally, but then he locks the door."

"And if someone needs a vial in his absence?"

"That someone has to contact the upper floor supervisor. They, of course, do not wish to be bothered over this sort of thing, and normally require the interrogator to wait until Brent has returned from lunch."

"And if Brent has to go to the bathroom?"

Gregory chuckles, his belly heaving. "I don't think I have ever seen him go."

"Surely…."

"Look," Gregory answers, disappointed that he has to clarify his statement. "If he has to go to the bathroom, then the person will simply wait a minute or two."

"I see. So, Brent is uniquely, solely in charge of the vial room."

"No question."

"You do know that the hantavirus that killed Alexandra Rosen came from that room."

"We know that for sure?"

Armand chuckles slightly. "You think vials of hantavirus are available at every drugstore? Come on, now, Doctor, let's be serious."

"I admit the likelihood of finding it elsewhere in these parts is remote."

"But you find troublesome the idea of that virus killing one of your workers..."

"Alexandra was a spot of sunlight," Dr. Gregory admits. "We looked forward to her being with us every day. Of course, we hate that it came from our room. I mean we hate that a drug attributable to us might have killed her."

"Or that she herself may have stolen it."

"Yes. But Brent says that there is no record of her having taken anything either in or out of that room."

"Then how could the virus have made its way into her house?"

Gregory pauses, swills his coffee stick. His face is now turning a pale shade of purple. "Someone got into that room despite Brent's caution," he concurs, his neck turning.

"Yes. Brent clearly didn't compile all the information, did he?"

"Clearly not".

"Talk to me about Brent and Alex."

Gregory giggles. "You mean as a couple? Impossible to conceive of," he smiles, his arms bouncing off his hips. "Quite impossible."

"And why do you say this?"

"Because Alex was a pretty girl. It was said she had a boyfriend. It was also rumored her boyfriend, true, was not a very nice person, but she showed no interest in Brent's attention."

"So, Brent was interested."

"Smitten is the word, I think."

"How do you know?"

"I saw them huddled together from time to time. I saw Brent's consternation when she held him off. It was clear that he was a pursuer and she was…well…not into him."

"And would this not have given him a motive to kill the girl?"

Gregory looks up, his smile fading. "Surely, you're not serious. Brent is a pussycat, Incapable of such an act. He would not injure a mosquito, much less the woman he cared about. Too farfetched to be a concern," he adds.

"Tell me, Doctor, about the talk on the floor."

"With regards to Brent?"

"Yes."

"Most people see him as a tad enfeebled. Not so that he cannot do a job for us, of course, but he often seems out of reach of…he hesitates… normal humanity. Somewhere dazed in outer space. Yes, he snaps back at once when challenged or when required to fulfill his duties. But for the rest, we all have noticed how unreachable the man is. The only one who had a chance to interact with him at a human level was Alexandra. Not only she was nice to him, but I think because she had a soft spot in her heart for the man."

"Impossible then for him to have hurt her," you believe.

"Improbable at the very least. Yet, little in this world is impossible," Dr. Gregory continues with a twinkle in his eye. "But I think you are barking up the wrong person. We, most of us, believe that Alexandra was having problems with her boyfriend, a man named Tal, and whether he threatened her or she was distraught due to their relationship, I do not know. Yet it seems clear that she brought that virus home and infected herself over a man who, to be honest, was not worth much of anything. She knew exactly what that virus would do to her. You do know, Mr. Desqueyroux, that men often murder themselves with a firearm, but rarely women. No, women prefer poison or some other less mutilating manner of disposing of their earthly remains. I suppose they don't want their corpse to be found disfigured. Vanity plays into their choice of suicide. That is, I guess what Alexandra did. Naturally, had any of us known her intent, we would have done anything to stop this. She was immensely popular with all of us on the floor. But she kept her sorrows to herself, the poor dear. She truly had nobody to turn to at the end, I believe, and because of it, finding herself alone and depressed, she could not take the burden any longer. But those," the doctor continues while scrutinizing Armand, "are quite handsome suspenders. Where ever did you find them?"

35

Armand and Keely Share Their Feelings

"There's an antique six-shooter to be auctioned off," Armand says to her over the phone. "Why don't you meet me at Brilliantine's Auction House. I can bring you up to speed on our mystery, and you might enjoy the auction."

"Anything offered besides firearms?"

"Yes," Armand says. "Lots of little porcelain figurines from an estate."

"Sure," Keely replies. "Sure."

The auction begins at five o'clock. In a seedy warehouse. Virtually crammed. Potential buyers appear less well-off, some quite elderly. Several need assistance to find and maneuver to a seat. Chairs are metallic, stiff bottomed. An elderly man lowers his cane underneath a chair with a clatter.

Keely is at the door awaiting Armand. Dressed in jeans and a tight sweater. Armand sees her at a distance as he mounts several stairs leading to the auction door. She looks appetizing and should wear tight sweaters more often, he thinks. Keely sees him hurrying in and is wondering what news he has. Armand takes her arm and leads her into the hall. They walk quickly over a greyish marble floor towards the back, towards two empty seats.

"Can you see?" he questions.

"Yes," she says. "If I crane my neck a little, I see fine. But if the figurines are small, I won't be able to identify them."

"The auctioneers bring the items around for inspection."

"Aaah," she says. "Well then, before the onslaught begins. Tell me what's new."

"So, Armand begins, I think we have narrowed all of this down to one or two possible conclusions. Your buddy, Brent was most certainly enamored of your sister. At the time, she was involved with her boyfriend, Tal. Even had she not been, she wouldn't have given two fucks for Brent. He isn't off-the-wall daffy, but certainly eccentric, maybe even a bit nuts. She knew this, still took pains not to hurt him as best she could, but when he came on to her...."

"He did? Brent?"

"Apparently in his own fashion. She snuffed out his ardor." Armand pauses. "Naturally, this is an historic motive for murder. That's one theory. At this time, I've got only speculation. But there's another side to this. Alexandra became depressed when she couldn't resolve her failing relationship with Tal. He beat her, if not physically, then emotionally. Tal is a swine, no doubt about it, but he didn't have motive to kill her. When he was done with her, he simply told her to go away which she did, her tail between her legs. The upshot is that she may have done herself in the way women do from time to time...that is, with poison. The handy one was the hantavirus which she could obtain either from Brent or, more likely, from the vial room when his back was turned."

"Interesting," Keely avows. But what now?"

"I don't quite know. I think I'll continue to investigate Brent

Sadowski as far as that trail will take me either to eliminate him as a suspect, thereby ascertaining that your sister did in fact snuff herself, or find conclusive proof that Brent was somehow involved. Had Alexandra asked him for a vial of hantavirus, would he have given it to her and not noted it on his computer log? There's nothing in those records. He's so fucking fastidious."

In front, the auctioneer is stepping up to the dais and speaks into a microphone, calling the room to order, quieting everyone. Wearing a white shirt with a blue bow tie. He has a round face, perhaps fortyish, with a pleasant, gravelly voice. He is starting the auction with a red and white plate he claims is Japanese Imari from the last century. He holds it up with both hands and begins the auction at $25.

"What do you think?" Keely asks him. "Would Brent have given her a vial knowing what she intended it for?"

"I don't know. I doubt it. She may have rejected him, but so gently, it appears, that it's hard to believe he would want to do her harm. But nothing is out of the question."

Fifteen minutes later, the six shooter is offered. A Magnum .357 holding six bullets. A boy comes by with it, pretending to holster it after he twirls it in his hands. Armand examines it carefully. Good sheen. The pistol has rarely been fired. The pistol is clean. The bidding is quick. Armand bids up to three hundred twenty dollars and wins the lot.

"Congratulations," she says.

"It's for my collection," he says with a pleased lilt to his voice.

Later, Keely raises her number on a Meissen plate from the 19th century, but she is outbid.

"Disappointed?" he asks.

"A little," she says, "although if I had won it, I wouldn't know

229

where to put it. I have too much crap already."

"We all do," he agrees. "Let's head out for a cup of coffee," he suggests. "There is a Starbucks on the corner." There, they locate a small, empty booth. Two coffees and two plum cakes. They settle in.

Armand is looking at Keely as he is holding a piece of cake. "I've been meaning to confide something to you," he says after a long pause.

She looks up, the coffee cup at her lips. "You seem perplexed."

"Not quite sure how to put this."

"Just put it," she smiles.

"Ok." He continues. "We've been working together on this case now for over three weeks," he begins. "My attention right from the beginning has been solely focused on what happened to your sister. True, I have had distractions. Clients asking me to shadow a spouse, someone else in a bribery situation needing documents for exoneration, but for the most part I have spent my waking (and occasionally sleepless) hours on your case."

"I do appreciate it," Keely flutters. "My sister, as you know, meant everything to me."

"But I noticed," he goes on, "more recently, that my focus has wavered somewhat. Really unprofessionally, I fear," he continues somewhat shakily.

"How do you mean?" she asks.

"I've been feeling comfortable with you. More and more, he says as our time together grows." Pauses. "I know that you are not seeing anyone right now.

She looks up. "I haven't been entirely mindless about this," she responds. "I see sometimes when I am not chatting, how you look at me. It is more, I assume, than just the inquiring glance of an investigator."

"Yes," he acknowledges. He reaches for and takes her hand. Warm, small. Her fingers curl up in his.

"Your hands smell soapy. Reach over the table," she says to him suddenly.

His other hand reaches over. "No," she says with a tiny smile. "I mean your mouth."

Leans over the table. She is leaning into him. Kisses him. He captures the kiss, holds her lips.

"Thank you," he grins.

She laughs, her eyes narrowing a bit. "I was able to overlook that bit of cold sore on your lower lip because your kiss was so intense."

"Shit," Jason Fierst shouts. "I don't believe a syllable of it. Roger, when you kiss the girl, make it look as if you really want to devour those lips of her. And Denise, please don't criticize him when he is about to seduce you. We may have to alter the line a bit to make you less critical."

"Is that what's he's doing?" she asks a bit angrily. "Anyway, you may not have noticed but the line is in the script."

"Yes. Step one or step whatever of the seduction sequence. Your mind should be spinning, girl, because it should be clear to everyone you have been pleasantly anticipating this moment for some time. You wake up in the middle of the night thinking, boy, I wish that Armand would place his lovely sweet French lips onto mine and clamp down until I squeal."

"You want me to squeal?" she erupts, giggling.

"You know what I want," Jason fumes. "Don't be cute. Make it work, that's all. And forget about his cold sore, for Christ's sake. Is it actually in the script?"

"Sure is," she complains. "Ok," she continues to Armand. "Reach over the table!"

Armand's hand begins to move over. "No, she goes on, I mean your mouth." She kisses him and he leans in to capture the full flavor of the kiss. Locked together, grappling lips on lips.

"Yes," Jason is stammering in the background. "This I believe. Oh, yes. Go on."

"I'm steaming," Denise announces, and then adds. "Keely is about to hyperventilate."

"It's fine. It's good," Jason says. "Let Keely dissolve in the boy's arms! Let the heat from this kiss scintillate throughout her body! Your fans, my girl, want you to be happy in the grasp of this adventurous and brilliant detective. And yet, the less desirable aspect of your personality, my sweet, has not yet made an appearance. Go on, Keely, go on!"

"Oh, Armand," she croons, contorting her face. "My face is burning. My heart is on fire. I hope you brought a fire extinguisher with you."

"Keely, my sweaty blossom, I wish to make sweet, mad love to you over the commode."

"Armand, how juicy is a toilet screw! Strip me of my garments, do! Grab any part of my body that appeals to you, lover, and if you feel like flushing, make that water steaming hot!"

"Boys and girls," Jason is shouting derisively, "the afternoon is droning on. Could we mosey back to the words on the script? The real script?"

"He thinks the script is real," Denise giggles. "What alternate universe is he living in?"

"Ha! Ha!" Jason shouts. "All right, get it out of your system. Go ahead. Be disrespectful, be less than charming. What do I care? It's only my career that is on the line here. All right, I can see the afternoon light is dimming and we are fucked. Go home everybody but be ready at 10 tomorrow morn to play the scene correctly. In the interim, maybe you two can develop some chemistry. But only if it pleases you!"

36

A Jazz Concert

(To audience) "I had three months to prepare for my sabbatical. I began to do the necessary preliminary research. At the same time, I tried to ready myself to the idea of doing without Marcella for several months. After several weeks, it began to sink in. Just then, another piece of trouble."

(Marcella entering. Her tone is different, defensive) "I know you don't much care for it."

Benjamin shrugs. "Jazz is entertaining, but not every day."

"You don't care about it nearly as much as I do," Marcella says. "I've never heard you once listen to any of my jazz CDs."

"Who is he?" Benjamin asks acerbically. "Who is the new star in your firmament""

"Joseph? He's the new clinical psychologist at the college."

"I've seen him. Bearded guy. Skinny, bearded guy."

"Yes."

"You're going to a jazz concert with this guy? You've already bought the tickets?"

"He did. They were hard to come by."

"Am I missing something in this? Aren't we engaged? (She looks at him strangely) It didn't occur to you to invite me?"

"Not your kind of thing," Marcella responds. "I didn't think you were hot on this."

"You didn't even ask. How did you and Joseph come to connect on this date?"

"President Jager asked me to show him around since he's new to the college," Marcella huffs defensively.

(Turns to audience) "Why is he making such a big deal over this? I'm just fulfilling one of my responsibilities as assistant to the President. Jager suggested I give Joseph a full tour of the campus. I did that. Well, during the tour, he mentioned how much he enjoyed jazz. One thing led to another, that's all. It's not as if I were being disloyal to Ben."

"I hope you both have a good time," Benjamin says, resigned.

(To audience) "This is a small community. Everyone will see her with another man and assume she's cheating on me. Maybe that's true.

(To Marcella) Do you find Joseph attractive?"

"I hadn't thought about it," she says, exiting left.

"He's kinda wimpy," Benjamin insists. "Short and thin as a rail."

"That's sad, Benjamin. I don't evaluate people by weight," Marcella responds.

"Attractive or not?" he insists.

"I told you I hadn't considered it."

(Benjamin to audience) "Typical answer. It doesn't mean either yes or no. So, they went to the concert and I stayed home trying to work, then nervously flipped TV channels, all the while fuming. After a while, I went out and found an antiques store opened late. I walked out of there with two Regency chairs. I don't even remember purchasing them. I was back before ten but Marcella didn't return until midnight."

(Marcella offstage, now entering left) "Thanks for everything,

Joseph."

"Have a good time?" Benjamin asks almost under his breath.

"The saxophonist was unbelievable. What did you do?"

"Bought a couple of chairs. Those over there."

"Nice," Marcella answers.

"And how did Joseph enjoy the concert?"

"Very much."

"And did he enjoy you?"

"Get off it," Ben, she snarls.

"A simple question, Marcie. Tell me whether the psychologist liked you. What did he say about you…about us?"

"He's never met us. (Pause. Suddenly she picks up one of the chairs and, with a scream, smashes it) Damn, sometimes you really piss me off."

(Benjamin, softly) "That chair which lasted not a minute in your hands, had survived for two centuries before you went bonkers."

(Marcella trying to calm herself, trembling) "What century are we in? I did nothing wrong, nor did Joseph. We went to a concert together. You're just jealous and possessive. I don't appreciate those traits."

(Benjamin to audience) "She really couldn't explain it. Confrontation! All of this only led to one argument after the other. We had words. We sulked. Then I would cave, cozy up to her to make it all better. Always me repairing the breech. Marcella didn't appear to know the behavior or the words to smooth things over. The following morning at breakfast she changed the subject.

"I had a look at that chair," she says. "It's been broken before. I'll see about getting it repaired."

(Benjamin reaches over and seizes her wrist) "Just once last night, I could have taken your little neck between my hands and broken it."

"You're hurting me, Benjamin. (He releases her wrist) What in hell is wrong with you? You're raising hell over a chair. It's nothing more than a chair." (Exits left)

(Benjamin to audience) "And that was that. No apology. No sense of loss. The chair could have been hit by a train or smashed in a tornado. Why was I surprised? The vehemence of her physical action shook me. I had already learned that this woman was unselfish and giving as long as her agenda was not derailed. Now I was seeing her other side. As for me, I had forgotten that I too could become enraged. I felt totally shaken with anger.

For a time, Marcella kept her distance as if, at any moment, I might harm her physically. Nonetheless, in fits and starts, life reverted to something like normality. Just when you are convinced it can never be healed. Two weeks later, content again in my own skin, I was sitting on the sofa reading when I heard voices as the front door opened." (Sits on sofa with book)

(Marcella enters laughing from left with Joseph) "You should have seen his face."

(Joseph enters behind her. A young-looking thirty-year old with a beard) "But I did see his face."

(Benjamin gets up). "Marcella! I expected you earlier. Dinner's almost ready."

(Marcella kissing him on cheek) "I ran into Joseph on my way to the car, and I convinced him to come home and have supper with us."

"I think we can arrange that," Benjamin says. "The roast is still in the oven. How are you?"

"Hungry," Joseph says. (He takes out a pipe and fills it with tobacco)

(Benjamin, to Marcella) "Well don't just stand there. Fetch the man a drink."

"Vodka?"

"Bloody Mary, Joseph answers. "No…"

"Salt," said in unison by both Marcella and Joseph.

"Nice duet," Benjamin says, restraining anger in his voice. "Been rehearsing long?"

(Marcella exiting left) "I'll be back in a minute."

"How are your classes>" Benjamin asks Joseph.

"Clinical is good, abnormal kinda abnormal," he laughs. "By the way, congratulations on your Fulbright."

"I am looking forward to time away."

"I've done some work on revolutions myself. The clinical side, of course, how individuals foment social violence to exorcise their own demons."

"Have you now?"

"I find collective movements as a product of individual derangement fascinating. Don't you?"

(Benjamin tries to keep himself in check) "How about Napoleon. Think he was deranged?"

"I've never studied Napoleon, Joseph answers, but I think the case could be made that he was megalomaniacal."

"That nuts, eh?"

"He did crown himself Emperor."

"Maybe there wasn't anybody else around to do it for him."

"You're pulling my leg", Joseph laughs.

"Who had a better mind than Napoleon? Who had a greater vision and the authority to pull it off? I think he was the right man to crown the Emperor."

"Still", Joseph argues, "what about the conventions that should have been observed?"

(Sardonically) "I hope you never forget them," Benjamin says drily.

"I don't quite take your meaning."

"I didn't think you could."

(Marcella enters from left with drink) "Benjamin doesn't like to be lectured about his field."

"I didn't mean to do that," Joseph protests.

"And I'll have one too," Benjamin says.

"What?"

"A bloody Mary," Benjamin says icily.

"I completely forgot to ask you," Marcella laughs in a self-deprecating tone.

(Joseph is now feeling the tension) "About dinner," he remarks suddenly. "You know I've neglected to let out the cat."

"Oh, please stay," Marcella pleads.

"We insist," Benjamin echoes.

"Perhaps some other time," Joseph responds, rising. (Returns the drink to Marcella) "Thanks for the drink. Good night." (Exits left)

(Marcella kicks him gently in the shin) "You were rude, Ben."

(Rubs his leg where she kicked him) "Just jazzing up the evening. I waited dinner for you. You could have called."

"I've explained what happened," Marcella responds.

"So, you have a friend," Benjamin says. "A clinical psychologist historian, and I have a sore shin, and an even sorer heart."

"Don't start up, Ben," Marcella rejoins. I won't take it from you."

"You're throwing your friend in my face," Benjamin erupts.

"Would you have liked it better if we hadn't come home and ate out? That would have suited you?"

"Love, respect, loyalty would suit me. What's happening here?

Don't you see I don't feel secure about you…about us…for me to sit calmly by while you sidle up to a young, attractive male."

"I didn't sneak around. I brought him home."

(To audience) A lot of good my forthrightness got me. Look at him. He can barely control himself. He's seething inside. It's monstrous. Because I brought someone home for dinner" What have I got myself involved with" I could slap his face silly!"

37

Keely Makes Demands

K eely and Armand shopping at their local grocery store. Pushing a cart down each aisle. "I can broil us a couple of steaks tonight," he suggests.

"I'm not much of a carnivore," she responds. "Why don't you allow me to make you dinner tonight?"

"Sure," he agrees. Checking the aisle. He observes her choosing a variety of salads. She holds up a pack of rigatoni, scans the label carefully, then returns it with a pout. Down the aisle, a Barilla pasta she prefers. He notices it is identical to the first, yet more expensive, but says nothing. Bananas! She is buying organic bananas. He cannot grasp the raison d'etre for organic bananas. He assumed that the skin of the fruit protected them against insecticides or other infringements. He reaches for a six pack of coke, but she shakes her head, informs him that this is terrible for him. "They use this to take off dried, stuck gum from metal when nothing else will manage," she says pointedly. "Think what it does to your stomach." It is dawning on Armand that he is connecting to someone unusual, ultra-special. Special in that she has learned to catalogue, maneuver around, even escape the poisons in the environment. And so, for the next half hour, he follows her in amazement as she picks out free range eggs, special breads, and the like.

"I've never bought so much healthiness," he says, exhaling deeply, but he is more intrigued than upset.

In her apartment, she is boiling noodles. Next to the noodles, a special sauce which she herself has concocted and stirred. "All lovely ingredients," she preens proudly.

They sit down at a round table she has laden with fine blue and white porcelain. At once, a frown slides down her face as she glances over at Armand who is taking his seat.

"Did you wash your hands?" she asks, sharply.

"Why, no," he admits. "No, I haven't."

She says nothing, but he understands that he needs to find the bathroom and cleanse his hands.

On the center of the table, Keely has positioned a candle which she lights. She places a glass over the candle. This dims the light somewhat, but also contains it. The meal is good, although less substantial than Armand is accustomed to. After dinner, he wants a coffee. Keely says she does not drink coffee. She suggests a Celestial Seasoning tea instead. Jasmine! He drinks it, finds it oddly flavorful, but lacking stimulation from caffeine. Armand is not assessing the pitfalls of dinner with Keely. Rather, he is thinking what a nice looking, slender woman this is, and, apparently, someone who is ready to give herself over to him were he to ask her.

Thus, after dinner, he is hovering next to her on her brown sofa. She asks him to wait a moment to sit while she removes a plastic coverlet. Chitchat, small talk. Waits an appropriate amount of time before lowering himself. Reaches over to kiss her. She takes his face between her hands, flutters eyelids. "Your breath isn't attractive," she says, clearly offended. "I have an extra toothbrush. Don't get me wrong," she adds. "I want to kiss you badly."

Armand returns to the bathroom, locates the toothbrush, and brushes. In addition, he finds a bottle of mouthwash. He sucks in some of this. Burns his tongue. Spits it out. Returns to the sofa. Keely is waiting for him. She tilts her face at once and he kisses her. She returns his kiss, and their faces are locked together for a moment or two.

Armand begins to undress her. He has located the zipper on her back and lowers it. She stands. Drops the dress to the floor. "Wait," she remarks without the hint of modesty. "Before we go any further. I need to ask you something."

"Shoot," he says, pulling back.

"Have you ever had an STD?"

Pause. Considering the question. "Well, no. Not really."

"Not really?" she asks concerned. "What does that mean?"

"When I was a teen-ager, I had a case of crabs."

"Crabs! How did you get rid of it? You did get rid of it, yes?"

"Yes. I took a bath in some acidic solution."

"Nothing else? There's a lot of chlamydia out there I am told."

"No."

"You have protection?"

"Well, yes, he admits. "I thought to bring some. Hoped you might…"

She interrupts him. "What kind is it?"

"You mean the brand?"

"Yes," she says.

He reaches into his pocket and pulls out the condom. Examines the wrapper. Looks up at her. "It's a Five-Star."

"I've never heard of that," she responds quickly. "Let me see it."

He hands it over to her. She reads the label. "Look," she says,

"I have a Trojan. Comes with a tickler. Would you like to try that?"

"Sure," he says. He does not remember when last a woman rejected his choice of protection and he is trying to preserve his patience.

While she has retreated into the bathroom, he undresses to his shorts. He is waiting for her impatiently now, his breathing more pronounced. She re-enters in a bathrobe. "Pull down your underwear," she says.

Shrugs. Never shy about this sort of thing, he complies. She falls to her knees, takes his member in her hands. "It's too soft to put on the condom," she complains, looking up.

"Hmm, maybe if you did things to it."

She strokes it gently for a minute and the member stiffens. She now applies the condom. "All right. Now," she continues. "Where do you want to do this? We can stand, recline on the bed or simply lie on the sofa, if you wish."

"Sounds good to me," he smiles. "All of it!"

"Well, just a minute," she answers him. "I want to put some towels under us to protect the fabric. You do understand that I need to do that?" The question has a tinge of nervousness to it.

"Of course," he agrees. "I always do." Now he is flabbergasted he has said this snarky thing and wishes he could take it back, but Keely has not noticed. "Good," she remarks. "It's always good to protect the furniture."

He is leaning her backwards on the sofa. "Stop just for a moment," she protests, her hands outstretched against his chest. "When is the last time you bathed?" she asks him.

"This morning, he responds sadly."

"That was over twelve hours ago," she says counting silently. "Maybe you better shower."

Armand is between seething and wanting and savoring. "A little sweat in love doesn't damage anything," he says laughing.

Eyes up defiantly. "The shower or the highway," she replies quietly, if firmly.

For an instant, Armand does not know which side in his internal battle will win. Finally, he rises nude. Does nothing to cover himself, strides as confidently as he can to the bathroom and into the shower. In a moment, he comes out. "For some reason, the condom stayed on," he relates.

"Come here," she says, her arms outstretched.

Now they are making love on the towel covered sofa. Armand notices at once the perfume in which Keely has bathed herself. In some ways, it is delicious, in others, overpowering. But he says nothing, soaking in her flesh. Keely's love-making, he finds admiringly, is never humdrum, always artistic. Armand knows how to undress a woman, how to apply hands and lips to various partner parts, but there is little thought, and even less creativity attached to it. Keely has managed to create a climate of seduction. She begins with small nibbles of her lover's earlobes, tiny caresses of her lips against his, stopping occasionally to indulge but never so long that Armand finds it ultimately satisfying. She clearly wants her lover to demand more of her. And so, it goes, her hands probing various curves of his flesh, reaching in for an instant, caressing his neck for another, then retiring to his thighs, until Armand feels that he must explode and, in that explosion, evanesce into the night sky. But then, just as he feels he can no longer undergo this exquisite torture, she offers herself wide to him and he is inside her, blending together in a rhythm that seems uncannily natural for both of them. Before he comes, she is matching the increase of his ardor. They climax in unison, movement for movement, breath for breath. In all his life, he has never experienced love like this. He has never been virtually debased, before the connection evolves into a real, powerful, and finally cataclysmic detonation.

In bed that night, spooning, he holds her in his arms as they fall asleep. But before sleeps finds him, he re-catalogues the events of the evening, worries that he is being molded, changed, even purified, as if readied for sacrifice on some bizarre altar of love. Satiated, trembling and bewildered, he finally gives in to asleep.

38

Embracing Marina

"I can sew your shirt back up to perfection," she giggles. "After all, I am a seamstress, aren't I?"

"Where did you really learn to do that?" Roger says, observing her at the sewing machine. Listens to the hum of it, watches her deft fingers inching along his shirt. "There," she announces with satisfaction, lifting it for inspection, "good as new."

"You are truly a wondrous seamstress," he says.

"Shucks, Roger, just doing women's work...."

At once, he is by her side, whips her around and begins to kiss her. As soon as his lips meet hers, she is pulling away. Not only her face. Her body is drifting. "Not now," she says firmly.

Annoyed, Roger grumbles. "Why not?"

"No reason," she shrugs. "Just not ready."

Roger is replaying the past two weeks in his head. First, the thrill of making love to Marina initially. True, lovemaking lacked intimacy, but he assumed that their stumbling, unfamiliar grappling would be quickly forgotten, and then refined, as time elapsed. That was two weeks ago. Since then, nothing. Marina does not initiate any physical contact except for an occasional hug or a brief kiss. Peck on the cheek. Sometimes, snakelike, wrapping around the nape of the neck. Like a bird settling in for a quick snack before flying away. Roger cannot understand this. He does understand sex at the outset lacking steam, but normally, closer encounters follow it, each one progressively more unifying than the last. Marina has not permitted a follow-up. Nor will she discuss it. Nights, while she brushes her teeth, Roger is already between sheets waiting, coiled, hungering for her, listening to her little tooth brush rasping against enamel. She dances into bed wrapped in a thin negligee, touches his cheek with her fingers for an instant, awards him a brief kiss, sometimes on the lips, then revolves towards her nightstand.

"Did I do something wrong?" he whispers into her ear.

"Not at all," she replies. "Not at all."

"But we are not together," he remarks with some anguish in his tone.

"Nobody can be as together as we are in this moment," she affirms.

"I meant we are not intimate."

"I knew what you meant. But from my point of view, I think we are classically intimate. Here we are in bed together night after night. We are virtually wrapped together. Classically entombed," she hums.

"I'm famished for you."

"Be patient," she says. "Patience!" In an instant, he can hear her breathing now subsiding.

But one morning, confused, at the breakfast table, Roger prods her about her past. At first, she demurs. "This is not fit conversation with a lover," she exclaims. Pancakes heaped in front of her. He brings her syrup. She is cutting pancakes with a fork. Looks up. His look is plaintiff. He brings her a glass of orange juice. She is drinking. Looks up, satisfied. Realizes that the moment is incomplete and will not end without some action on her part. Now speaking. Something about their initial encounter which he does not quite understand. Just as he is dissecting her meaning, she goes on with words he does not put together in any comprehensive way, pushing her plate away, settling back into her chair. Pause. She confesses that she has had sexual encounters with actors at parties.

He looks at her uncomprehendingly. "These meant nothing," she protests. "They satisfied an itch at that time. Maybe I had a drink too many."

"And this happened?"

She turns to him and sits up. "From time to time. When I was without an ongoing lover," she adds. "Sometimes I felt the urge to have sex."

"What did it feel like?"

She gives him a questioning look. "You really want to know this?"

"Yes."

"It is a gnawing in the abdomen, something to do with the mind directing blood flowing in that direction, and it begs the body to bring about relief."

"With actors you worked with?"

"Not necessarily," she says. Then adds: "In fact, most of them were simply guys who paid attention to me. We actors would sometimes position ourselves between curtains and do it standing," she laughs.

Roger is not laughing. "This is maddening," he blurts out. "You boast about a pattern of random sex, obviously meaningless sex in the sense that there is no follow-through with men whose names you may not even know….and yet you are living with me and we are fucking celibate. I said that badly. We are simply celibate."

"I get that it doesn't make any sense to you," she says almost sadly. "Anyway, no sex is meaningless. Just doesn't make sense to you right now."

"No! No sense at all."

"Well, don't get upset."

"Not upset. Furious is more like it," he huffs.

"Heah, buster," she becomes agitated, "this is my body we are talking about. I use it as I wish. You have no control over me or it."

"Clearly," he spouts.

"Look," she responds seeing how hurt she has made him feel, now settles into a gentler tone. "My past had to do with lust. I get horny. Not just you. Not just men. Women feel it too. But relationships like ours have more meaning than just a quickie now and then. I want to work myself into ours slowly."

"You don't find me attractive?" he asks.

"That's not the point," she responds. "The point is that intimacy is different. It takes work, understanding. I have to find a level of comfort."

"So, what am I to do?"

"Jerk off," she responds, exasperated. "Do what all men do when they can't get pussy."

"Wow! Is that all? Between angry and bewildered."

"And be patient. Be loving of me. But above all, exercise restraint."

In this fashion, days pass. Marina's theatre gig is coming to a swift end. She partakes of several auditions without obtaining a role, and rushes to Roger in angry and disillusioned evenings.

"You're the one who needs patience now," Roger says. He is looking into the weepy face of a disheartened woman.

"I thought I would have the road paved for me after I played the seamstress lesbian," she says. "I received such glowing reviews! Instead, the road seems rockier than before."

"You're an actor," he cautions her. "This means that there will be lean times. Everybody suffers through them."

Face in her hands. He is caressing her as she sobs. Hands her a handkerchief. She blows her nose, then eyes lift up at him. "There is a little theatre of less than seventy-five seats which is holding auditions for a new play. It's some trite alien nonsense," she adds. "Some fucking Martian comes to earth and has a relationship with a fucking nun, and can't quite figure her out even though he has traveled millions of space miles in his own ship. I would play the part of the fucking nun. Pays peanuts," she adds.

"Not even a lesbian nun?"

"Not even," she smiles sorrowfully, and settles back into his arms.

39

Pascal Makes an Admission

(Benjamin at center stage to audience) "Look at Marcella! (She is standing to right) She's angry that I uncovered her deceit. What is this world coming to? (Marcella exits)

It's coming to dying. Suddenly, Marcella's dad was taken ill with a heart attack. I don't even remember who called to tell me, but I got out of bed at midnight and raced to the hospital. Marcella and her mother had already left. I managed to enter the intensive care unit and looked at Alberto hooked up to a spaghetti of machines. He could not speak, but he saw me and tried to raise a hand. The nurse would not let him open his mouth.

Marcella spent the next days at the hospital. I hardly saw her. She would come in at night and leave before I got up in the morning.

A week later, they released Alberto. Marcella moved into his house to be closer to him and to her mother. I saw her at work shortly afterwards."

(Marcella enters from right, pensively) "It doesn't look good. He may recover entirely but it's not certain."

"What do you intend to do?" Benjamin asks her.

"We can't afford round-the-clock supervision. Mother and

I are watching him alternatively. If he doesn't improve, you'll have to go to Nice alone."

(Benjamin to audience) "Weeks passed. Sometimes days elapsed without our seeing one another or even speaking on the phone. I was sympathetic but also increasingly anxious.

(To Marcella) There must be some other way. You're killing yourselves watching him in endless shifts, and trying to manage a day's work on top of it."

"We have no choice. Anything can set him off," Marcella says grimly, "and somebody has to sit with him."

"Let me help."

"We can handle the situation," Marcella says without intended cruelty. (She turns away)

(Benjamin to audience) "Periodically, some organ would give way and Alberto would find himself back in intensive care. Medicare ran out for any special nurse coverage, and Marcella tried to take up the slack.

(To Marcella) I haven't seen you for three days."

(Marcella Turns to Benjamin) "You know my situation. I wish you were more empathetic. While he's in the hospital, I could have stayed at your house. It's so much closer than mother's. But it never occurred to offer, did it?"

"You've hardly seen me or called me in the past weeks," Benjamin says irritated. "I thought you wanted me out of the way."

"What an insensitive jerk!" she cries, trembling. (Moves away from him towards center stage).

(Benjamin to audience) "I didn't deserve that, but given Marcella's fatigue, I chalked it up to nerves and lack of sleep. As her stress mounted, she looked worse. The doctors released Alberto again, and this time he perked up. Marcella decided to come to Nice with me after all. I thought it would be good for her, and we intended to meet up with Pascal. We would have his company for several days.

On the plane over, Marcella was in better spirits. I had rented a studio apartment in Nice on the Promenade des Anglais. We found Pascal in the hotel. That afternoon, we took the bus under a spectacular Mediterranean sun, and rode up the hill to Saint Paul de Vence. It's an old fortressed, walled city. Its streets are too narrow for traffic, so the bus stops outside of the walls.

We walked the cobblestoned city and then watched several old men in berets playing petanque in the dirt next to a café. After a while, both Pascal and Marcella asked whether they could play as well.

(Pascal entering, speaking to Marcella) "The object is simple. I throw out a tiny rubber marker. Each of us has two metal balls and we roll them as closely as possible to the target. (He throws out the marker. Marcella tosses her metal balls but they are not close to the marker). Not so hard, he says."

"Let me do it again."

"Just wait your turn," Benjamin says (He throws balls which land closer)

"Child's play," Pascal says. (His balls are closest of all)

"You cheated," Marcella exclaims. "You've been playing this game all of your life."

"I cheat by being the best," he boasts. "Now I'm going to show you how to do it. Hold the ball this way. (He takes her hand, stuffs a ball into it and forcing her to throw underhand. This way you can use backspin. (She throws another one away from the rubber) No, No! Pretend the marker is the heart of someone you wish to capture. Space in love is everything. Think the ball closer to the marker.: (She throws again)

"I think Marcella is getting it," Benjamin says, "but if we're going to have lunch and climb the hill to the museum before end of day, we need to leave."

"Then let's go," Marcella says. (They move to center stage where there is a table with four chairs)

(To audience) "A great idea for Marcie. She already looks years younger."

"What a beautiful place," she says.

"It is where Picasso and Chagall came to eat," Pascal remarks. "They often bartered their paintings in exchange for food. In the other room, there is a museum of their work."

(Benjamin to audience) "We drank a lot of wine and ate up a storm and chatted one another up as if we all truly loved one another. For that moment in time, we surely did. After lunch, still tingling from wine and talk, we started the climb to the Museum." (Marcella leads the way right)

"Hurry up, you old men," she yells back. (Exits right)

"I need to stop for a moment," Pascal says, breathing heavily.

"Are you all right?"

"No," he says out of breath. "Do you remember all those colds, the bronchitis, even a pneumonia I had?"

"I thought you were over those," Benjamin says.

"I was. But on morning I found lesions on my back and glands were swelling. I had a slight fever, so I visited my doctor. The news ain't brilliant."

"You're indestructible," Benjamin laughs. "What are you talking about?"

"I have AIDS."

"There must be some mistake."

"It happens to everyone else, of course. Are you afraid?" Pascal asks.

"Afraid?" (Benjamin embraces Pascal) "You are really asking me that?"

(Marcella from off-stage) "Come on, you old fags. Hurry up!"

"Please don't tell anyone, not even Marcella. I want to exit gracefully and without pity."

"You talk as if it's fatal."

He winces. "They tell me the new drugs are great as long as I stay on them, and yet others have died anyway. I figure I have between seven months and three years, depending on how well I adjust to the drugs. I'm supposed also to visualize my system fighting off the virus," he snickers. "Hell, it gives me something to do. My business runs itself now anyway." (He arises and they move off-stage)

40

The Unravelling of Brent Sadowski

J ust after five o'clock of a Friday afternoon, the sun beginning to settle below the horizon in an orange and peach sky, Brent Sadowski takes the elevator at the Pharynx Corporation. As he mingles with the hordes of workers hurrying home, he reaches into his briefcase and pulls out his pair of earphones, adjusts them around his head. Listening to Dvorak's Serenade for Strings. His goal: to block out humanity. He does not care for people. He does not care for Dvorak either, nor is he particularly fond of classical music, but Keely likes it. Therefore, he feels he must learn it to understand what Keely enjoys. For Brent, the music is an assortment of erupting squeals, sometimes diminishing which, while somewhat musical, leaves him cold. He does not understand how Keely can appreciate such noise. Now, he changes to a popular music station and catches Adele. This he can relate to. This he understands.

Behind Brent, Armand is walking step for step. He is wearing a rain coat on an afternoon devoid of rain. But the coat has high cloth which can shield his face to avoid detection were Brent to turn suddenly. After several weeks of relentless investigation, several pursuits, a myriad of interviews, it is clear that Brent Sadowski is deeply involved in the death of Alexandra Rosen.

Unable to link the vial room, Brent and Alexandra in a fashion that would lead to arrest, Armand's intuition tells him that the man he is following has, in some fashion, a clear responsibility in this case.

Suddenly, Brent turns down a side street. Clearly, he is not going home, Armand thinks, pursuing the chase. Brent turns left at the next intersection, crosses a major intersection with flying, bristling traffic speeding by, crosses at the light and continues down a street known to Armand. "He's going to Keely's," Armand thinks. Quickens his pace slightly.

Within ten minutes, Brent halts before Keely's apartment building. Enters, presses a bell. Buzzed in. Through the etched glass door, Armand observes Brent awaiting the elevator. Its door opens. Brent steps in. Armand buzzes several numbers knowing that Keely is not home. He is buzzed in. The elevator register shows that Brent has stopped at the fourth floor. Keely's floor. Armand runs up the stairs. Breathless, opens the emergency door to the fourth floor, looks out. Sees his prey. Brent has a key in hand, lets himself in.

Now Armand hurries to Keely's door, his face is burning from racing up the stairs and anxiety. Keely has given him a key. He turns it softly in the lock, opens the door silently. At once, he perceives Brent lowering himself under the kitchen sink. Brent is reaching into his case and retrieves a vial. Stops. Pulls out a gas mask, covers his face. Slowly, unstops the top of the vial, and sets the tube upright underneath the sink. Then he gets up and turns, his face totally covered by the mask.

"I bet that's not cocaine," Armand says.

Brent gasps, trips over his own shoes and falls to the floor, dislodging the mask. Armand tugs at his clothing and yanks him up. "How much time do we have before the hantavirus is activated?"

"Not more than a half hour," Brent answers sullenly, brushing himself off. "I guess you caught me, eh"

"Take a seat," Armand says. "How did you get a key to this apartment?"

"Wasn't difficult," Brent replies. "I made an impression and copied one of Keely's."

"You've been a bad boy, Brent", Armand continues. "Tell me why you killed Alexandra."

Brent is stone faced. Breathing becomes slightly labored. Face flushing. Armand repeats the question.

"She pulled back from a lovely relationship," Brent responds, eyes down. "I thought she cared for me, but she made it amply clear that she had no regard for me. Yet I alone loved her. Me alone! Not her lousy dope addict boyfriend."

"How did you do it? I mean kill her?"

Silence.

"Brent, it's over. Too late to stonewall now. The time has come to answer some questions."

Brent sighs and nods his head. "I placed the vial around Apepi's collar knowing that when he went upstairs, eventually he would bang into something and release the contents. Pretty good stuff, eh?" He continues now smiling with satisfaction.

"Fascinating," Armand agrees.

"I thought about it for a long time," Brent confesses. "She was once a wonderful girl and then she went back to that guy, Tal. I spied on them once. She was standing in front of him nude. He was in an armchair snorting. I couldn't take it."

"But she never offered you a relationship, did she?"

"You're wrong, Brent replies looking bewildered. Why would you say a thing like that? She clearly loved me. She liked to

259

nibble my earlobes. We cuddled. She adored me."

"You had sex?"

Brent clearly confused. "Our bond was never that crass," Brent cries out, almost in disbelief at the question. "Never."

"I get it. Fucking would have been bad form. So, she didn't reject sex. She just rejected you."

"Yes."

"So, you got pissed. Very cleverly, I admit. But what about Keely?"

"Keely is her sister," Brent responds as if Armand would have no knowledge of that relationship.

"Yes."

Brent looks up, his eyes red, his eyebrows raising. "I commiserated with that woman. I told her my dreams. I got so I liked her. Better, I was sure she liked me, and then one day, out of the blue, she turned me away."

"She rejected you."

"Bitch!" he cries out. "No," he remarks angrily, shaking himself, "I don't mean that. Keely is the sweetest of girls, but she did bad. She said we must not be together. Held my hand while telling me that above all we were friends. But I felt her commitment. Her hand was burning. I thought it would turn to fire and, if I held it long enough, would smolder into an ember, it was so fierce. How could she hurt me like that?" And this coming from a girl who has no boyfriend. Hardly any friends at all. She had nobody but me. She once turned to me, and then when it suited her, she tossed me aside. What was she thinking? Never once did she consider my pain. Didn't she deserve retribution? Of course, she did. In her own way, she asked God to cure her bad behavior."

"You mean cure her with death."

"Putting words in my mouth, Mr. Desqueyroux," Brent snaps. "I mean that I wanted to teach her a final lesson. To reject me is to reject all mankind."

"Because you are…."

"I am a model for humanity, Brent says seriously, humbly. "Not druggies like Tal or even guys like you. I am simple. Direct. I know that. Maybe too direct. I know who I am. I try to hide nothing with the grace of God. But that is what God intended for man. Not that a human be loud mouthed and insensitive to others. He ordained that we love one another. I loved Keely. She said she did not love me. Ergo, she broke a commandment that God laid down. You know God meant for women to be subservient to man, but when I tried to control Alexandra, she stubbornly resisted. That was not what the Almighty intended. Nor was her sister any the less forthcoming. She too defied me, despite my rights over her."

"We need to get out of here," Armand says, looking at his watch. "Time is not on our side."

"You go," Brent answers quietly. "I would like to remain in this apartment. I always liked it here. For a time, I found affection here."

"You understand that I can't let you do that."

"Look, Mr. Desqueyroux, I mean you no harm, but if you interfere, I would make it my business to crush that vial right now and we both will hurt. You do understand what that means, no?"

"I do," Armand shrugs. "You want to stay here? Suppose I call the cops?"

"Too late for them to do any good," Brent says, his face screwing up. "I control this situation," he adds with a grin.

"Yes, you do," Armand says rising. "But you have missed your mark. As soon as I step out of that door, I'll call Keely and make sure the apartment is disinfected before she sets foot in it."

"You wouldn't do that," Brent says darkly. "You give me time. You converse with me. I can see that you truly care. After all, you are the only man I know who would be sitting in a chamber marked for death and chat with me until the end. Anyway, you must know God has a plan. Keely will get what she deserves," he goes on. "If not from me, then from the next man she engages with. So, if you value your love of the Almighty, don't call the cops. Let nature take its course."

Armand decides not to confuse the issue. "Of course, for a buddy like you," Armand says soothingly, heading for the door, "maybe I'll just go down to the corner bar and down a beer in your honor. See you!"

"In the sweet afterlife," Brent shouts after him. "We'll meet again there, I so trust."

41

Marina

She does not know that he is standing there watching. She is in the shower with a waterproof radio. Volume is turned up high. The Eagles. She sings along with them. Then she stops. Checks her knees. Soaping herself. The panes of the shower stall fog up. Still, there is an aperture between the panes for him to see. He is looking at the body he craves but is not allowed to touch. If she catches him observing her, she will be furious, but Roger no longer cares. Looking at the curves of her body as she swoops down to soap her knees, ankles, then turns so that the jets spray onto her lower legs. Stops. Moves her body closer until the jets are focused to her nether region. Immobile, she stands, her chin lifted slightly. Three minutes slip by. In another moment, she places a hand between her legs. When she removes her hand, the jets spray onto her vagina. Then her hand slowly returns. After a time, her body curls upwards and she emits an unearthly sound. The sound of a wounded beast. The tone is woeful, mysterious, primeval, and is followed by a strident, shrill laugh. This prompts Roger to retreat hurriedly out of the bathroom. Even into the living room, the volcanic laugh following like some malevolent wind.

Roger goes to the theatre. More rehearsals. When he comes

home at night, he finds Marina sprawled over the sofa chewing popcorn and watching game shows. She hardly notices him as he enters. She is watching, giggling, sometimes applauding. He asks her what she has been doing all day. She sits up and, with a pat of her hand, smooths out her hair. Stops to think. "I went to the mall and drank coffee," she says. "Some kind of cappuccino with a shot of caramel in it. Then I stopped at the Nordstrom's resto to grab a bite. They're dying to have you buy one of their overpriced salads. Later, I stopped by Auntie Anne's and watched them wrap a hotdog in a pretzel. They call it a Pretzeldog. Will wonders never cease? That is the sum of my grand afternoon. Is that what you wanted to know?" she asks defiantly.

"Yes," he says, with a hangdog look. "Think I'll fix a drink."

"You do that," she says.

They have been together a month now. Marina continues to await the results of her audition. They tell her that she sounded religiously sexy in the role of the nun abducted by the Martian. Apparently, a good way to sound. She has mixed feelings. On the one hand, she would like the work. On the other, the plot is so shitty, she wonders whether the role would move her career in the right direction. Probably not, she judges. So, in a way, she hopes they will reject her for the role. Still, nothing else on the horizon right now, she admits, dejected.

"Have you been checking the actors' site?" he asks.

"Sure," she responds, but not convincingly.

She doesn't get the role. For two days, she lolls about in a depressive state. Then she arises, cleans up for the first time in days, dresses carefully and sprints down to McNichol's Burgers and Fries. Accepts the position they offer behind the counter. She will be taking orders.

After the third day, she becomes incensed. "You see this guy standing in a line," she complains. "He's been in the line for ten minutes. So, when he comes to the counter, wouldn't he be eager to order? Not at all. He stands there as if he has never seen the order board, although you suspect he comes in every other day. He is reading it, his lips following along, as if it were a children's book. After two minutes, restless people behind him shifting feet and arms, he finally decides. But then his debit card doesn't work. Can't scan it. He has a chip. So, I show him what to do with his chip. No, not this way. Put it in that way. This guy has a face with nothing in it. Not gratitude, hunger, longing, nothing. The face of an empty vessel. He could use his mouth to piss. Probably does." Roger grins.

Two more days pass. Lunchtime on the third day: man enters, orders a burger with fries. Cash transaction. She gives back change. He looks at it with open mouth and says. "Miss, this isn't enough. I gave you a twenty." "No, sir," Marina says, "you handed me a ten, and I've given you the change. The exact change."

"No, miss," the guy continues, "I know what I gave you. I never carry ten dollar bills. I only carry twenties. I gave you a twenty."

"Sir," Marina responds with just a touch of irritation, "I am looking at the ten dollar bill you gave me and which I deposited in the ten dollar slot. You did not hand me anything else".

"I demand the manager," the man cries. Marina shrugs and calls for the manager.

The manager appears. He is a black man with acne and a dirty shirt. "You say you gave this girl a twenty?" he asks the guy.

"I just told you that," the guy responds with steel in his voice.

The manager turns to Marina and says: "Give the man the correct change, please."

"I did," she says, her eyes wide open.

The manager is thinking. Marina knows this because his eyes are uplifted towards some unknown metropolis near the ceiling. Finally, he lowers his eyes and hands down his judgment. "The customer is right," he confides to her. "You need to return the correct change."

"Which I did," she repeats quietly.

The guy now is agitated. "I want my fucking money."

"No need to speak this way," the manager says, scratching his ear, "you will get what is owed you."

"Yeah, but I want it now. I'm not waiting until tomorrow."

The manager counts out change and the guy leaves mollified. Now the manager turns to Marina and explains how the customer is always right even when he is wrong.

"This is a strange notion," she says. "It's like saying that there are several versions of the truth."

"Nonetheless," the manager insists, "I'm telling you what Mr. Boulbay has told us". Here he has invoked the name of the owner of McNichol's who likes to hand down edicts to his employees. An offering like the ten commandments. Each one is accompanied by a stern paragraph. "It's like saying that white is black and black is white," she resists.

"Marina, I'm not gonna fight with you. Things are what they seem, not what they are. You have to accept it." With this, he retreats into his office. Marina, however, is upset. She cannot digest what the manager has told her. It uproots all learning deep within her. She contemplates the dictum that the customer is right even when he is wrong, and the tussle within her leads her into sullenness. For the rest of the day, she takes orders without conscious awareness of her work.

At home, she decides to test the proposition for herself. When Roger comes home that night, she asks him whether he has enjoyed his dinner.

Looks at her strangely. "No," he responds, "for I have not yet had dinner. And you must know this because you are the one who told me that you were cooking dinner for me tonight. Spaghetti and meatballs, I believe."

"So, you insist that you have not eaten," she says.

"I personally don't insist. My stomach, however, is addressing the matter."

"So," she continues, "you think you are right about this even when I am certain you have already dined."

"I just came from the theatre where we played a matinee," Roger responds. "Afterwards, I rushed home because I was hungry."

"Still hungry," she prompts.

"No," he responds cautiously as if speaking to a mentally deranged person. "Just hungry."

"So, you contend that you are right in this even if I disagree with you. Not only I, but the facts."

"Well yes," he says, "I don't know what you've been smoking this afternoon. Nor do I need to make a federal case out of it. Instead, how about some dinner."

She shrugs. "All right, if you are still hungry…if, in fact, you need to eat again."

Roger is now tugging at his blond hair. "Yes, he says. I need to eat again. Give me food," he begs, "and please just shut the fuck up."

"Just checking," Marina grins.

Nights, they slip into a humdrum routine. The now familiar negligee swishes as she slides between the sheets. Roger is in the bathroom flossing. Wearing shorts. Marina lies in bed, lightly perfumed. She is reading a novel, some romance opus with swords and balustrades and girls with swirling long dresses and big earrings. Daunted, his heart imprisoned, Roger can think of nothing more to say. After a few moments, she places a bookmark in her novel, turns out the light, leaving Roger confused, smoldering like a lightning-struck log. Marina closes her eyes, falls asleep quickly, effortlessly.

Another week passes in this manner. Finally, of an evening, Roger can no longer retain his tongue. "I think", he says to her as she bookmarks her novel, "that we need to do something about us."

"And what is that?" she asks evenly.

"We have been together for weeks on end. I have been lusting for you day after day. You know this, but you go on blithely as if my feelings did not matter."

"Of course, they do," she says. "I'm simply not ready for sex."

"And tell me again why?"

"You don't have the most desirable face or body," she quips.

"Trying to be lighthearted? Maybe even funny?"

"I do try," she replies.

"I intend to pull out the sofa into a bed, "he continues. "Starting tomorrow, that is where I will be sleeping."

Her face devolves seriously as if he were about to plunge a knife into her. "Now why would you do that? You can't even be patient with me until I feel more comfortable with your body?"

"I'm tired of waiting," he confesses.

"I see," she says. "But I don't believe you."

"What?"

"I don't believe it's fatigue. It's not even about sex…it's your insatiable need to dominate me."

"Excuse me?" he asks, his mouth open in wonder.

"You say you care for me…that is shorthand for you love

me…yes?"

"Yes," he says, his speech muddled. "I do. I think so. Sort of."

"Then if this love were real, you would be as patient as I require to make me happy, and for us to be joined sometime in the future."

"That's a laugh," he replies. "What's so hot about the future?"

"Ripeness is all."

"Great. Well, I'm so ripe, I for one am about to rot."

"That's just one of us," she responds evenly.

"So tomorrow," he forges on, "you'll have the bed all to yourself. It won't change anything for you."

"That's a lie," she retorts angrily. "A fucking lie. I'll be in your bed without you."

"You are in my bed with me right now without me."

"We may not be having intercourse…that doesn't mean that I am ignoring you," she says with fire in her eyes.

He throws up his hands. "We aren't even speaking the same language."

Marina sits up, positioning a pillow behind her back. "If you do this, I will leave."

He says nothing. "You hear me? I'll leave," she repeats loudly.

"Then you had better go," he drones flatly. "Yes, it will be a relief for me. If I can't have a full relationship with you, then I suspect we won't have one at all."

"You're a child, she spouts. "A child!"

"A nasty child with a boner," he shouts at her.

42

Benjamin and Marcella in France

(Marcella at center stage, to audience) "I feel better in Europe. There are no pressures, no stresses, and Benjamin and I are doing well together. But I haven't heard from mother. Wonder how daddy is doing?"

(Pascal enters from right, walks over to the stocks, and puts his head in it and giggles) "A most comfortable fit."

(Benjamin, entering from right) "Punishment? For what?"

"You've got me wrong," Pascal says. "It's not punishment I want, but a speedy, uncomplicated death. Do you recall the pact we made when we were younger? Whenever we became a burden to others and didn't have the wherewithal to do ourselves in, the other would assist. Just another project for two old school chums."

"I do hate to see you suffer," Benjamin replies.

"It's not bad yet. Sometimes, I admit I am scared shitless. But that's a kneejerk reaction. It's because I don't know anything except life that I don't want to leave it. But in my heart, I do know that I am going towards zero. But is there anything wrong with that? We spend much of our time lying to ourselves that the road eventually ends. The drugs are helping. I seem to be walking on air. For the most part, when I think about my future,

I just stop thinking."

"So, what do you need?"

"Like a good soldier, to fade away quickly, quietly. I have a right, just as you do, to choose the moment of my passing."

"Pascal, as long as you are feeling all right, don't give in," Benjamin replies quietly.

"I've lost my sense of mission, future, hope," Pascal goes on. "Well, then, buddy, if you're too middle-class to take this life from me, I suppose I'll just have to plod along a little while longer." (Arises with Benjamin's help, and he exits stage right)

(Benjamin to audience) "I said nothing of this to Marcella. We finished our trip placidly, Pascal in amazingly good spirits. Marcella returned home to her bedside vigil. At first, she called several times with bits of news. The content didn't matter…the contact did. But after a month, the calls were fewer, emails and texts less frequent, and I began to grow anxious." (Exits stage right)

(Marcella entering from stage left, to audience) "Things are deteriorating. I couldn't dissuade President Jager. He won't renew Benjamin's contract because he doesn't have his doctorate. How do I tell him that? (Moves to center stage. Sits on corner of bed) And then my father. In one moment he looks great, the next wretched. The doctors say that his organs are too weak to sustain his life, that he could die any day."

(Alberto enters in a hospital gown from stage left, edges towards the bed). "Marcella!"

"I'm here, daddy."

"Didn't you leave for France?"

"I'm back early," she says rising and walking over to him.

"How could you be here and also in France? Help me into the bed, please."

"You shouldn't walk around alone."

"Marcella, do I really have false teeth?"

"Your teeth are real, daddy."

"I was worried for a moment," he says. "They pinch from time to time."

(Tucks her father into bed, now faces the audience) "Day after day of this. I love my father, I think. Or maybe I stay with him for other reasons. I was never adept at finding these things out. I have an email from Benjamin. His research and writing are going well. Why does he feel so distant?

And Joseph. My psychology professor! What do I do with him? He follows me around like some dog looking for a bone." (She moves to a sofa)

(Joseph enters from stage left) "I brought you some flowers and a standing offer to help. You look done in."

"Flowers! That is sweet of you, but there's little anyone can do."

"I'm here for you if you need me," Joseph says, kissing her.

(Marcella lingers with the kiss, but then moves away nervously. To audience) "Should I accept this now? Still, I'm not married. I am free to do what I want. I need some company, something outside of work and the slavery my father's plight demands. I think I am bringing on a migraine. It's so hot in here. (To Joseph) Take me home with you." (He kisses her hand and they exit left)

(Benjamin entering from right) "Poor Marcella. I wish I could alleviate her burden. What am I doing in France when she needs me with her? I'll talk to the commission and maybe they'll let me cut my stay short." (Exits left)

(Gabriella entering from left) "He's just the shell of the man I married, but how do I go on without him? He could die any hour, they tell me, but the thought is absurd. For decades, I have only known my life with this man next to me. We have been together too long for him simply to vanish."

(Marcella follows her mother on stage) "I'll take over later."

(Alberto from bed) "Don't go, chicken."

"I'll be back tonight."

"Don't leave me now."

"I'm here, Alberto," Gabriella cries out.

"Don't leave me. I can hardly see."

"He's on the drugs," Gabriella says.

"I know," Marcella says.

(Benjamin enters from right and makes his way to the center. Calls on his Iphone) "Janice, I'm glad I finally caught up with you. What's happening with Marcella and her dad?"

(Janice entering from stage right with phone to his ear) "I've hardly seen her myself. Occasionally in the hallway."

"How does she look?"

"Like she just walked out of the pages of Vogue. She manages very well. You needn't worry."

(Benjamin, on his phone) "Then why don't I hear from her?"

(Marcella enters with Joseph) "Does my dress have wrinkles" I should have changed it."

"I couldn't wait," Joseph says.

"Poor Marcella," Benjamin says, replacing phone in his pocket)

(Janice, hanging up) "Should I have told him about Joseph? He must already know. The college is so small, someone may have texted him. But our girl, Marcie, needs a little sugar in her life. It can't be all about worrying and stressing." (Exits left)

"No one will know," Joseph says, grinning. "I'm so in love with you."

"I'm glad," Marcella says, still examining her dress.

"And Benjamin," Joseph asks, pulling out his pipe. What are

you going to tell him?"

"I have other worries this moment," Marcella replies.

"An email would do it," Joseph thinks aloud, a nice, farewell email.

"Let me handle this in my own way, please," Marcella replies sternly. (Joseph exits left)

(Benjamin, in an aside) "I haven't heard from her in almost a month, just that little text in which she tells me that my contract won't be renewed. I'm not concerned about that. Not much. So, is she sleeping with Jager? Not likely. He's too strait-laced. Like a minister. I did hear that he and his wife were separating. So what? Still there is always Joseph to keep her company. Why do I infuriate myself like this? We are engaged after all, committed."

"I don't know what to say to him," Marcella says entering from left with Janice.

"Do you intend to do nothing? That's not fair either."

"I can't think about Benjamin now. Not with these pressures."

"Not with Joseph in your life, you mean. Benjamin deserves a word of condolence about his career even if you have nothing else to say to him. He's sitting in Nice mooning over you, and you can't even call to wish him well? If you won't, maybe somebody else ought to do it."

"It's none of your business. Stay out of it, Janice."

(Benjamin on phone) "I don't know what to do. She doesn't return my emails, my texts, my phone calls. What the hell is going on?"

"I'm not permitted to say anything," Janice says on the phone.

"That sounds serious," Benjamin answers.

"Her father is still gravely ill."

"Tell her that I desperately need to talk with her."

"I can't even do that. She's gone out of town for a week and won't answer her phone."

"Left town? I don't understand. What about her father? I'm totally confused and miserable."

"She was not alone," Janice adds.

"Not alone? Where did she go…with whom?"

"Benjamin," Janice continues, "you are about to lose your job. Maybe you need to focus on finding another one somewhere else. Marcella has a sick father and, right now, she is confused about her priorities. If I were you, I'd forget her."

"Forget Marcella? I'm coming home as soon as I can.

(To audience) Ten days later, I did. I had to lie to the commission about my health. They commiserated with me, released me. But I might as well have stayed in France for all the contact between Marcella and me. I thought she might pick me up at the airport, but instead Janice came with a note from her that she would be out of town for several days, and that she would call me as soon as she returned. Janice said nothing, but from her tight-lipped expression, I knew I needed to prepare for the worst." (Exits stage right)

(Joseph entering stage left with Marcella) "I'm in love with you."

"I love you too," Marcella says.

"I think we ought to get married."

(Marcella pointing to the sofa) "Sit down, Joseph. Whatever there is between us, it cannot lead to marriage."

"I don't understand," he responds plaintively.

"It's freedom I want…freedom to love…not the bondage of love. Doesn't anyone understand that?"

"I must have misunderstood," Joseph says slowly. "I thought you said you loved me."

"But I do," she protests. "Now let's just leave it at that and please don't complicate my life further. My head is already spinning." (Joseph exits left)

(Marcella returns to the bed where her father is sitting up) "How are you feeling, daddy?"

"Like a spring flower. It's good to be back home."

(Marcella, to audience) "I'm glad too. Today is Benjamin's birthday and he has been calling me every half hour, but I don't answer my phone anymore. I don't know why I don't want to see him. Jager made it clear that it would be in my best interest to stay clear of him. Benjamin knows my job is important to me. There's nothing I can do...or say.

(To Alberto) Let me help you to the sofa and we'll play cards." (As she does so, the doorbell rings, but she does not answer it. It rings repeatedly)

(Benjamin appears from left) "Hello, Alberto, how are you?"

"Like a spring flower."

(Benjamin turning to Marcella) "Sorry to break into your house this way. I remembered you always left the rear door open. You and I need to talk."

(Marcella, irritated with him) "I have to pick up mother from the grocery...I'm late as it is."

"Just a few moments," Benjamin insists. I've been trying to reach you for weeks."

"You know how trying this situation has been,} Marcella complains. "This move of yours is terribly upsetting for daddy. What is the meaning of this erratic behavior?"

"I love you. I came back from Nice early to be with you, to help you, to see you through whatever awaited you."

"There's nothing you can do", Marcella says almost bitterly.

"Not even take you out of this misery from time to time? To lunch. To a movie, to life? I bet we could even find a game of petanque in town (For the first time she smiles and he takes her hand) Let me back into your life. I worry about you so much. I'm losing weight, smoking again, smoking myself into an early grave. I'm totally miserable without you. I'm dying inside."

"I can't be what you want," Marcella responds. "Not right now. For the sake of our long-term relationship, you need to go on with your normal, ordinary life until this situation is finished. Underneath everything, you and I have a deep friendship. You have to give me space. I'll call you. I know I owe you a birthday dinner." (He kisses her. She leads Alberto out left)

(Benjamin to audience) "That was the totality of our conversation. Even though it was short and I hadn't learned very much, I felt better about us. She was after all not rejecting me. Still, she did not call as she promised and we did not go out to dinner.

Since she was not answering her phone, I texted her or emailed her every so often. I wrote about my jealousy, because I now fantasized that Marcella was involved with somebody else. And yet, I also wrote of my love and support because I could not be sure. It was possible that she was telling me the truth, that this horrible situation with her father had caused a temporary rift for reasons that neither of us could understand."

(Janice enters from right) "Look at this poor boob. He wants so badly to believe the best because he doesn't want to be hurt…he still believes she loves him."

(Benjamin to Janice) "You know Marcella in ways I do not. She did send me a note. She texted me. In the text, she said she had forgotten exactly what happened in the pork roast incident and asked me to refresh her memory. She wants to know who came back to whom."

"All I know," Janice retorts, "is that she is terribly confused. But then aren't we all?" (Benjamin exits right while Marcella enters from left, Janice crossing to meet her)

"I don't know what to say to Benjamin. He thinks I am having an affair with Joseph, but that is no longer the case."

"Release this poor son of a bitch," Janice cries out. "Can't you see he's pining over you to his grave? He looks almost as bad as you".

"I know," Marcella assents. "Even Jager suggested I get over him...quickly. But I do have feelings. However remote."

"And you give in to that?" Janice snarls. "Some gall. I thought you wanted freedom, independence. These notions are only a front to help with your career, to sleep with whoever makes you feel good at the moment or advance you. Is that what it amounts to?"

"You have no right to judge me."

(Janice to audience) "Shoot! The girl isn't fighting a war of independence. She lacks responsibility. She's a guerilla littering the college with broken hearts, and for what" Is that the price others have to pay for her to stay on an even keel." (They exit left as Benjamin re-enters from right)

(Benjamin, to audience) "I haven't slept well for a month. This must stop. It's my own fault. I clearly got involved with the wrong person. They say that women are more sensitive than men, but women cast aside relationships with ease. I didn't demand this bond with Marcella. I knew she was lacking an important attribute for a titanic bond. Well, after a time, I lost my compass and like some dog strayed right into her confusion. She's still got me on her leash.

Yes, I'm feeling sorry for myself. I may love Marcella, but I refuse to be played by some woman whose heart is sealed, who can't generate even minimal caring or decency. What does it take to say goodbye kindly to someone to whom you were committed? Instead, she pretends that I don't exist. A rock in her path. She can't even kick the rock out of her way. I'm lonely, upset, my work is suffering. I'm not writing. I'm not even looking for another job with the school year ending. I've given her ample opportunity to act decently. I have but one goal now. I'm going to make this bitch pay, and pay dearly for her effrontery."

43

Keely and Armand Reach an Understanding

Both sit fidgeting in the courtroom as the bailiff calls for the jury's verdict. The air feels heavy, taut. The foreman arises. He is reading from a paper. He is speaking about the first count. When Keely and Armand hear he is guilty, they both breathe a sigh of relief. She presses his hand. Brent Sadowski arises, turns, sees their hands enclasped. "So, this is how you betrayed me," he whispers to Keely as he walks by. She is about to answer, but Armand grasps her arm. Weeks later, they learn that Brent will spend the rest of his days in prison. "I only knew him as a gentle soul," Keely says. "I can't really judge him, and yet he admitted to killing Alex and wanted to kill me as well." "And," she continues, looking into the eyes of her man, "he would have succeeded had it not been for you."

Armand reaches over to kiss her, but she turns her face away and his lips land on a cheek. With any other woman, at any other time, he would think nothing of this, simply a quirk of the moment. But with Keely, it has meaning, a reservoir of meaning. His spirits decline as he sits next to her.

"Did you fully understand how Brent murdered my sister?"

she asks.

"Yes," he replies. "He removed a vial of the hantavirus and, one day at Alexandra's, fixed the vial around her dog's neck. The vial was closed then with a cork, but he knew that any kind of bump Apepi made during the next hours would release the virus. Then all he needed was to return to the apartment, retrieve the empty vial and dispose of it. That would create a mystery. The first clue as to what was going on was Apepi himself. He came down with a sharp fever and lolled about for several days. As for Alex, she took the dog to the vet's, was given an antibiotic for him without further testing. The vet had no test for hantavirus. The pill probably had no effect. Apepi recovered from this virus by himself. Animals are able to do so. People cannot."

Keely shivers. "What a ghoulish plan."

"And the plot was meant to extend to you had I not followed him that day."

"Thank God for that! But I still don't understand his motivations. I was never going to love this man and, if I knew my sister, neither would Alex."

"But Brent could not know this. For him, love takes on a different hue. He assumed, because both Alex and you were gentle with him, even respectful of him, treating him as a friend, that this amounted to love, and when he thought it was removed, he fell into a depression which only murder would cure. Your murder," he adds.

"Lovely," she cries, shivering once more.

Armand suggests that they go his local gym and work out the remnants of the Brent Sadowski story through exercise.

"I'm not much for things like that," Keely replies.

"If nothing else, there will be treadmills which you can walk on while I'm doing weights."

"Ok," she says. "I'll need some time to change." They agree to meet later in the afternoon.

At the gym, both wearing shorts, Keely watches Armand lifting weights. "Wait," she exclaims, "this is not possible."

Armand lowers the bar.

"You need to disinfect it before using it," she says scornfully. "My God, surely you know that!"

Armand has a silly smile playing about his lips. "Really, Keely, caution is not necessary. I will wipe it down with disinfectant after I'm done with it."

"But that is for the next person," she says. "Please do this for me. Otherwise, I cannot watch you."

He walks over to the nearest pillar containing a solvent, sprays it on paper and disinfects the bar.

"Happy now?"

"So much better," she replies happily. "How heavy is that weight, anyway?"

"Less than you," he says, grunting as he lifts it.

In a moment, she has turned and finds an unused treadmill and begins to amble on it.

Huffing from exertion, Armand finds her. "Hope you disinfected this," he says with a mean smile playing about his lips.

She looks at him as if he were a fool. "Are you kidding?"

At the end of the afternoon, Armand is about to take an important decision. Despite Keely's intelligence, grace and beauty, her constant griping about his lack of cleanliness has finally plunged a death mark in his heart. Drives her home. She gets out of the car. He follows her to the door.

"I think this is where I say goodbye," Armand says.

She looks up, totally unaware of what he is implying.

"I mean," he adds purposefully, "I think we should stop seeing one another."

"Oh," she says, her mouth wide open. "Oh!" Fumbling in her purse for the key. Swearing under her breath as it eludes her.

"Too difficult for me," he pleads. "Just too hard. It's as if we were constantly tussling in some Olympic competition." Face screws up from the effort of telling this woman his truth.

"I get it," she smiles. "You need to exercise more control than you can find in my world." Locates the key. Holds it up. Tries to smile. "All you needed was to say so," she goes on. "Look, here's where I can prove this to you. Let's go inside," she adds mustering a faint smile. "Strip me naked, tie me to the bedpost and do whatever you want to do. You'll have total mastery here."

He smiles, leans on the metal bannister. "I know you too well," he remarks at last. "Halfway through, you would be suggesting ways for me to modify the game of abusing you. Impossible for you to allow me to run the mile all the way through without interjecting."

Her face is blanching. "Simply a control issue," she repeats. "That's all we're talking about. It's not the end of anything."

"If that's your perception," he says, not certain this is truly the main issue.

"Yes, it is," she says firmly. "I'm sorry about this decision. I thought we were good."

"For a time, yes," he acknowledges. "But to be clear. It's not about control for me. It's about being in a relaxed environment with someone I love. Not worrying about everything I say or do. That's where the gold is for me."

And then he turns and walks to the car. Silence.

A ripple from the audience. Swelling. Applause in the theatre from Jason Fierst. Leaps up onto the stage. "Good ending," he judges. "I think you nailed it. We get that Keely pours cleanser down her clothes every morning, evening, and night. And Armand...a poor dude incapable of either finding or giving in to love! Babylon Revisited thanks you for playing the dysfunctional characters you truly are in such purposeful style. Of course, I realize that you both find yourselves at the end of lucrative storyline, one you have lived with and nurtured for months. But we've exhausted the tyke, haven't we? So now, we're leaving Babylon in the dust to pursue other half-crazed characters, moving on to bigger and better things. Rehearsals for *Wars of Independence* start soon. Here's an idea! Why don't the two of you take a week away from the city. I seem to recall you met in Nassau. Go back there and unwind. Strip yourselves of Armand and Keely. Be yourselves, a boy and a girl. Yes, run around naked! The detective and the control freak are going to give way to the college prof and his fickle girlfriend. But please don't bring a script with you. Take the time to let muscles stretch, relax, to pump new thespian blood into your veins. Bon voyage, my sweeties!"

44

A Question of Integrity

(Pascal enters from right) "You called?"

(Benjamin crossing to meet him, embracing him) "You look good, my friend. You remind me of the boy I met in military school. Lean and trim and…"

"Cut it out," Pascal, says. "You're hurting. You always gab too much when you're hurting."

"I haven't been able to talk to anyone," Benjamin admits.

"So, she finally did you in. I knew this would happen," Pascal crows. "She never had her shit together. Did you think you were going to convert her to loyalty or decency? What a jackass you are!"

"I made my bed," Benjamin replies with steel in his voice. "Now I plan to clean house."

"You are in a bad way."

"You and I both are," Benjamin insists.

"I've got several months before I'll need help to climb out of bed. Seems to me you're already there. You took the wrong path, Ben. The way of the bayonet, as Marcella knows, is the only way to cut through the crap. You opted for the soft road."

"I've learned that," Benjamin admits. "I hoped to find caring, and learned that caring is far down her list of priorities…not when it conflicts with need."

"You've come to me for some reason. What can I do?"

"With your help, my friend, Benjamin says with a gleam in his eye, I intend to right the balance."

"Just tell me what you want me to do. You have my full attention."

"I have an agreeable chore for you. Wish I could do it myself, but I can't."

"Name it."

"I want you to wield your bayonet one last time."

(Pascal laughing) "It's in my job description. I'm at your service." (Exits right)

(Benjamin, aside) "Think of it. Gender roles reversed. She is hard and inattentive and I am soft and obsessed."

I can't say which of us I hate more. Marcella for her disdain of love or myself because I am weak. We are both vulnerable, but my weakness is my problem alone to solve. Hers has killed us." (Exits right)

(Marcella entering from left. Leading father out of bed) "You mustn't try to get up on your own. That's why I'm here."

"I think I overdid it," Alberto says shakily.

"Please call me before you get up again."

"What are you doing? Who the hell are you? You're here to steal my money? I know a thief when I see one," Alberto exclaims with disgust.

"I'm your daughter, Marcella says with confusion in her voice.

"I know who you are," he cries, and begins to strangle her.

(Marcella breaking free from his grip) "Daddy, it's me, Marcie. You are hurting me."

(Alberto, standing shakily) "I think I need to take a leak now." (Exits. Pascal enters from left) "Forgive the intrusion. I hoped to visit your dad. How is he?"

(Marcella, in monotone) "The same. He's in the bathroom, now."

"That will give us a minute or two to talk. Can we sit? (They sit on bed together). Do you recall the conversation we had at your engagement party?"

"Yes."

"I have tried all these months to resist my need to see you again.?

(Alberto, off-stage) "Can't find any toilet paper."

"You're very sweet," Marcella says evenly to Pascal.

(Alberto, off stage) "I'd like some goddamn paper now."

"I would never have presumed to talk to you like this, except that I gather you no longer are involved with Benjamin."

"You presume a lot," Marcella responds testily. "I do care for him. I just can't seem to fit him into my life."

"I understand."

(Alberto, off-stage) "My ass is waiting," he yells insistently.

(Marcella shouting) "Look under the sink, daddy (To Pascal) "Then what are you after? To criticize me for how horribly I've acted towards him?"

"I'm not here for recriminations," Pascal says.

"I'm surprised again. What do you want?"

"You."

"Oh! And Benjamin?" she smiles insidiously. "Your lifelong buddy? Aren't you the surprise… You're truly callous." (But she is pleased)

"He would understand."

"You've seen him, of course."

"Do you want to know how he is?"

"He's sent me texts. Lots of texts!"

(Pascal trying to keep himself in check) "But you haven't been in touch with him. Someone who worries about you, who adores you and whose best friend you once claimed you were."

(Defensively)" There are pressures here you don't understand," Marcella says.

"I do understand the meaning of friendship, and how a gesture from you might make his life a little less agonizing. In the meanwhile, he's trying to recover."

"I don't think I need all of this. So that is why you are here just as I guessed….to tell me how awful a person I am. (Pause) All right, since you persist in wanting me to know, how is he, really?"

"In mourning," Pascal retorts. "Suffering because of you, but getting on with his life. (He touches her hair) It's time for us to see what there is between us."

"Where's my pipe?" Alberto cries off-stage.

(Marcella raising her voice once more) "You haven't smoked in months. Call me when you're ready." (To Pascal) "There's nothing between us."

(Pascal reaches into pocket, pulls out executioner's mask and dons it) "I don't accept that for a moment. Nor do you. We are thrilling together."

(Watches him, trembling) "Who the hell are you?"

"I am your murderer," Pascal replies smiling (He kisses her and she responds. His movements from now on are savage)

"Gently, Pascal, or you will murder me."

"Stop it. I recognize lust when I'm this close to it." (He takes her by the hair and forces her towards the stocks)

Get on your knees where you belong, bitch."

(From off-stage, Alberto cooing) "A spring flower!"

(Marcella enters the stocks with her head on the half-moon)

"To be honest, I did feel something for you, she says," her voice insipid. "As long as Benjamin was in the picture, I wouldn't allow myself to do anything about it. But my hair's a mess. Do you still want me looking like this?"

(Off-stage) "Could it be a daffodil?"

"Don't move," Pascal says. "It's your father. (She starts to lift upwards) I said, don't move."

"He's calling me."

"Too late for that. A whole lot too late. I'm going to fuck you like a canon."

"I have to go to him," she pleads, but does not move.

"Of course, you do. (He holds her in place) In all wars, there are wielders of the bayonet, and there must always be a soft spot to receive it. Lift your skirt!" (She complies)

(As Pascal moves behind Marcella, she begins to moan between syllables) "I've been in bondage too long. Let it…let it happen… (Pascal feigns savagely penetrating her) My father's death is evolving slowly, but if I am honest, I crave it. (Her voice becomes shrill) I hate him. Let him croak. I need my freedom. (Voice rising again) I will have my independence at last."

"You don't even enjoy sex, do you?" Pascal sneers. (Takes off the mask and speaks to audience after a momentary pause) "I just adore progress. My weapon has turned invisible. High tech is what we're about these days. I can severely damage or kill silently like some invisible intruder. Don't you just love this century?" (He exits left while Marcella pulls out of the stock and exits).

(Pascal to audience) "Marcella and I had several encounters. Each one clearly indicated how little suited we were for one another. Of course, I was simply using her. I was simply honoring Benjamin's bidding and fucking her to death." (He exits).

(Marcella re-entering) "Oh Lord," she says. "Thank God, it's passed. (To audience) A week has gone by since daddy died, and it seems as if everything now is different. I feel my numbness fading as if some obstacle pressing against my chest had lifted. I sense my blood flowing again."

(Benjamin enters from left with two epees) "It's finally over for you."

"He is asleep for good."

"And how do you feel?"

"Honestly? As if some weight had been lifted from my shoulders."

"I haven't seen you for months, Marcella, but you've rarely left my thoughts."

"I've often worried about you," she says softly. "These days after the funeral caused me to re-evaluate my goals. I hadn't realized to what degree father's condition had enveloped me. I hardly saw my own child during that time."

"You were loyal to your father."

"Was I? If so, at the expense of a lot of people, including myself."

(Benjamin pausing, rubbing his eyes) "You hurt me badly, Marcella."

"Not intentionally. I was muddling through the best way I knew. I had responsibilities, you know."

"Of course, you did. (He gives her the epee and holds one himself) One more time. Or have you forgotten what you learned in fencing?"

"I can't do this anymore. No more games (She returns the epee to him, and he lays both down). What happens to you now?"

"I haven't looked for a new position," Benjamin says. "I've stopped writing my book."

"That's not good."

"I've decided to leave teaching."

"Ben, there are thing I need you to know," Marcella says.

"It's too late now. (To audience) Why did I come to see her? Yes, to pay my respects for her father. Maybe to see whether the ravages had begun. But there is no sign of them yet. (To Marcella) Tell me how you're feeling these days."

"Strange that you would ask. I've had a persistent fever and my lymph nodes are swelling. Feels like a flu, but I'm not sneezing or coughing."

(To audience) "So it begins." (To Marcella) "Pascal is quite ill."

"I saw him a while ago. He looked ill, thin, shaken."

(Benjamin, to audience) "I wanted vengeance! But now that I see her again after all this time, my fantasy in the flesh, she's only the wisp of a woman. Like the rest of us, always struggling between the left and the right, just trying to get on with life. Is it her fault she couldn't find the right path? What have I done?

(To Marcella) I remember many a night when I slept in this bed with you. Awakened in the morning with you by my side. I thought I had stumbled into heaven." (He goes to one side of the bed towards the nightstand).

"I loved our time together," Marcella intones. "Benjamin, I'm so tired. I feel superficial, dissonant. Have I done something stupid?"

(Benjamin opens nightstand, pulls out a pipe. At once, this changes his demeanor) "Yes, smoking a pipe would put you out of whack."

"That was my father's," Marcella replies quickly.

(Benjamin to audience) "Or Joseph's. (Momentarily, he is beaten down) I can't stand…I can't stand it anymore.

(Sits, staring at audience, speaks pensively) Suppose these

brittle bits of history had never taken place. Take our civil war. Had it never taken place, would we now have more racial discrimination and conflict? I doubt it. Recreate our America without the war of independence. Imagine the worst result. We'd be Canada. Would that be so bad? Look at Lenin. Had he not roused the people and the Romanoffs continued to reign, the upshot might have been a slow fade to constitutional monarchy, just as in much of Europe. How about the cold war, the arms race, the endless sniping and killing. Without it, where would the Russians be? Worse off? I doubt it.

People, like nations, have an essential task. To grapple with and to overcome the burdensome effects of their childhood.

Look at Marcella and me. Unresolved dilemmas led us to this moment to destroy one another, to grievously wound our souls." (Replaces pipe in nightstand)

"I've never lost my feelings for you," Marcella says hesitantly, and yet with some emotion. "Maybe I was sidetracked by daddy's illness, by events of the moment, but the feeling remains. I need you again. I need you now." (She unbuttons her blouse)

(Benjamin slowly removing shirt) "Do you know how many times I hungered for this moment? How many white nights in which I thought I might explode in the insane, torrid fever of wanting you?"

(To audience) "What the fuck am I doing? How weak am I? This sick slut has soiled my character beyond recognition. So, what am I looking for? A final acceptance? The little and the big death to blend together in one momentous climax? Will that help her forget? Will it help me be more congruent, more honest? I don't know whether I can deal with integrity just now. (Pauses) God, I still love this bitch.

(To Marcella) Yes, let's make love one more time. Like you,

I am also very tired and so very sorry." (They embrace on the bed).

Curtain

45

Back in Paradise

Roger leans forward in his chair to view the stern of the large cruise ship exiting the harbor. The day bodes well. Cool in the morning, the kind of cool that augurs a warm afternoon, containing within itself the germ of burgeoning afternoon heat. A scant breeze blows in from the waterway. Next to Roger, a glass stand on which he has placed an ice pitcher of water. Pours himself a glass and drinks slowly. Then he turns to his companion on the balcony.

"I'm glad you came with me," he begins. "But I am also surprised. Truly, I thought you would turn me down. Particularly since you were not quite over your flu."

Denise smiles, shifts the pale green and white sarong about her waist. "Believe me, I considered it. You know that I felt betrayed by you. We were undertaking a relationship which, at least from my point of view, had neither run its course or even run halfway. There was much more that each of us could learn about the other. Ultimately, we would see whether we wanted to stay together over the long term. But you short-circuited the process. You short-circuited us."

"I don't deny it."

"And all because a pretty face turned your head."

He shifts uncomfortably in his seat. "When you put it that way…."

"Yes…. kind of venal, isn't it?"

"I have no excuse. I fell hard.?

"Your ultimate excuse I take it is that you have balls. Ergo, this affords you privileges that your lover does not have. For when a man wants to stray, he can always justify it as part of the evolutionary process. Men are meant, even required, to spread their seed, isn't that how the song is sung? Women are supposed to spread their legs and humbly receive it. I only need to be faithful to one man to fulfill my destiny. You, on the other hand, need to fuck everything that pleases you to promote evolution.

"Well said," he applauds with a grin.

"You don't even deny this?"

"Not a word. And it doesn't have to do with the usual excuse we men offer: can't see myself settling down with the same vagina day after day. That doesn't do justice to the argument."

"I agree. Come on, lazy bones," Denise says. "Let's go for a walk while it's still cool."

They get up and press the down elevator button. "Still selling four dollar bananas," he complains as they pass the bar.

"Yes, but this time I was smart," Denise laughs. "I packed a dozen with me."

"Clever you", he says, squeezing her arm.

They head towards the lake where they locate a couple of plastic lounge chairs, set them up and stretch out. In front of them, young mothers with children playing lakeside. Men following their kids down a waterslide.

"So why did you ask me to come with you?"

"Well, this is where we met," Roger begins.

"You could have returned on your own and found a new

dolphin master," she says, laughing.

"No," he replies seriously. "I wanted to spend time with you. To explain myself, I guess, and to see what else might develop."

"But you had already broken us up."

"Yes," he replies, "but I felt for some reason that I was wrong. That I hadn't allowed enough time for us".

"You mean after you kicked your new girlfriend out of the house," Denise remarks playfully.

"I feel like such a shit when you put it that way."

"And so you are," Denise replies, and now she is not smiling.

"And so I am," he agrees.

"What happened with Marina?"

Pauses for an instant. "She didn't put out," he confesses.

"That's it? That's all?"

"No, that's not all, but it capsulized what was happening between us."

"And what was that?"

"That exactly was the problem...not much. Marina was happy to fuck strangers at conferences she attended. But she nixed sex with me because it was.... how do I say this? intimate."

Denise now laughs. "A girl afraid of giving up her most potent weapon."

"Well, maybe that's it. Once you use it, you can't withhold it, at least not using the same argument. You can't not be intimate once you screw, right?"

"Well," Denise counters, "women aren't always reasonable, logical in these things. She may have been afraid to hand over control to you."

"Look," Roger claims. "She said she wanted to be with me. She lived with me. These are already concessions of intimacy. But to go the next step, to have sex was a bridge too far."

"She just wasn't ready for you. And I could turn the argument around by saying you left me because you weren't ready for me. Ripeness is all, sayeth the bard."

Scratches his head. "Yes, no doubt."

"But there was enough residue so that you called me after Marina left….."

"Yes. I don't really know how much. Not something you can weigh or even reasonably observe. Yet, there is something valuable between us. Our connection enables us to do things that I have not often found possible with other women. You and I can talk about anything. That is marvelous. We can discuss our craft which is beyond marvelous. And furthermore, when we want to make love, nothing interferes.

"Still, something is missing."

"Yes, but I'm trying to wade through it, to sort that out."

In a few moments, Denise falls back into a doze. It allows Roger time to think through their conversation. Why had he brought Denise along, in fact? On the surface, he could justify it on the grounds that he would interact with her in the new play, *Wars of Independence*, for as long as the show ran. Still, that did not mean that he needed to connect with her at a more intimate level. And it is clear to Roger that this is what he is asking. But why?"

He rises and goes into the bathroom, washes his hands, looks up at himself in the mirror. Yellow hair flowing about his head, still unruly now and lightened further by the fingerprint of the sun. But the face! He draws his head closer to the mirror. For the first time, he bears witness to a wrinkle about one of his eyes. He examines it more closely. Not much of a wrinkle, but a harbinger of lines to come. Upper lip receding somewhat. Christ, getting older! The tangible proof in his eyes. Suddenly, he realizes that he has matured these past months, grown tired of fucking for the sake of fucking, of seducing for the sake of manipulating. Not that his sexual drive diminishes an iota, but that he no longer wants to wield it as before. Nor does it matter that his bond with Denise might not be as sexually titanic as Armand's with Keely, or Benjamin's desperate sexuality with Marcella. Roger's torrent of hot emotion is beginning to flow into a more manageable drip. Like hot coffee from an espresso machine. Powerful yet measured.

In the mirror, he is studying a new Roger, the youngster redolent with illusion and depravity regressing in favor of an older, sager individual. I love Denise, he speaks suddenly. Even though she may not be everything in the universe. She is enough, more than enough. A woman who could dissect the pretty lines of the play, a pretty, intelligent actress with whom he has soldered.

As for Denise, mounting through slumber into the warmth of the late morning, awakening, she searches for Roger, and not finding him there, feels a nibble of concern. Then relief. In an instant, she sees him exit the men's room walking towards her. Thinking how catlike he strides. Concerns linger nonetheless. Will she trust him again? Not for a long while, for she fears his erratic nature. And yet, tentatively she promises herself like a child to take his hand, to grow, if growth is possible. Perhaps, one day in the distant future, to interact totally with Roger, once tensions are unwound. Replaced by the touch of her hand on his. No guile, no game, no hunger. Simple ease.

In their bathroom, she stands before the mirror carefully applying lipstick. Pats her lips with a tissue. Stands in the doorway of the bathroom looking out onto the balcony. There, on the chaise longue Roger stretches out, his thin, long legs basking in the morning sun. A slight frisson plays up and down her spine. Only then does she venture out.